QUANTUM SAGAS

THE LEGENDS ACROSS TIME

ANKIT SINGH

BLUEROSE PUBLISHERS
U.K.

Copyright © Ankit Singh 2024

All rights reserved by author. No part of this publication may be reproduced, stored in a retrieval system or transmitted in any form or by any means, electronic, mechanical, photocopying, recording or otherwise, without the prior permission of the author. Although every precaution has been taken to verify the accuracy of the information contained herein, the publisher assumes no responsibility for any errors or omissions. No liability is assumed for damages that may result from the use of information contained within.

BlueRose Publishers takes no responsibility for any damages, losses, or liabilities that may arise from the use or misuse of the information, products, or services provided in this publication.

For permissions requests or inquiries regarding this publication, please contact:

BLUEROSE PUBLISHERS
www.BlueRoseONE.com
info@bluerosepublishers.com
+4407342408967

ISBN: 978-93-6452-545-9

Cover design: Daksh

First Edition: October 2024

INTRODUCTION

The threads of time are all interconnected and the time is being watched. Any small wave in the threads can have a repercussion which impacts the timeline over millions of years. The past builds the present, the present impacts the future, but can the future impact the past ?

"In string theory, all particles are vibrations on a tiny rubber band; physics is the harmonies on the string; chemistry is the melodies we play on vibrating strings; the universe is a symphony of strings, and the 'Mind of God' is cosmic music resonating in 11-dimensional hyperspace."

-Michio Kaku

About the Author

Ankit Singh is a corporate professional and "Quantum Sagas: The Legends Across time" is his third book. He has dabbled in different genres before this. His first book was on interview and CV preparation by the name "Give the Interview You Can Be Proud Of" which had reached the Amazon best sellers in its category. His second book was a novel in the young adult genre "Singlehood Pandey" which was loved by the target audience.

Ankit is a Mechanical Engineering Graduate from NIT Durgapur and MBA from XLRI Jamshedpur. He loves history and science fiction and, "Quantum Sagas" is an attempt to merge the two.

Prologue : The Walls

Earth, Year 3200 AD

The World that we knew of had ceased to exist.

Human race always was aware if there was one thing which could lead to its destruction and that is the human race itself. The progress made on the shallow peace of the early 21st century was short lived. The destruction caused by the great war was so huge that the once most dominant species on the planet was struggling to keep itself alive and it lived hidden like mice . There are no countries in the new world, only city states often separated by hundreds and sometimes even by thousands of Kilometres. The human population which had once reached 10 billion in the year 2050 was reduced to a few millions and most of them lived in cramped walls of these city states, scattered all over the globe , most of them were under the control of warlords and monarchs.

The citizens lived and died inside these walls and for them nothing existed outside, the dire lack of basic human needs, diseases and wars with other cities made sure that the human population never increased beyond the walls , some of these mini civilizations perished without leaving a trail of their existence. The "half humans" living inside the walls never knew that once upon a time there was a World which was connected together and people moved around the continents and even planets. The contact most of the states had with each other was rarely anything friendly. An ambitious warlord trying to obtain the resources of the other city would try to run over the walls of the city and the citizens were either cannon fodder in war or slaves who would live miserable lives under one ruler or the other.

The life inside these walls was hell but the walls were sacred; it protected the ones living inside from the things that roamed outside. The ones who lived outside these walls were on their own. Some called themselves the free citizens, some were called nomads but most of the men who stayed outside the walls were dreaded by those who lived inside. The citizens of the walls knew these men outside the walls as Pirates, thugs and even cannibals. They often attacked the citizens who ventured beyond the walls but the threats beyond the walls were more than just the men, there were the most inhospitable terrains and then there were creatures whose true tale no one ever lived to tell.

Table of Contents

Sr. No.	Chapter	Page No.
	PART-1	
1.	The Seed Of Destruction	2
2.	Revenge A Dish Best Served Cold	6
3.	Beginning Of The End	14
4.	Giant Leap For Mankind	17
5.	The Future	22
6.	The World Within The Walls	26
7.	Fallen In Love	34
8.	Revealed	40
9.	The Quest Begins	46
10.	The Quest (2)	57
11.	Quest (3)	62
12.	Recoup	69
13.	Finding Ashmit	85
14.	Vikram's 9	96
15.	When The Libraries Wept	104
16.	The Portal	107
17.	The Journey To Home	115
18.	The Training Ground	117
19.	Welcome To Hell	129
20.	The Two Of Many Worlds	132
21.	The City Of Ghouls	142
22.	Hell Coming	148
	PART-2	
	THE UNDEAD ARMY	156-235

PART - 1

Chapter - 1
THE SEED OF DESTRUCTION

Islamabad, Year 2048 AD

The 100th year of Inter-Services Intelligence (ISI)

Pakistan Prime Minister's Office. 10:30 A.M

The Defence Minister was waiting for the Prime Minister, Anwar Khan. Also present was the Head of Armed forces Yakub Ashraf, Director General of Inter-Services Intelligence Abdul Rahman and top ranking military officials. The 100th year was an important milestone and the Government wanted to cash on it and create a wave of feel good factor in the masses, the general elections were about to be held next year and after a long time the elected PM was about to complete the full term.

Rashid Ansari's phone buzzed. He had a quick look at the message and put it back. He took out his laptop, as he always would before any meeting and recorded every detail of the discussion. General Rahman quipped "Janab, seems like you have brought a 100 year laptop for the occasion. This wasn't his usual laptop, it seemed a bit too heavy. "Yeah my old laptop had some issues, so I decided to use this old thing today. Anyways I have always been a fan of the retro".

"Hazraat", PM Anwar Khan entered the room "Good to see all of you gathered together in peace time". "But before we begin today's discussion let us have a cup of tea."

"Ansari Sahab here seems to be ready with a big presentation for this" Anwar Khan said while sipping his masala tea.

" Janaab, here is the presentation I have made for the 100 year celebration, just let me connect this laptop to a power source, the battery is drained" he connected the laptop with a power source and immediately there was a voltage fluctuation. "This ancient relic will probably eat the entire electricity of Islamabad" Anwar gave a loud laugh.

Rashid looked at his phone - a girl tied up in a dark room. A gunman was standing behind her.

But something else was louder than that laugh, an explosion, and the entire room was blown to pieces. Even the dead-bodies could not be recovered to provide them a funeral

The Country was put in a state of emergency. The position of PM was taken over by the Home Minister Jahangir and Lt General Omar Javed, the second in command in ISI was made the interim head of the armed forces and the ISI. But before anything else his first responsibility was to look into these explosions. Often the killings of Pakistan Prime Ministers were by the Army Generals but this time even the general was a victim of the explosion. This kind of attack was the first of its kind. Two major theories were floating around the explosions: the first theory as always blamed India for this and the second thought that this was a work of the Balochistan separatists who were said to have received funding from some unknown sources. Another theory which was doing rounds was of Chinese hand in it as the PM was trying to distance itself from China owing to the increased influence of China over everything in the Country.

Omar Javed, now General Omar Javed, made a task force involving the most experienced operatives of the ISI to enquire into the mess. The initial reports post the explosion had suggested presence of strong electrical charge in the area and even nearby area. It was discovered that the laptop which Rashid Ansari had brought to the meeting triggered the explosion. It used the electricity of the building to create a powerful explosion, such an explosive was still unheard of and using it for such a high profile assassination was certainly the work of a big organisation. The use of this device disguised as a laptop ensured its easy entry into the premises without being detected, it just seemed a little odd and looked like a laptop of a very old time but nothing which would draw suspicion, and it was a fool proof idea.

Javed and his team went deeper into the case and while checking about the family members of the former Defence Minister they got to know that his daughter was studying Law at King's College London and had been missing her classes a week before the blast. She came back to Pakistan after hearing this news and was inquired about the events that had happened a week before. She denied any foul play and produced a medical certificate that she was suffering from high fever. Was she lying and the Defence Minister pushed into this to save his daughter or was he unaware of this plot? The team still had many unanswered questions.

The tensions on the borders had increased and Pakistani forces were violating ceasefire on a regular basis. It seemed a tactic by Javed to escalate the trouble to divert the attention of the country from these events.

Many Pakistan and International News Agency took this as a sign that India had a role to play in the assassination. Meanwhile the emergency situation had given a lot of control to Omar Javed and the interim PM, Jahangir knew that he had to be in his good book to ensure not to get overthrown. Jahangir had many cases of corruption running against him but he used his position to get favourable decisions from the judiciary.

General Javed was known for his hatred towards corruption, he had court martialled many army officers who were caught in corruption. Talking to trusted subordinate Lt Gen Akhtar he said" I cannot allow a corrupt politician like Jahangir to run this country and to risk its internal security especially when we are at our most vulnerable stage"

"Are you planning a coup?" Akhtar asked

"The country is going through a lot of uncertainty and a coup at this time will make the Army power hungry" Javed replied, looking out of his window at the night sky of Islamabad which had few stars shining.

"But then what is the solution?" Akhtar was perplexed

"I will make an offer to Jahangir, he knows that he is on slippery ground. Making him the Home Minister was an unpopular decision of the Late Prime Sahab and it is very likely that Jahangir will not win the next election. He is also wary of coup. I will let him be the face of the government, allow him to take the decisions of the day to day affair, even if it means…. " he took a pause " he is able to fill his coffer with dirty money"

"So what is in it for us, he gets what he wants and runs everything and we will be running around fighting his opposition ?" The Lt Gen was still not able to fathom his superior's plan.

"You will know soon," Javed told him calmly.

Next morning Javed had a meeting with the PM "Janaab I suggest you enjoy the fruits of chairs but let me take the pains of ensuring the security. My decision with regards to internal and external policies concerning will be final. If you agree to this then you can rest assured that you will not have any trouble from the army."

"But why are you doing this?" the acting PM questioned him

"I don't want the people of this country to suffer any more and I cannot allow someone with a tainted reputation like you to mishandle the security of the country"

Jahangir stood up from his chair, went up-to Javed. "You have my word"

"Pakistan Zindabad" the General said and left.

Few weeks later, the team working on the bomb blast case was able to get leads. They were able to track down a group of Baloch fighters who were operating out of London. They had kidnapped the daughter of Rashid Ansari. To set her free they wanted him to show a presentation to the PM on the laptop they had shared, to protect his daughter Ansari agreed, last year Baloch fighters had killed the son of an MP, he did not want to risk it. He thought it would be a presentation, at worst it would be offensive but at-least his daughter will be safe. He was quite wrong in his assumption, it was a presentation to the entire country, and the old laptop he was given hours before the meeting was an explosive. He was given the instruction not to open it before a chip fitted inside it will let the Baloch fighters know of it and his daughter will be blown to pieces.

The Scotland Yard helped the ISI to nab the suspects in London and many more of the rebels were captured across Pakistan. The motive was simple, the former PM was tough on the Balochistan situation so eliminating him and creating unrest would help them to strengthen their operations.

The case was brought to closure, the tensions with India also mellowed down, at-least for the time being.

Javed lived a solitary life, he never got married and did not have many friends. People said that the Army and the country was all that mattered to him, looking at the picture of his mother Noor. She had brought him up with great difficulties and had died many years back, and he remembered his father.

CHAPTER - 2
REVENGE A DISH BEST SERVED COLD

Born in Muzaffarabad in the Pakistan controlled Kashmir, as a child Omar moved to Karachi with his mother who was afraid of the safety of her son because the city was often caught in crossfire between India and Pakistan armies.He did not know much about his father, he just had a few photographs and some hazy memories. His mother had told him that his father is away on a mission and he had lived with that throughout his childhood.

Omar went on to do his Masters in Physics from The Quaid-E-Azam University of Islamabad soon after that he was recruited by ISI in the Department of New Weapons development. He had a hobby of collecting rocks , something which he had picked as a kid living in Kashmir. When he was moving to Karachi with his mother the one thing he begged her to take was the collection of his rocks which weighed more than his weight but only few of his precious rocks made way into the luggage.He wept for days for it. As a young man he often searched for minerals and rocks for this, he would plan trips to the sea side and to the mountains and the river valleys.

Post his graduation he and his friend wanted to go for a small grad trip. His friend Sakib suggested a Dubai trip but it wasn't possible for Omar due to limited means. "Every other person is going for a trip to Emirates , let's do something unconventional. Let's visit some place which would be an adventure to remember and we may anyways get to travel to Dubai in our professional lives, but before we become working slaves let's go on a trip to remember " Omar suggested to Sakib.

" I think you make a solid point my friend. It's a done deal , but you have to come up with such a place" Sakib agreed.

So Omar convinced some more of his friends to visit Astola Island which is a few miles from the coast of Balochistan,it is not much of a tourist spot as it is a small island and quite far away from the shore so maybe a dozen odd people come there every day for a few hours and return. But Omar believed that this would be something unusual and would be a fun trip for his friends and for him another rock scavenging expedition.

Off he went with his friends Sakib and his girlfriend Laiba, Mubarak and his girlfriend Shifa. The five of them hired a motorboat which Shakib was driving as he had fair bit of experience in driving motor boats and he did not hire a pilot because he did not want any stranger to be a part of this trip. They had got stuff for an overnight stay over although staying was generally not advisable due to high tides but the couples wanted to have some cosy time and Omar just wanted to explore the island , find rocks and observe the laws of physics in the island.

They left for the island early in the morning from the Pasni district , it was a 5 hour journey. The sea was calm with gentle breeze flowing over the waves. On the journey they came across a pod of Dolphins which was noticed only by Omar. Laiba was standing near Sakib and would sometimes hold him from behind and sometimes played with his hair. " Jaan, you will make us all drown" he smiled and said to her. " My love I would be happy to drown if i could be in your arms" she laughed and kissed him on cheeks. On the back of the boat Mubarak and Shifa were making out. Omar was single and he was a classmate of both Sakib and Mubarak , he was mild mannered and always helped them in studies. The three had become good friends and they would always tag along even if Laiba and Shifa were with them.

The island was almost empty except for a couple of foreign tourists. They rested for a while and had lunch. Mubarak played a song on his guitar and the two girls danced. Later Sakib did some beatboxing and Omar gave a shot at street dance on the beats. "Brothers , I don't know where life will take us now. Responsibilities often bring distance in friendship" Mubarak was getting emotional. "There will be no distance and soon I am going to come to your and Shifa's wedding" Omar said, putting an arm around the shoulder of Mubarak. "I am planning to move in with Laiba. She has got a job in Lahore. I will also find something there or else will handle the family business operations in Lahore but don't you worry guys we will plan getaways to whichever city you are living in " Sakib said cheerfully. The boys continued talking and reliving the moments they had spent together. The two girls were taking a dip in the sea.

As it got a little dark, all the other tourists left the island. The boy set up three small tents , two for the couples and one for Omar. They lit a bonfire while the girls came back from the swim. It was a starry night." You are wet , come in the tent and change" Mubarak told Shifa. She went in the tent and he too went inside. Seeing this, the other couple, Sakib and Laiba too, went into their tent. Omar decided to take a stroll around the island while the couples were making love. He took out his torch and started walking. He could clearly hear the sounds of love-making coming from the two tents, "Wish I too had someone to hold my hand and love me" he thought. Throughout his college he had only focussed on studies "But I have to become something for Ammi. She never had happiness in her life. I want to make her happy by becoming successful and giving her all the comforts" as soon as the thought of having a romantic partner came to his mind it went away the next minute. This was the major reason why he had always remained single , despite being an attractive and intelligent young man.

He went on the small rocky hill to search if he could see any hidden treasure to add to his rock collection. Contrary to the popular belief he said " night is the best time to look for rocks, you get the brightest and the shiniest ones which get hidden in the daylight. And yes of course you can get to encounter some elegant serpents and scorpions in your quest" while talking to a group of other rock collection enthusiasts he had met in a meeting of rock collection enthusiasts. He had his big boots and rubber gloves on to avoid any fatal connection with any reptile or arthropod. He kept on searching for almost an hour but did not find anything significant except a few bird nests and soon he was on the top of the rock. The waves were high and the water had reached well inside the island , fortunately they had their tents fairly away from the coastline. No movement or sound was coming from the tents, "I guess they are done and asleep". The stars were shining brightly and the sea was lit by their lights. The breeze was cold and strong.

" Never have I felt so close to nature". He stood there for a few more minutes looking around and feeling the nature. The wind got stronger and then there was a strong lightning in the clouds. " It can start raining any minute, I should hurry up and get inside the tent. The weather report was all fine , hope this is not a strong thunderstorm, otherwise we may get into trouble". He picked up his bag which he had put down and tried to run, but his torch slipped from his hand and it went in a small crevice. He put his hand into it , got a small rock in his hand which by the shape of it seemed like a crystal but covered in a lot of mud. He was in a hurry and would have thrown it away in a normal scenario but the crystalline shape got his attention. The rain had gotten harder and his hat had water filled in the rims which fell down on the crystal and removed some mud. He saw some shine and he rubbed it against his jeans , the dirt was removed and it was an electric blue crystal, something which he has never seen in his life." This is a piece of beauty and must be very valuable. There must be more of it. I must take some more samples before the weather gets worse." He took out a small trowel from his bag and started digging the area near the crevice , a lot of water started flowing in it along with mud "this means that this is hollow" even before he could process what to do he heard a strong lightning strike and slipped, the land inside him caved in and he fell inside. The very next second a strike of lightning hit the island and a blinding flash and explosion knocked him off his senses.

He opened his eyes and saw a tube light above him" This is not the island" he jumped up from the bed. It was a hospital room , he was tied up in bandages and IV was being administered. " Is anyone here?" a feeble voice came from his throat which no one could hear ." How did this happen? How did I come here? What happened to my friends?" The questions were blasting his head but he did not have the strength to call anyone , till the time the door was opened and a middle aged nurse walked in " What happened?" She went out and called the doctors who came rushing in " Son, you are lucky to be alive. You have woken after a week from coma"

" What are you saying? How did this happen?" still in shock Omar asked the doctor. "You were found almost lifeless floating on a piece of wood in the sea. Some fishermen saw you and brought you here" The doctor told him. " Rock? But I was on Astola island" Omar was still not able to make any sense out of this. " You were on Astola? Ohh. The island was hit by multiple lightning bolts in a storm and the entire island exploded last week. The geologists are still trying to figure out how this happened" The doctor had seen this on the News.

"And what about my friends? Do you know about them?" Omar had tears in his eyes worrying about the safety of his friends. " I am afraid no one else has been seen around the island. The island was so badly destroyed that nothing exists around it. Even the fishes and corals around it were floating all dead. It is Allah's miracle that you survived"

"It was my idea to go to that island. I killed them all" Omar cried in agony and tears rolled down his cheeks. "Don't think that. No one in their wildest of dreams could have predicted that. You are not at fault. Now take some rest, your body has not recovered enough to talk long. Also please let us know if you need someone from your family is to be informed"

He gave the phone number of his mother. She had not been eating or sleeping for the last seven days since she had known of the lightning strike at the island. " I am going to Hajj next year, i would have died if something would have happened to you my son" she had tears of joy in her eyes while speaking over phone to her son. " Your prayers have saved me Ammi. I will be discharged in few days and I want to eat sheer-maal from your hands"

After another couple of weeks Omar was discharged from the hospital. While being discharged he was handed over the clothes he was wearing and his bag. " You still had this bag in your hand when you were found" the hospital clerk told Omar. The khaki colour bag has turned dark and had burn marks visible. " Here is my bag, it remained safe in the accident but my friends….I wish for a miracle that they are alive somewhere" he thought to himself. He thanked the clerk and went away.

He took a bus to his home and his mind oscillated between zero thoughts and thoughts about the time he spent with his friends and the last day he spent with his friends. He was so lost in thoughts that the bus conductor reminded him to get down. He reached his home. The door opened within seconds of pressing the bell. " My son!" his mother exclaimed and she hugged him tightly. She had lost considerable weight and he noticed that" Ammi you haven't been eating properly in the last few days" he said. " Now you are here , I will become fat. Get freshened up. I have made all the dishes of your choice"

After dinner , Omar went to his room but the guilt of being responsible for his friends' death was haunting him. "I don't deserve to live. I should die. I can't live my life with this guilt. I should die" He went into a hysteria and picked up a scissor to stab himself in the neck. "Do not be stupid. There is a purpose that you are alive" he heard a voice. It seemed like his own voice but he could feel as if some present in the room was talking. He held his head and tore his hair, " I am going mad". The voice responded " No you are not. You are getting better. You will now have a purpose to live. You have to stay alive for your mother". " Yes , I can't abandon my mother. I have to stay alive for her" He calmed down and fell asleep.

He looked into the mirror and he could see his reflection appearing different to him. " I am tired," he said. " No you are not, " the reflection said. He ignored it and took a sleeping pill and went to sleep. Next day in the ISI lab , while crossing the data room he could see his reflection standing inside the room , the door was ajar. He ignored it. Next day he saw the reflection running towards the data room. " I have to get inside the room, there is something. It is my subconscious or is it a sign I don't know but I have to get inside the data room" . He stole the access card of his senior.

He logged into the system and started looking for files, he felt someone was telling him which folders to look into.

He asked for a break and he went to the Hindukush mountains. He was wandering around and clearly standing out as a foreigner there he was spotted by a man while he was having tea. When the evening came he decided to set up his tent. Few men walked up to him and threw a blanket over him. Omar tried to resist but he was taken away. These were the terrorists of the famous terrorist organisation J.E.U, which had its base in these mountains. He was taken inside a hideout which was in a cave in the mountains where he was tortured and questioned by the terrorists because they were sure he was a RAW agent from India or a spy of the FBI. They asked him his identity but he kept on saying he was a scientist for ISI.

He was beaten and he went unconscious and then when he would get up he was beaten again, finally his body gave up , his heart stopped beating. " Either we picked up the wrong guy or he was too tough to open his mouth," said one of the terrorists to the other ones. " We should dump his body," the other one said. They threw him in the valley to be eaten by the vultures. They then went back to their regular business.

Next day they saw a shadow outside the cave. One of them went out with his AK 47. He fired his gun but it went silent, he did not return. Then two more went outside, they saw the dead body of his friend. One guy turned around to see his partner but he too was lying dead. His heart was beating hard and he started firing his gun in all directions till he ran out of ammo and then a stone hit his knee and he went down in pain and he was met with a kick in the face and he was beaten till he begged for mercy " Tell me what do you want?" " I want to meet your leader and take me to him." it was Omar who they had left for dead but he did not die he got up and he was a different man. He could hear the whispering way more clearly, he knew they were guiding him and he could feel a different strength inside him. He walked up in the den. He was surrounded by gunners, the leader came out to see him " You have killed my men. I am sure you are no civilian. What is that you want? You will not go out alive if you fool around" He asked Omar in his roaring voice

Omar heard the voice and said " I am the son of Nasir" he repeated the voice and everyone was stunned

His father was killed in a special operation by Mossad as he was helping the Palestinian forces with men, money and weapons. He met the current chief of J.E.U Tareek who was once the lieutenant and the right hand man of his father Nasir He told the story how Nasir sacrificed his entire life, even the elder brother of Omar was killed in the fights and operations. The US, Israel and India were responsible for these losses. He swore revenge. ISI had always supported JEU in their operations, though they never admitted, but this was common knowledge. Over the years the ISI had supported many other terrorist groups especially in the proxy war against India but the support to JEU was much more. JEU with support of ISI and funding from many Arab countries had become very active in many parts of the world.

Nasir AKA Tadmir (Arabic for destruction) was the founder of the World's most notorious terrorist group and its leader was the most wanted by World's top investigating agencies right from CIA to Mossad and RAW.

Nasir was an orphan and a bomb expert who was raised by radicals to die for their cause of Jihad. At the age of 19 he joined the Taliban to be a part of the Jihad against the United States army when the US attacked them in the year 2001. He operated like a ghost, swift, silent and present at the place of action. He was said to have killed 80 US soldiers by deploying landmines. When the Taliban forces were falling he was made the commander of the Bamiyan province, the same Bamiyan where the Buddha statue was destroyed by the Taliban guns. Karma got to him and the entire force under him, constituting Of Taliban fighters, mercenaries and Jehadis from different parts of the World was killed. He and 4 of his close aides survived but while trying to run away he stepped on a landmine and lost his right leg. His life was saved and he hid in the Hindukush Mountains where he met the biggest terrorist of 20th century Osama Bin Laden. Though disabled in one leg he served Osama and became his trusted aide. Few years later, because of his poor health, Osama was shifted by Al-Qaeda and ISI to Abottabad, Pakistan where he was finally killed by the US forces in the year 2011. During these years when the US and allied forces were busy searching for Osama, Javed was silently building another terrorist army. Many other fighters too reached the safety of caves Hindukush Mountains. Javed's operations in the Afghanistan war and his closeness to Osama earned him respect of these fighters and he formally named the group as *Jaysh –e- 'uwnadd*. He expanded the activity of the group and made many camps to find new recruits. Many teachers were inducted in JEU, sometimes by their choice and sometimes by force to brainwash young men to join the JEU.

It was during one of his missions in the Pak Occupied Kashmir where his entire unit was eliminated by the Indian army and he struggled to stay alive that Nasir met Noor who took his care while he recuperated from the injuries. He fell in love with this orphan girl who believed in his jehad. He kept a low profile over the next few months and married her during this time. Over the next many years he kept on moving around the world carrying out attacks and radicalising youth all around to make them terrorists but managed to spend a few days with Noor. Over the next few years he had two sons. The eldest son Asif wanted to be a fighter like his father and the father was proud of his son. When he turned 13 Asif joined his father and soon became a dreaded guerilla fighter. The younger son Omar was only 3 then.

Chapter - 3
BEGINNING OF THE END

Omar was now the head of ISI, he had killed so many to rise the ladder. Agents of Raw, Indian civilians and so many Pak civilians were killed to blame it on India and the men of his own organisation who knew his secret or were a threat to his ambitions of becoming the Chief of ISI.

But to be the Chief of ISI was just a title for him, the money, the perks were useless, all that mattered was just one thing - The nuclear warheads and now he had the access to the nuclear weapons of Pakistan. Using them was insanity but all he knew he wanted revenge. He dropped nuclear warheads on Palestine. "My father was killed in saving you. Now all you can die and go to hell"

The world thought it was by Israel. It led to a full scale war by the Arab countries on Israel. He supplied them nukes, most of them were gunned down by the Anti-Missile tech but one hit. The US joined in. Oils supplies were cut, also this was a great way for the US to control the entire oil in the Middle East. But they burned their oil fields. NATO joined in. He dropped another in Pakistan itself. India was away from the imbroglio, and was now dragged into it. North Korea supported the Arabs. China saw it as an opportunity to topple the US and crush India. Chechen fighters attacked Russia after stealing tech.

The World was split in two groups- The Alliance which was led by the US and India. Russia,Israel, Japan, UK , France and Germany were also part of this.

The second group called themselves the Jury was led by China. Pakistan, North Korea and Arab Countries were part of it.

The Alliance was much stronger in terms of technology but the Jury had countries all around the globe and they were able to wage war across various fronts which were led by the radical Jihadis who never cared to die. Chemical and dirty bombs and releasing new viruses was the plan of warfare which they knew they couldn't win fair and square.

The war was not only restricted to Earth, this was the first time there was a battle in space. China developed satellites which have laser guided missiles and guns to destroy other satellites. These were like the German u-boats of the previous world war, sinking any ship that came in their path. In a day over a dozen satellites of the allied nations were shot down. Communication was taking a hit, what was not known to the Chinese was that Russia and US too had these weapons installed in some of these satellites. They had not used it so far but after this provocation they started destroying the satellites of the enemy countries. Soon more than a third of the satellites were destroyed or became dysfunctional. Communication ad come to a stand still

India had developed a technology of using radio wave cannons to destroy machines and impair enemy soldiers, it was launched in the last days of the war and it helped to overpower the enemies.

This was the final straw, it led to nuclear warfare. All the countries emptied their nuclear arsenals and by the time war ended there was so much destruction that some of the smaller countries were erased from existence. Farms and industries were destroyed.

World War 3 or the last war, destroyed everything that humanity had built in thousands of years.

The war owing to the nuclear and chemical arsenal that every country possessed lasted for only 2 years but the destruction was unimaginable. The Alliance won but the costs were huge.

Due to the direct impact of this a fifth of the world population died and the major metropolitan cities were reduced to ashes. The pathogens and viruses released in the air aided by the widespread radiations further mutated and waves of epidemics haunted the surviving population. Destruction and pollution of water resources and farm lands created mass famines. In the next decade another tenth of the population died.

All the countries were engulfed in civil wars due to lack of food and amenities. The Governments did not have resources and armies to keep the law and order in control, one by one every government toppled. Soon every state and city was managed by a different political entity who fought with the neighbouring areas for resources.

Over the next decade temperature increased so much that all the low lying and coastal cities were inundated in floods in the thirty years after the war. London,Mumbai,Bangkok all were under the sea now.

Most power stations were destroyed in the wars, the communication channels kept on breaking down. The Internet was now a thing of the past. Humans were no longer a global species but divided and separated living in their own small geographical area.

The man who had all started this, Omar, was known to have been killed in the battle of Islamabad when alliance forces captured the city. When his hideout was captured he tried to flee while firing at the alliance forces. He was shot multiple times but kept on firing till he was hit by a mortar shell and was blown to pieces.

But unknown to all he was still alive not as a human but as a shadow, surrounded by many such shadows and controlling them to control the minds of those still living making them ravage, plunder and kill even their kins.

Chapter - 4

GIANT LEAP FOR MANKIND

Year 2012 Headquarters of NASA:

Special research team on Extra-terrestrial power resources is about to submit its findings to the Administrator and the Deputy Administrator of NASA. Some other senior scientists and their assistants were also present in the meeting. Team is headed by Dr. Sullivan who along with his twenty scientists has been working on this project for the last 10 years.

"The World is reaching a stage where they will soon run out of fuel to power the ever increasing industrialisation. Renewable energy, bio fuels, everything has been tried but the results are still not promising enough for the future. Nuclear energy comes with its own hazards and no country can afford a Chernobyl like event ever again. Our answer to the infinite power source is in the direction of our journey, it lies beyond. Beyond Earth"

"I along with my team have been looking out for minerals on the other planets which can help us to solve our problem. We have been using the images and signal sent by our space probes and satellites to analyse the composition of various planets and space bodies to find out a fuel source which can end all our energy problems. The search seemed endless till the time we came across, ladies and gentlemen – "he switches on the big screen "Electronicium", on the screen appeared a sparkling blue crystal like substance. "This is our solution to all the energy problems of earth."

Sullivan then opened his bag, it had his 3D projector which was the size of a book "And in case you are wondering what this substance really is then to your amazement this is electricity in solid form so we have decided to name it Electronicium, perhaps the rarest mineral in universe", the projector showed a 3D image of a small crystal of the size of human palm. "I know most of you are amazed but then you will be further amazed if you see this "he pressed a button on the projector and the crystal opened and the entire room was filled with a bright light. "This three inch crystal has enough electricity inside it to power the entire New York City for a day and there is enough of it on the natural satellite named after a character of Shakespeare play The Tempest"

"Is it Caliban?" asked one of the senior scientist present in the meeting

"Yes Doctor, you have an amazing knowledge of literature. It is indeed Caliban, one of the moons of Saturn. We have been getting information from the Cassini Space probe which was sent to observe Saturn and its moons. Since the time we started getting observations we have seen lightning around this moon. For a lot of time this was assumed to be just ordinary lightning. But five years back further observations of Caliban revealed that the lightning was not generated in the atmosphere but was coming from inside the surface of Caliban. It was from that point onwards it was included in our list of the probable energy sources and soon it emerged as the sole winner when we realised that beneath the surface it is composed of solidified electricity"

"But Doctor, how is it even possible? Electricity is basically electrons which are carrying charge moving from one place to another. How can they be in the form of a crystal? This is beyond comprehension" administrator John Harvard asked.

"I truly appreciate your concern and I am sure everyone listening to this must be thinking the same. So have we been thinking. But all the test results have pointed to the same results that the mineral inside the surface is generating this electricity" He asked his assistant to handover a file. "Here Sir, are the reports" he handed it over to the administrator.

Yes there are some questions regarding how this mineral was formed in the first place and how could it remain stable and not blow up the entire moon is beyond our understanding and perhaps once we have the mineral and recreate it on earth we will be free of our worries of running out of fuel ever".

"But you realise that obtaining it is almost impossible. We have only been to observe Saturn from a certain distance but landing on it and then getting a piece of it back will be a gargantuan task" Harvard said after having a glance at the report.

"Not today but certainly if we start a project dedicated to it, maybe by the start of next decade we will be able to obtain this mineral. We can even mine it if we are not able to recreate it on Earth".

"Dear Doctor Sullivan" Harvard was still unsure about the idea "do you realise how much it would cost to land on the moon of Saturn?"

"As I said, Doctor, it will take time and money but there are two aspects to it. Anyways we have been trying to explore and reach planets beyond

Mars. So not only this is an exploration but an exploration which will reap heavy dividends. A few kilotons of the minerals if extracted can power the whole world for years and with zero pollution. And the best part is" he stopped for a few seconds, "the presentation showed the images of the collapsing of twin towers and then moved on to scenes from the Afghan war" we counter the growing clout of the Arab countries. They have nothing to offer except oil and not to name but we very well know that some of them have been actively funding terrorist organisations across the World. This single mission will be a death blow to it. We have the biggest mission of NASA, we get the fuel for years, we solve pollution and we tackle terrorism. So even if the cost of getting and using Electronicium is more than the fuels we are using today I think it still makes sense to obtain it. This single mission will make America forever great." Sullivan had made the perfect pitch.

There was a loud clapping in the room hearing this and now it was impossible to ignore his idea.

Harvard still had his doubts but he decided to have a further look into the proposal" Doctor you do have the basic proposal ready. I will assign a committee to look into it, they will do a feasibility study and will also look into the finances. Since the project will involve a huge investment I will need to take it up with Mr. President himself."

"Thanks a lot for considering it Doctor Harvard" Sullivan smiled.

There was another round of cheering in the room. The team of Doctor Sullivan started giving hugs to each other. "Congrats fellas for this victory. You all did a great job. Drinks on me today" Sullivan said to his team

The special committee got into action. Within 3 months they came up with the detailed calculations.

Harvard called Sullivan to meet him in his office. Sullivan had all his reports cross checked and ready for review. He said a silent prayer before entering the office, it was the biggest project in the history of NASA, it would make him immortal.

"Mr President has approved this project but this information about Electronicium and the project remains classified and only on a need to know basis. Every individual team working on it should know only their piece of information, the full story should be known only to us and Mr President." In parallel a secret lab was conducted for experiments on Electronicium and to use it to generate electricity for the country. The biggest capacitor bank was to be created for storing and transferring the electricity that will be released from the Electronicium brought to Earth.

Harvard briefed Sullivan's team and other senior scientists who would coordinate the project.

Special funds and additional manpower was put into the project and it went ahead of the schedule.

15 September 2017

Cassini Space Probe is deliberately destroyed by making it plunge into Saturn's atmosphere. This was the information that was made available for the general use. But it was actually getting more information to find the correct coordinates for the safe landing of Voyager Cal-E. It was hit by lightning coming out of the surface of Caliban and lost control and fell inside the surface, but it did its job before going down. In the past 7 months it was confirming the spot where a heavy spacecraft can make a landing. The Southern Pole of the moon was the place which had ice solid enough for the landing of the vehicle.

22 Aug 2025

Dr. Sullivan is palpitating, his pulse is 150 and face is flush, Cal E is about to land on the surface of Caliban. It had been more than a decade since he had revealed his discovery, the landing was impeccable.

The entire craft was made resistant to the strongest lighting impacts, it had two rockets one for taking it to Caliban and the other one for return and a large vault in the middle to collect the sample. The landing is successful, NASA HQ is getting images of the surface of the moon of the Saturn. A small robot rover came out of the vault and Over next few days it collected samples of Electronicium and loaded them in the vault.

15th September 2025

Cal E sets off for the return to Earth, NASA awaits the prize treasure

21st Feb 2027

"Dr Sullivan, would not be around to witness the fruits of his discovery. He left us last night due to a cardiac arrest. His contributions to NASA will never be forgotten.", the current administrator Wong Chu continued" The success of the mission and harnessing the power of electonicium will be the true tribute to Doctor Sullivan" the speech was followed by a 2 minutes of mourning.

21st Nov 2028

CalE is closing on the surface of Earth, this has been the first time that such a large extraterrestrial sample is being brought to Earth.

Cal E enters the atmosphere, the temperature increases due to friction but everything seems under control till all the readings go blank. The people on ground witness intense blinding lightnings and it causes cloudburst.

No sign of CalE.

Search missions are launched but to no avail, the mission fails.

July 2035

E2 is launched to reach the surface of Caliban but it gets destroyed by the electricity bolts before it could hit the surface of the moon.

No further attempts are made to tame Electronicium.

*****

CHAPTER - 5
THE FUTURE

Year 3200 AD Earth. Orca City, Northern Antarctica

Server Control Room

"The engines are working fine and servers are running at 90% capacity" a man wearing a radiation proof suit said over a button sized communication device attached to his wrists.

Another man in the control room heard this. "Okay, you can handover the random key codes for tonight to the night shift officer" . The man in the control room had a badge- Dr. Bhaskar, Head Server Management HRP Ltd. HRP - Hyper reality project , a start-up a few years ago it has now become the biggest and the most powerful company on the Earth.

The early part of the 21st century witnessed the rise of social media and within a few years it became an integral part of everyone's life. By the quarter of the century online existence , appearance and acceptance had become apparently more important than the real world but the real world was facing a different challenge. The rapid industrialisation in the underdeveloped countries in the last quarter of the 21st century brought the fresh wave of global warming.The implications were many, the average temperatures increased by 5 degrees.The higher temperatures caused a sharp dip in fertility which was accentuated by higher levels of education. On the other hand the polar caps completely melted and more than half of the world was consumed by the floods. Venice, the city of canals was now submerged in water, Mumbai the financial capital of India had witnessed the same fate.

This led to a global crisis and entire humanity suffered. But something good came out of it. The world came together to fight this. They made new settlements in the highlands and the once uninhabited poles became the most conducive to life. Over the next few centuries the population continued to drop due to floods, pandemics due to these floods and drop in fertility. Over 60% of civilization was now concentrated around the two poles and a few cities stationed around which mainly acted as transit hubs for ships and planes moving between the two places . Antarctica became the biggest and most prosperous country on the planet.

Almost 50 million people lived in the country. It was governed by a democratically elected government but it was not a party system like that of today's democracy. People would choose their representatives and there was a separate election for every ministerial post including the Chancellor - who was the leader of the country. Arcticland, the second biggest country, had a population of about 30 million and was a multi-party democracy. There were strong ties between the two countries and the rest of the 40 million World population was scattered in small countries all over the globe. The agriculture was mostly indoors owing to the six months of sunset and sunrise in both these countries.

After continuous decline in the world population for over a thousand years the situation became stable in the 10th millennium and it remained stable over the next many years. People did not die of diseases and all natural catastrophes were taken care of. There was no war and all the countries co-existed in peace . Only extreme old age and major accidents resulted in deaths. Automations reached a stage where there was no manual or blue collar job left, even when machines broke down they were repaired by other machines and not by humans. This mandated changes in the work rules. People worked 3 days a week there and most people did not have enough work to occupy their days.

" Video games and VR both were born in the later days of the 2nd millennium, but over the next many years they had taken a backseat since humanity had more pressing concerns to save itself from imminent destruction. In the war against nature humanity came victorious" Professor Staurt Mcgrath was giving the tour of the Virtual reality Museum to school kids.

" So finally, a hundred years ago video games and VR merged. No longer one needed consoles to play a game like it had always been. Gamers no wore special glasses to show them the visuals and gloves or suits which would mimic their actions in the game. Those who were not into gaming used the VRs to get into meditation to soothe their minds" Professor Mcgrath continued " But the biggest game charger was HRP- hyper reality project." He walked up to a device which was the size of a washing machine. "This was the first prototype made by Samarth Narayan 30 years ago. Samarth was from the country of Himkhand, while he was in the final year of his college in the Antarctic National University. All you had to do was take the two receptors" he held two wire-like things coming out from the device " and stick them to your temples and switch on the device. The infrasonic sound waves from the device will take you into deep sleep like trance and you get connected with the server. His project got multi million dollar funding and the subsequent devices became smaller in size and you can choose which server you want to be in. You want to fight the baddies or explore the oceans for sunken treasure. Every experience is as real as it can be.

The children happily came out of the tour, they woke from the deep sleep. The tour was being undertaken in the hyper reality world.

Almost every individual on the planet used the HRP box and it became the biggest corporation on Earth. It had diversified into a lot of other segments. It was possible to order anything from the HRP commerce where you can order stuff by seeing ,touching and testing them in the hyper-reality and get them delivered via drones within minutes.

HRP Corp started universities where you can be a part of the class without being physically present.

The corporation was so big that it launched expeditions to discover the lost treasures of Earth before the great flood. The Net worth of the company had crossed the GDP of Antarctica, it was like the internet of the 21st century being owned by a single company , it could control everything in people's life.

Over the years many other companies tried to venture into it but either their product failed or they were bought out or shut down by HPR corp. Some who managed to succeed did it so late that it was impossible to poach the people who were already hooked on the HRP's product which had created a world of its own.

To change the systems meant to change your entire world, it was like moving to a new planet, so except for some of the occasional enthusiasts no one really tried the other systems. The combined timeshare (the total time spent by all users in Hyper reality) of the competitors of HRP was less than 1%. HRP Corp was there to stay

And every year there was a gaming championship where contestants fought in the hyper reality world and the winner would win a prize money of 10 million coins. Contestants from all over the world trained for years to be a part of this and win the event. An entire parallel industry was booming due to the championship. There were trainers and coaches, nutritionists and psychiatrists who helped the contestants win it.

Surrounded by hundreds of boats around him, he looked at his own ship. .All of his crew was dead,he was stuck in the moment and a cannonball was fired at him and hit him. He hit the mast of the ship , his right hand was blown to smithereens. The enemy wanted him to be captured alive to break the morale of his people; they threw ropes and started into his ship. The captain was metres from him with his men laughing and shouting. He picked up the sword with his left hand and used it to stand up. His long mane had covered his face, and blood was coming from his eyes. He looked up at the captain and laughed " The echoes of immortality, Valhalla is Calling me" . He ran at a speed faster than the reaction time of his enemies and cut down the head of the captain. He fixed a shield in whatever was left of the right hand and danced the dance of death on the sounds of steel and agony, he was Odin himself the God of War. Men kept on coming towards him and he kept on cutting them to pieces , the sea was red and winds had the scent of adrenaline. The falling of heads continued and he started moving the Queen ship. The Lieutenant decided that they can't capture him alive and if he doesn't throw caution to the wind he too will be rolling dead. He ordered his men to aim their arrows and start firing towards him , " our men will also get hit," said one of his subordinates , "Just do it. Do it if you want to live"he shouted ,more in fear than anger, hitting both him and their own men. All his body was covered in arrows and all the enemy men lay dead around. " Why don't you die?" the lieutenant shouted at him. He laughed again and shouted "Valhalla , here I come", he picked a spear and threw it at the lieutenant with the last left breath, the spear pierced the heart of the lieutenant , the two men fell down at the same time.

The contest had come to a close, Jose Martinez was declared the winner securing the maximum points in this year's contest game called The *Valhalla,the heaven of the fallen soldiers*. He emerged from the hyper reality, took a few moments to adjust to the reality of the things around him and let the feeling of winning the biggest tournament on Earth sink in.

He was surrounded by his friends and family members who started to hug and congratulate him.

The spectators too were a part of the Hyper reality to witness the contest and they were awed by the spectacle they had seen.

*****

CHAPTER - 6

THE WORLD WITHIN THE WALLS

The sun was shining and the sun rays were coming through the tarpaulin tent which was half torn, it was past midday and he had a bad hangover from last night of drinking. He looked at his side, there was still some leftover food and whiskey from the previous night's celebration. He was unemployed like most men of his age and did odd jobs for the people who could pay. These jobs often bordered into the territory of illegality, Joe lived a life of carefree abandon.

Last night he had to steal a consignment of bottles of whiskey which were being taken to the castle of the King Janashan. The King was just a namesake title for the man who ruled over only fifty thousand people, the city of Rajgarh; Janaashan was more like a warlord and had recently taken over the city after executing the previous ruler. He was the commander of the army and with the support of his men he had planned this coup and took over the throne.

There was a celebration in the king's castle where his trusted men were invited along with dancers and performers, it was the first year celebration of his coronation. He had also lined up all those who had been opposing him or were suspected to do so so that he and his guests could enjoy torturing them.

The liquor bottles were being brought via the roads from the small godown where it was being stored, the major business of the city was that of liquor. They sold or traded it with the nearby cities for the goods produced by them. The citizens got the low quality liquor, the best ones were sold outside the cities or were reserved for the powerful people of the city.

Joe had laid out an ambush, he stopped the carriage carrying the booze by breaking the sewer line which was flowing under the main street. The horse carriage had to take a detour and use one of the bylanes. It was always dark in the bylanes, as there were hardly any street lights. The letters " In Duty of the King" had been painted in bold on the van , no one would try to attack a vehicle like that.

Van had a driver, a coolie and 2 guards in it.

Suddenly crackers started bursting near the horse, and it got agitated. The coolie got down and tried to placate it but he wasn't able to. One of the guards also came down to help him. From the shadows came two darts which hit the guard and the collie and they fell down unconscious.

The driver shouted to the other guard, " we are being ambushed, both the men have fallen down"

The other guard remained inside and said" Let the horse calm down and we will move ahead. It is better to remain inside, the next checkpoint is close by"

He had drawn out his sword, guns were not known in this part of the world.

He saw a soldier running towards them. " I heard some bursting of crackers and the noise of the horse. I was on patrol so came running to see if everything is fine"

"It seems we have been ambushed" , the driver said pointing to the guard and collie who were lying unconscious.

" These thugs are becoming bolder everyday" said the soldier

" We are waiting for the horse to calm down so we can start moving," the guard inside said.

The horse calmed down, the new soldier asked them " Let me in, I will get down at the checkpost"

The guard opened the door of the carriage and was about to let him in but the new soldier sprayed a liquid at him and he fell down. The soldier threw the guard out of the carriage. The soldier put a sword on the neck of the driver "get down and run away" . The soldier was Joe. He looked at the shirt that he was wearing, "stolen uniforms always come in handy"

He took the carriage to a dilapidated house where some men were waiting, they emptied the entire stock and burnt the carriage and took away the horse.

Joe took his payment from the leader of these men and went away doing a small salute. He went away and smiled, he had tucked away a bottle inside his clothes " Bonus of the honest work of the night"

Later in the night something bigger was happening in the castle. The King was infuriated on knowing that the finest liquor has been stolen and he will have to do with the ordinary liquor. He asked the guards and the commander in charge of the night patrol to stand along with the enemies of the King. "You will be met with the harshest of punishment for ruining my party" he growled at them with wrath in his eyes.

The party started and the guests started enjoying themselves, there were skimpily clad dance girls pouring out drinks, some men played with their bodies. The guests were given bow and arrows and in front of them a curtain was raised.

The King announced, "It is time for some games my friends, here are the men and women who have dared to rise against their Lord. They are condemned to the most painful death" All these supposed sinners, twenty in number, were painted like a target and tied on poles. The heart was the bulls eye , carrying maximum points followed by the head.

The guests gleefully started shooting arrows, some of them hit the bodies, many others missed. One man noted the points. Those who were hit tried to scream but they could not, their mouths were tied up.

The bows were loaded again and released, but before they could hit the curtain fell down and their arrows were stopped by the heavy curtain.

"Who the fuck is managing the event today? Bring him to me" , the King shouted at the top of his voice.

The head servant ran up to him and other servants were trying to lift the curtains back up but the rope had been cut down and they were not able to open the curtains.

" You fool, you are ruining this evening" and he took out his sword to cut the throat of the head servant, who was weeping and was begging for mercy with his hands folded.

The sword came down with a great force but before it could reach the neck, the hand stopped.

Janaashan was hit by a metal boomerang on his wrist and he could hear the bone cracking, he dropped the sword and grimaced in pain " catch this bastard"

All his soldiers and the guests immediately became alert and started looking around for the intruder. Some of the soldiers covered the king to protect him from any projectile attack and started to take him out of the courtyard to a secure room.

Suddenly there was smoke all around before everyone realised the intruder had put fires to the tapestry and this fire was spreading around the castle. The intruder came from behind the pillars and started knocking down the soldiers using fire and smoke as cover. There was commotion all around and using this he freed the prisoners, who made a dash outside the castle and they picked up the weapons of the soldiers who had fallen.

They started cutting their way, some got killed in this but fifteen of them reached the gates. The intruder kept on killing the soldiers while remaining in cover of the commotion and smoke and overpowered the guard and opened the gates and ran out.

By morning the news spread like wildfire in the city. Janaashan asked his men to find the perpetrator of the crime. They started rounding up all the people who had been involved in any criminal activity in the past , the hunt for the escapees was also on and heavy rewards were declared on them.

Joe took a sip from the bottle to help him get to senses. He was taking a bite of the leftover bread when he saw four men standing outside his tent.They caught hold of him " Time for buggers like you is up", they tied his hand from behind and took him with them to the market square.

These men were part of the secret police which was scattered all around the city and would spy on the citizens.

There was a huge gathering and many other folks like him were tied up on a raised wooden platform.

The Commander in Chief of the King's army was at a distance standing on a pedestal looking at all this. The King did not come because of his injury and he thought it was dangerous to go out in the presence of such a big crowd after last night's incident.

The Commander in Chief addressed the crowd" See this is what happens to those who try to betray our Lord. Witness these executions and remember it if any such thought of betrayal comes to your mind".

Joe was captured because while he was coming back home past midnight one of the spies saw him drinking the expensive liquor on his way home. It was unusual to remain outside after midnight and Joe had a history of antisocial behaviour. He was picked up along with all those with similar background and were outside last night.

Walking back he remembered his earliest memory, it was of some men chasing him and his father was screaming at a distance, he did not remember after that. The world within the walls was all he had known. But he suffered from a condition, he would often forget recent incidents and his memory about most of his past was hazy. He thought it is due to alcohol or may be due to the beatings that he would get as a part of his job.

He reached the gallows, a noose was put around his neck. " So it's goodbye then, it all ends today" said the man next to him. " Not today" Joe whispered

The hangman pulled the lever and the platform they were standing on opened up and the bodies started hanging by the neck and went under the platform. Joe had dislocated his thumb to loosen the rope from which his hands were tied, and then he opened the noose and came on the ground. The man next to him had died by this time, he closed his eyes " Hope you get a better life next time."

Two soldiers came after a few minutes to remove the bodies and they saw one of the nooses was empty. They looked at each other and knew it's better to keep mum or they will be the next to face the hanging. Joe had slipped in the crowd.

The other dead bodies were burnt except for this man, his body was paraded throughout the city. He was declared as the spy of another city kingdom, Ashrafinagar and a board with traitor written on it was hung over him and supposedly the one who had helped the escape of the prisoners. The news of the escape of the prisoners from the castle has spread in the city, some of the residents were hopeful that king Janaashan would be soon overthrown. Their lives were always miserable but last year was even more so. After knowing the one who had helped the prisoner to escape was caught and killed they were disheartened.

But they did not know that this was just a ruse. The advisor of the King suggested that the news of the incident in the castle could result in rebellion and also suggested a way to counter this. One of the men who was hanged who had no known relatives was portrayed as the spy and his body was paraded.

It had been a week, Joe was in hiding. After running away from the gallows he hid in an unoccupied house. It was at night he heard some noises, outside in the alley. He saw some men dragging a girl who was trying to resist them. The men were holding bottles in their hands, one the man hit the girl and she started to bleed from her lips.

"Today we will feast on you, don't trouble yourself by resisting us" , he said.

The other two men grabbed both her hands , they pinned her to the wall, the first man unbuckled his trouser and went closer to the girl. A soldier was passing near the alley, and the girl shouted" Please help me."

He overlooked and went ahead " I have better things to do than protecting low lives like you."

The man came closer to the girl, she could feel his alcohol stenched breath, she closed her eyes and tears fell down her cheeks. From a distance someone was taking an aim, a stone fired from a slingshot hit the man on his temple. He collapsed immediately.

The other two men took out their knives, " Come out you coward and fight us like a man".

"Just the way you were showing your manhood to this helpless girl?"They saw a figure running on the building, and he jumped over the alley to the other building.

"Who are you? Come out in the open."

A brick came down on one man and he too fell down. The third man let the girl let go and started running away. On his way out of the alley he was hit by a rod on his head . He was about to collapse but he was holding the man who had hit him, it was Joe. The girl came out of the alley, she still had tears in her eyes. "Thank you for saving me"

She tried to walk but she limped, "Let me take you to home" he said

Joe helped her to her home , she stayed about a mile from that place . Both of them did not speak during the walk , they were only worried about the people gazing at them. It was a decent middle income house unlike the slums which covered a large part of the city. He came inside with her and helped her lie down " where is the antiseptic , you have badly hurt yourself"

"It is in the bathroom, it's on the left."

While he was putting antiseptic on her wounds, she said " I wish there were more brave men like you in the city. I wish someone could have helped my parents"

"What happened to them?"

"They worked for the earlier King in his office and continued to work for the new King too. But they were taken away a couple of months ago by the men of the new king on suspicion of treason. Few days later they were killed." She started sobbing again.

" I am so sorry", he did not know what else to say

"What about you? Do you have a family" she asked him

"I had, a long time ago"

"I never asked your name, my name is Tanvi"

" I am Joe"

She cleared the blood and dirt from her face with a towel and tied her hair back.

He had not noticed her till then, " She is beautiful" he said to himself. Her face was brighter than the moon and she had big eyes and dark curly hair. He did not realise that he had been staring into her eyes for a while till she blushed and looked down.

" I am so sorry, but .." he did not have words to say.

"Where do you live?" she asked

" Actually… " he did not want to tell her that he is a homeless and wanted man

She understood that he did not have a place to stay

" I understand that you are going through some tough times. You can stay here for the time being" she said, putting her hand on his hand.

"Are you sure? I don't want to bother you" he got a bit nervous.

"I feel safe around you" she smiled at him

He stayed back at her place, there were some clothes of her father he changed into.

Over the next 3 days Tanvi told Joe many things about her childhood and how she wanted to become a doctor. Joe did not have much to share about his life but he was always happy to hear her stories and help her with her chores.

By the fourth day she had recovered and was able to walk more freely.

" I have stayed quite a long time, I think I should go," Joe said on the fourth evening.

She packed him some food " take this and remember me"

" I will" he went outside the door of her house, she was looking at him and was about to close it, but she stopped and waited for a few seconds and then asked him " what is that one thing you want the most from life?"

" I just want to be close to you"

She held her hands and pulled him inside and closed the door.

They kept on looking at each other for a few seconds, she put her hands behind his neck and pulled him closer and kissed. Time froze.

Chapter - 7

FALLEN IN LOVE

Tanvi took him in the bedroom, and they kissed again. Joe still could not believe that this was happening and started to kiss her passionately, " slowly" she said and pointed towards the bed.

He lifted her in his arms and got her on bed. They helped each other get undressed and made love.

"I have never been so close to anyone, " Tanvi told him.

"Life was such a struggle that I did not even imagine being with someone and to be with you is like a dream. A dream I never want to wake up from. You are the most beautiful thing I have ever seen" Joe hugged her and she hid in his arms.

It was getting dark outside and they fell asleep.

A few blocks away two soldiers were beating an old man who asked for money after they ate from the small eatery that he owned. The passersby did not help the man and he kept on pleading to let him go " How dare you ask money from the soldiers of the King. We shall teach you a lesson that everyone will remember.

Few moments later both of them were lying in dirt after being hit by a man who was wrapped in a shawl and hit them hard with a stick in a single shot. He came with such great speed that no one could notice him and he vanished before anyone could react. The old man thanked God, his wife closed the shop and went away from the scene while the soldiers were still lying in pain.

Tanvi woke up, it was dark and she did not find Joe around him. She got dressed and came out of the bedroom to look for him. Joe was coming into the house.

"Where were you my love?" she asked him

" I had gone out to get some food, did not want to disturb you"

He came closer to him and she wrapped him in his arms and kissed his cheek.

Joe took up a job in the city, security guard for a ration godown, he would some days work in the day shift and on some other days work in the night shift. The next days passed like the most beautiful dream for Joe and Tanvi.

Sightings of the vigilante were seen at various places in the city, the king was trying everything to catch him but no one ever saw his face or knew where he came from.

It had been a month since the day they had met, Tanvi had made Joe's favourite dinner. He came home and saw the dinner table laid out and the room was lit with fragrant candles.

After the dinner they slept in each other's arms.

Suddenly a noise woke him up and he saw some masked men in their house. Two of them were holding Tanvi who was trying to free herself and calling Joe to wake up. Before he could get up he was hit by a rod on his head. " He tried to reach out to Tanvi, "Tanu" was his last word before he became unconscious.

Joe was tied to chains, his hands were stretched and the chains were tied to the pillar of the prison. He was in a large room, which he thought must be in the castle.

" Your trick of dislocating your thumb won't work this time", he saw the King Janaashan walking towards him, everything appeared red to him due to the blood trickling into his eyes.

" One of my men had spotted that you had managed to escape from the gallows so we decided to keep an eye on you. So tell me what is your agenda? Are you a spy of another Kingdom or a rebel who is trying to overthrow me?"

"I don't know what you are talking about. I am just an ordinary man"

"'Ordinary , oh yes you are an ordinary man who thought who would overthrow the ruler of this Land. Do you know how many people I have killed to reach the throne? And you think you can rise up against me all by yourself?"

" Tell me what I want to know, or I will kill your girl" Janaashan said while putting a burning rod on the thigh of Joe. The physical pain of this seemed nothing to the pain of losing the only person he loved " Don't do anything to her, I beg you"

"She is still alive, but she will remain so only if you tell me the truth"

"I am telling you the truth" Joe pleaded

"Keep on beating him till he reveals his secret" Janaashan ordered his men and went out of

His men continued beating Joe.

Few hours later Joe opened his eyes, he was still tied up.

The guard gave him the clothes of Tanvi, they were blood stained, "What Have you done to her, you bastards?" He cried out loud and he tried to break free but he could not.

" Me and my friends just had some fun with her. She is a beauty" the guard grinned.

Joe broke down and started crying.

"She is still alive, used but alive, and now is the last chance for you to speak up" Janaashan came in the room and gave him the last warning " I am counting till three and if you don't tell then I am going to order my men to finish the girl"

" I am a criminal and have been doing petty crimes but I don't know who you are trying to find . I was the one who stole the liquor bottles which were on the way to your party." Joe said while crying

"So you are not the one who entered my castle and helped the prisoners escape?" Janaashan was confused

" I am not, I do petty crimes and I am a drunkard" Joe confessed

"Commander in Chief , bring the coachman who was driving the carriage carrying the liquor that day

The driver came after a few minutes " Is this the man who took away the liquor?"

"It was dark that day, but that man did appear like him" the coachman said

"Yes, I was wearing a uniform which I had stolen a few days ago during another robbery"Joe reminded him

"Yes, he was wearing a soldier's uniform and tricked us and took the van"

"What time was it?" Janaashan asked

"It was about 8 PM , he asked me to get down and run away, I reached the nearest check post and gave them information"

"The attack in the castle took place at approximately 9 Pm" the Commander in Chief said

" You would have come to the castle in the next one hour and you are using this as an alibi" Janaashan grabbed the neck of Joe .

"After that I took the van to the place I had to deliver it to it was on the other side of the city"

"We found the van in the other part of the city" Commander in Chief concurred.

"This is all his trick" the King was still not ready to believe.

" At 9 Pm I was in the bar which is near the slums. You can check with those people. Please let Tanvi go, kill me for my crimes" Joe begged.

"I will kill you, but the girl's life depends on you. You saved her once from those men who were trying to rape her , but alas her dignity has now been taken away by my soldiers" the king mocked him.

" I did not save her. It was God's grace and some unknown man. I was in hiding after I escaped the hanging when I saw that some men were trying to force themselves on a girl. Someone was hitting them using projectiles. I had not got a drink for many days so I thought I would use this to snatch a bottle from one of these men. After two men fell down and the third man was running away I caught hold of him. After some struggle I kicked him in the balls and he fell down and then he hit him on the head, the man fell down and the bottle too. Before I could react it fell down and was broken and by that time Tanvi was in front of me. She thanked me thinking that I was the one who had helped her. I walked her to her home and then we fell in love" Joe told everything that happened.

"And you were often missing from your house and your work?" was the final question of Janaashan

"Tanvi did not like people who drink. So I would slip out to drink. If I don't drink I get strong withdrawal symptoms and blackouts" Joe replied with remorse. He understood that the spies around his house might have correlated his going out and sightings of the vigilante and this has jeopardised the life of his beloved.

Janaashan paused for a few moments, he understood that this man would not put the life of his girlfriend in danger to protect himself. He was disappointed that even after so much effort they have not been able to capture the vigilante.

" He is telling the truth, he is a petty thief and drunkard.... but he has wasted a lot of my time. So kill him by giving him the maximum pain and chop him into pieces and feed it to the dogs." he told his men. " But I want the real vigilante caught immediately, else next will be you" he warned his Commander in Chief.

Janaashan started walking out of the room, he paused the door and turned "Ohhh.. one last thing.. I promised that I will let his girl live, so keeping my promise even to a low life like him I will hold my end of the bargain. Bring his girl."

Joe wanted to see her one last time and prayed to God for her safety. She walked in the room, Joe thanked God and smiled at her through his pain. She was wearing different clothes and there was no blood on her, she was looking as fresh as she was at home and had a smile on her face.

The truth dawned upon him. There were no spies around the house. Tanvi was the spy.

Janaashan tapped on her back, " no more failures now" and went out

"You toyed with my feelings. " Joe shouted in pain. This pain was more than the physical pain. He started getting unconscious and his head fell down. Two soldiers came close to him and raised their swords to cut through him.

Joe raised his head, there was no expression of pain, anger or fear on his face now. In fact there was no expression on his face or his eyes. His eyes had gone blank, the pupil had disappeared.

The soldiers paused, but the Commander in Chief shouted at them" Just get done with it" before they could raise the sword an explosive laden arrow hit the chain and Joe's right hand got free. He grabbed the sword of one soldier and slashed the throat of both of them in a single motion.

"The Vigilante is here", another soldier shouted. The Vigilante had disguised himself as a soldier. Joe broke the other chain using the sword and started moving ahead.Half of the soldiers attacked him and the other half of them went towards the vigilante , meanwhile Commander in Chief sounded the alarm and a swarm of soldiers started to rush inside.

*****

CHAPTER - 8
REVEALED

The Vigilante used his bow and arrows and other projectiles to stop the soldiers. He was using pillars to shield himself while shooting at the soldiers. But Joe was heading straight at them , his eyes still blank. No was able to touch him and even if many soldiers attacked him at once he was able to fend off their attack with extreme swiftness. Even when multiple arrows were shot at him he was able to dodge them or cut them using the sword , it seemed as if he could predict what would be the next move of his enemy and would react before that . He was moving faster than the wind. Tanvi had run away seeing the massacre in the room.

In a matter of a few minutes all the soldiers were dead or maimed. Janaashan got to know of this when the Commander in Chief ran up to him " My Lord, the two of them are cutting down our men like grass"

"What? Who two?" Janaashan was furious

"Joe and the other person seem to be the vigilante, he broke the chains of Joe." The Commander in Chief told him.

"Your incompetent men can't handle two men at once and you tell me you will defeat armies of other cities. Useless " Janaashan shouted back at him.

" My Lord , you know how sneaky that vigilante is and this guy Joe, it seems that…. he is possessed. He is able to handle dozens of men all by himself and no one can even come near him", there was fear in his voice.

" This opportunity has presented itself, kill them both. Burn down the entire block of the castle if that is needed. I want both of them dead and don't show your face if you fail and send my personal body guards here immediately."

Explosives were laid out in the southern part of the castle where the fighting took place. There was a huge blast and the walls shook. The ceiling started to come down, the soldiers tried to run out but were unable to save themselves from the falling debris. The vigilante followed Joe's lead and they were able to come out in the open courtyard of the castle. A few soldiers who chased them were killed by the vigilante.

After coming out Joe's legs started trembling and his eyes became normal and he was about to fall down but the vigilante caught hold of him. "Don't worry. I am here my friend". He tied Joe to his back using the cloth which had covered his face and he took out suction cups from his pocket and climbed up the wall of the castle.

Next day Joe woke up and saw bandages all over him.. The Vigilante was sitting close to him and gave him a bowl of soup as soon as he got up. "We are safe now, this place is outside the city walls' '. It was a wooden house and by judging the sounds of birds he was sure that this is the jungle beyond the city boundaries.

He looked at the face of the man who had rescued him, he seemed familiar but he could not recall but before he could ask the man himself told him " Remember me? Bodhi, Bodhisattva, your partner and friend. "

Joe seemed to remember now, he had known this person but the memory seemed hazy. " You have lost your memory, you were attacked during your meditation. This is the same reason why you had blackouts."

"Did you know everything that was happening around me?" Joe asked

"Yes" he replied without any emotion

"Yet you did nothing to stop it?" Joe was a bit angry.

"I have been searching for you for the last 15 months. We were meditating in the forest near the Gurukul and it was the final stage of your training where you could go into your past lives, and in that moment you were hit on the head by one of us and it scrambled your brain. I tried to take you away with me but you fell down in a river. I tracked down the entire path of the river, the jungles, villages and cities. I was not ready to give up on you"

Joe held Bodhi's hands and put them on his eyes as a gesture to thank him . He remembered now, he woke up one day in the city with tattered clothes not remembering anything. He was standing in the middle of the road when a man said" Step aside Joe". He thought his name was Joe, later he took the life of a thief and smuggler and the blackouts and the jumbled up memories made him a drunkard.

"Manav, that is what my name is" he remembered it now

He was happy ," I remember now. I was a student at the Gurukul."

"Yes, you were " Bodhi confirmed

"But why did you not tell me all this so far?" Manav AKA Joe asked

"I was looking around for you for many years, I reached this city a month back and spotted you. I realised you had fallen into a life of crime and drinking and you remembered nothing of your past. I was waiting for the right time to tell you otherwise you would have not believed me and during this time whenever I encountered injustice I fought against it."

Manav remembered the life he had been living" But why did you not save me when I was caught by the King or even before that when I was about to be hanged ."

" I wanted to know if you are still worthy because the life that awaits us Joe could not survive that."

"Worthy?? What does that mean?" Manav became slightly angry.

" We two were the most powerful warriors of the Gurukul. I had my Ninja skills, and you had mastered a siddhi, a superpower."

"What superpower?" Manav was puzzled.

"You don't remember how you fought the soldiers?" Bodhi asked.

" It is hazy , I remember fighting them but I don't know how I could. It all seemed like a dance in a dream" Manav told him.

" You have the power to view the present and the immediate future and hence during a fight no one can touch you because you know the next move of your opponents. Due to the injury on your head and your immoral life your power was lost but yesterday you got it back because of the extreme conflicting feelings that got generated in you. The happiness to see your girl alive and the pain of her betrayal. Such strong opposing feelings are like electricity and this triggered your superpower when you were face to face with death."

" And once you saw that you broke the chain of my right hand" Manav continued Bodhi's sentence .

"Yes, because I knew, the rest you will manage on your own" Bodhi patted his shoulder.

" She at least gave me something worthwhile," Manav said with dejection.

"I hope you are not planning to go back to her?" Bodhi asked

"Oh no, I am done with love." Manav smiled at him.

"Good for you and good for us" Bodhi smiled back

" How is our Gurukul, Bodhi?" Manav asked him

"It is nothing but ruins, we were attacked by people from outside and inside and everything was destroyed. Pradhanacharya Tatva lost his life and so did most others.... You take rest and recover. We have a long journey to complete."

Manav was still tired, he went to sleep and Bodhi stayed on the lookout for any possible danger.

— Manav —

Manav was the son of a priest who lived in a city where an evil tyrant ruler had banished religion, which was the case in many other kingdoms too. Most of these Kings asked their subjects to worship them as their God or to follow the religious belief which they had. Any deviation often resulted in the death of non obeying subjects and their families. One such massacre had happened in the city where Manav was born.

On the occasion of Holi, the community of the priests and those who still followed the Hindu tradition had gathered in the house of Manav to celebrate the festival, which was outlawed by the King Butshikhan.

The family members were putting colours to each other , Manav's mother had made gujiya and thandai for all of them in the spirit of old traditions. The Kids were splashing colours over each other. There was a knock on the door, "Must be other guests, I will go and bring them," Manav's mother said to the guests, and as soon as she opened the door she was hit by a baton and fell down with a scream. " Run it's army of the Butshikhan" shouted one of the guests. Everyone started to run around. The officer asked the soldiers to kill all of them.

The soldiers took aim using their cross bows and started shooting all those who were in their vision . All were soon dead.

"Search for others and kill them. Destroy any idols or religious artefacts that you may find. These are infidels who chose to not worship our King, there should be no mercy" the officer ordered them.

It was a two storeyed house, the soldiers started spreading around and looking for those who were hidden. They were taken out of the hiding and hacked to death. The religious books were burnt, one of the priests tried to save the idol from being destroyed by covering it. The soldier killed the priest and then went ahead to destroy the idol. The holi was red, the house was covered in blood. Manav's father took him in his arms and went outside using a hidden door. He gave him a thing like a compass and a book. " Son, follow this device for directions, there are people who will protect you and give this book to them. Now run away my son. Don't look back."

The compass and God's protection helped him to reach the Gurukul. Manav was eight when he reached the Gurukul . He was raised by the teachers of the Gurukul where he learnt from them and trained to be a warrior.

He was now about twenty five years old standing at 5'10 athletic build, with deep eyes and a thick brow.

—Bodhi—

Faraway on a secluded island of the Indian Ocean, a facility was being made for experimenting on humans and animals. The children were given sometimes voluntarily by their poor parents unable to afford food or stolen away by professionals who supplied kids to this lab. The experiments were of different kinds, sometimes trying to look for cure of genetic diseases and some other times these were to create humans with extraordinary powers. They more often than not resulted in the death or disablement of these kids, who were generally thrown into the sea to die.

One such disabled kid had somehow managed to survive and had reached the shore, he was found begging by some of the students of the Gurukul who was on the task to find a rare herb, the boy had no name, they named him on the herb they were trying to find, Bodhisattva.

After bringing him to Gurukul the *Vaidya*, doctor, looked into his condition, he realised he was suffering from chemical poisoning which had resulted in his physical deformities. He was treated with medicines and yoga. Soon the boy started to recover, the experiments had resulted in the side effects and once they were removed the boy became extremely strong due to the intended effect of the research on him.

Bodhi was two years younger to Manav . He was 6'3, thin but extremely strong and swift, he could stop a raging bull with his hands or chase a panther. This combined with his skill of stealth warfare made him an unstoppable force.

*****

Chapter - 9
THE QUEST BEGINS

Manav was able to recover well enough to be able to travel in the next four days. Herbal medicines given to him by Bodhi and meditation helped in the quick recovery.

"So where are we headed to? Manav asked Boddhi.

"After we were attacked the Gurukul was destroyed. Most of the people were killed. Pradhanacharya had talked about the great purpose but never said what it really is. Whenever we asked he told us that we were not ready yet. We need to find out what it was and who were those people who attacked us?" Bodhi told him.

"It was a day prior to the attack that he said that tomorrow he would tell us what it is, he told me that" Manav remembered.

"Someone would have got this information, and betrayed us. They did not want us to know what was it that Pradhanacharya wanted to tell us" Bodhi guessed

" Or it may be something else. Do you remember that he was working on some documents?" Manav asked Bodhi

"Yes, I saw that there were a lot of maps and blueprints of some devices , and lots of drawings with him. He was being helped by Acharya Prajwal who was the master of the sciences" Bodhi

"Bodhi, What happened to Achara Prajwal?"

"He too passed away in the attack?" Bodhi told him remembering the sad day

"And those documents and drawings?" Manav was trying to reach to the reasons behind the conspiracy

"The building was put on fire. I went there after a few days. There was no trace of it" Bodhi told him the after events

" We learned in our class that the papers which were used in the Gurukul for important documents were coated with Alum, making them more fire resistant" Manav informed him

"Yes Manav, absolutely. I did not think of it then due to the grief but now, I can see things clearly. There were not even traces of burnt paper. The documents would have been stolen. So that was the motive of the attack. To take away all those documents."

" and the timing of it , just a day before we were to be told of the mission meant that the blueprints must have got completed" Manav pointed out the timing of the attack.

" There was one person apart from the two Acharyas who knew about this. Assistant to Acharya Prajwal, Ashmit. I did not see his dead body after the attack, I thought he might have run away. But now it seems that he was the one who sold us out" Bodhi was certain of it.

" We must track him down. It could be the first clue" they both said in unison.

"I did not know much about his background, but there are still some people of the Gurukul who are alive. After the attack some people managed to escape. We should start by first reaching out to them and see if they might know something about Prajwal" Bodhi suggested

"Yes, that seems the right plan" Manav agreed

"But one thing before we start this journey"

"We are now in the open world, it will be much more dangerous than the city and you are still not fully fit and in complete control of your power. So be cautious" Bodhi warned him

" I will need to practise and meditate to be in control of my power. Hopefully it will be fine before we start the revenge against those attackers. Anyways I don't need to fear, the master of stealth and mystic warfare is with me. The King of Rajgarh was lucky, he did not see the potential of your true powers" Manav put his arms on the shoulders of Bodhi.

Bodhi took out the map of the region, he had marked the routes he had taken while trying to look for Manav. He had marked other information too about the places he had visited. He pointed out to a village, one of the record keepers of the Gurukul lives in this place. I saw him while I was looking around for you but did not establish any contact with him then."

"Let's go there and see if he can help us" Manav said with enthusiasm

They gathered some stuff needed for the journey. Bodhi managed to get hold of two horses "This will ease our journey" and they went to the village called Athila. It was in the middle of a Jungle, with a very small population. It was under the jurisdiction of the City state of Masaan. Masaan was not visited by Bodhi earlier as it was some distance away from the river hence the possibility of Manav being there was less.

They had reached near the end of the jungle, it had been a journey of more than a day and it was already getting dark. The village could be seen from a distance because of the fire torches which were lit.

"It is a small village , barely 100 odd residents. We can easily find our guy, ask him what he knows and be away by tomorrow morning."

When they came closer to the village, They got down from the horses and started walking as the ground was slippery due to the rain . After walking some distance they saw a man who was carrying some wood on his back on the path leading to the village.

"Chacha, what are you doing so late outside the village and so close to the jungle?" Manav asked him.

The old man got startled seeing the two old strangers with him and dropped the wood he was carrying, Manav picked it up " Don't worry we are not here to trouble you, we are only looking for an old acquaintance who lives in this village."

"Oh.. thank God. I was afraid that it might be the bandits, "the old man said in his crumbling voice.

"Don't worry, as long as we are here no bandits will trouble you" Bodhi assured him." Could you help us to find our friend?"

"Certainly I will help you to do that. Can you tell me the name of your friend?" he asked

"Shahid, his name is Shahid. Do you know him?" Bodhi asked him

"Oh yes, I know him very well. Let me take you to him" the old man told them.

The three of them started walking towards the village." Do you have families?" the old man asked them

"We two friends are each other's families" Manav smiled at the old Man."What about you Chacha?"

"I have a wife who lives in the village with me."

They kept on talking about the life of each other, for sometime. Then the old man told them about the history of the place. The times when there was a tree at the centre of the village which would glow at night and there were mythical creatures who would come to rest on the tree. The stories engrossed both Manav and Bodhi.

The sun was about to rise, they were still walking on their way to the village. Manav was getting tired, but the stories seemed so interesting he did not disturb the old man. Night fell again. They still kept on walking, the village still seemed near to them.

Manav, who was no longer used to the rigour of intensive training, fell down due to thirst and fatigue. Bodhi was about to pick him up and wake him" The old man said, " Your friend is tired, let him sleep. You and I would continue on the journey to the village."

Both Manav and Bodhi were still at the same point where they had met the old man. There was no one with them, Manav was asleep and Bodhi was standing and seemed to be talking to himself.

Dehydration was setting in for both, it was a matter of time that even Bodhi would give in to the exhaustion.

The first rays of the sun had fallen on Manav and Bodhi, the stories of Old man were still continuing"

People say before the great war this place was a big city where they used to make big vehicles of steel which used to run on oil. Thousands of people used to work in this place. Could you imagine that glory, but today this is just a small village with a handful of people living in it."

Whenever a new kid was inducted in Gurukul their skills and the latent abilities were gauged in the first few years of their education. Over the later years their primary skill was developed to the maximum. The training duration could be anything from 10 to 20 years, this was for the Acharyas to determine. The training would complete only when the Acharya would feel that his student has reached his potential, and then after the completion of the training they were assigned various roles.

These roles would include jobs in the Gurukul like teaching, administration, security or some of them become members of the fighting units such as the reconnaissance, retrieval and attack teams which would carry out various missions in the outside world while keeping their identities secret. At the end stage of the training the students identified for these teams would intern and work with the other members so that they are ready if any important mission arises.

Even the members of the fighting units had their unique strengths and abilities, just like Manav and Bodhi had. In the last days of the Gurukul, before it was ransacked and destroyed, the members of the fighting units were very few and Manav and Bodhi were the strongest fighters despite the fact they were still in the last stage of their training.

Manav's training had been a lot focussed on channelling inner strength and connecting to elements. This over the years had helped him develop the siddhi of viewing the incoming attack of the enemy, but due to sudden attack on him and his time in the city of Rajgarh his control on his power had greatly reduced.

The day Gurukul was attacked Manav was doing his meditation, every morning whenever the first ray of sun would touch him he would meditate and do Surya namaskar. This connected him with the cosmic energy, and now his body was so used to it that the first sun ray would act as a charger for him.

The sun rays fell on Manav and this was time for the Surya Namaskar and to do that he had to get up. Now with his partial memory back his body went back into the old routine and he woke up and did Surya Namaskar even while being only partially conscious, while doing it he remembered the time he was attacked while doing meditation and a burst of energy happened within him. He started shouting" Save the Gurukul, save the Gurukul Bodhi."

Bodhi even in his trance noticed that they had been for so many years and whenever either was in trouble the other one was always around to help them except for the time when Manav was attacked and Bodhi could not save him.

This made him alert and he came in his Ninja mode, ready to fight but he noticed there was no one around and both of them had been standing at the same spot for many hours.

His instincts kicked in and he came out of the hypnosis, meanwhile the power of Manav made him see the immediate move of his enemy and the move was there was no one around, he too came out of the trance " What was this?" He asked Bodhi in a state of shock " Did you also remember talking to an old man while we were on our way to this village" he asked him back "Yes I did , I think someone or something was playing tricks with us."

They spotted the old man at a distance, sitting under a tree and smiling at them. "There he is, he tried to kill us by putting us in this spell" Bodhi was about to throw a boomerang at the old man but Manav stopped him before he released it.

The old man got up" You two are splendid, no one has ever been able to break free of my spell before today."

Bodhi confronted the old man" and then they would die in the trance itself"

"Sometimes they do," Old replied plainly.

Manav was more in control of his anger than Bodhi. "So you wanted to kill us too. But why?"

"My name is Sudama and I live in this village…" the old man started

Bodhi stopped him" he is starting his stories again and now he will hypnotise and kill us. We can't take chances "

"Yes, we can't. Don't go near him and don't look at him" Manav asked Bodhi

The old man continued"It has been almost a year now since this village was pillaged by the army of another kingdom who were attacking the city. They needed food for the men and animals to carry the arms. They used the village for their supplies. The granary was run dry by them, the cattle were slaughtered and the horses taken away.

Used to run a small school in the village for the kids. I was out of the village for a few days at that time. I was collecting medicines in the mountains to treat the diseases which villagers often contracted . When the army looted the village, some of the kids from my school tried to stop them.`` He seemed to choke while talking and his eyes were getting wet.

Manav and Bodhi were still cautious and not looking directly at the man.

The hands of those boys were chopped off, they gave them punishment worse than death. After the war was over and the enemy were defeated the city celebrated but this poor village suffered with pangs of hunger and many died. Those kids whose hands were chopped some of them were orphans and there was no one to take care of them.

It was that day I decided that I will never let any stranger with arms ever enter my village.

I had the power to hypnotise and put people in trance which I had learnt during my younger days and have used it to heal people suffering from mental trauma or illness , but after the tragedy my village went through I decided to use them to safeguard the village.

Bodhi went on his knees and did a pranam to the old man " Please forgive me for trying to use force on you" . Manav also bowed down to the Old man. " My sons you are honourable men bestowed with great power and mental fortitude else it was not possible to break free from the spell. There must be a great purpose that drives you here."

"We were students of the Gurukul which is situated at the heights of the mountains. It was attacked by some unknown men when we were about to start a mission that our Guru, our Pradhanacharya was about to tell us. We are trying to find the attackers and know what they were after. I saw the Gurukul's record keeper entering this village with wood and his cattle, I understood that he lives here. We want to meet him if he knows about the person who we suspect could have been the snitch" Bodhi told the old man everything

"You boys lost your Guru and your Gurukul, I lost my students. I will help you to meet this person. He lives here and I will give you something else too." He wrote down a mantra using a special ink and gave it to them. "Keep this mantra with you and no one will be ever able to mind control you".

He then gave the two boys some food and water and took them to the record keeper Shahid.

Shahid was surprised to see the two boys "Cannot believe my eyes on seeing people from Gurukul… so happy to see you two. At first I thought I was daydreaming but it is really you two."

"We are happy to see you too old friend" Manav said

" What brings you here? And how did you know I was living in this village?" Shahid asked them.

" I was searching for Manav for a long time and I came across this village a few days after the incident at gurukul and I saw you" Bodhi told him.

"We are trying to figure out about the events that took place on the fateful morning and find the people behind it" Manav told him.

"And we think that the assistant of Acharya Prajwal might be behind it. Since he had an idea of what was being built by the Acharya, he might have sold the secret to someone. It is a long shot but it seems the only starting point" Bodhi continued.

"So what do you want from me?" Shahid asked them

" You were the record keeper for a very long time, if you remember anything about this man, where he lived. Any records you might remember about him?" Bodhi asked him

"The attack at the Gurukul was such a trauma, I have forgotten a lot of things which were even day to day things. Details about his past before coming to Gurukul… yes I might have seen that but honestly I don't recall a single thing about this guy…. I am so sorry. I can't help you guys. I really want those who killed my friends to be punished. But I can't help you." Shahid sat down disappointed and buried his face in his palm.

Manav went to him and put his hand on Shahid's shoulder " Don't worry Sir. We will think of something else to find the culprits. But we won't stop till we find them."

"I pray to god for your success" Shahid wished them.

So we will take your leave now" Bodhi said and the two friends started walking towards the door.

"Wait, you guys have travelled a long distance. Rest here today and you can leave tomorrow .

morning. I really insist" Shahid requested them.

Manav and Bodhi looked at each other and nodded " We anyways don't have any plan now. No harm in staying here for a day."

" We will be your guests for a day and we will be away tomorrow at sunrise" Manav smiled at Shahid.

Both of them stayed there, after a while they went to the school, the one which the old man had talked about. The old man was there and there were some kids of various ages.

It was lunchtime and the old man had got some food for them. It was plain and simple porridge made of cereal. The kids were happily having the food, and old man started feeding one boy who wasn' having hands. Manav came and took some porridge and took it to the other boy who wasn't having hands. " What is your name?" Manav asked the boy.

"Sir, I am Ajay", the boy smiled at Manav.

"Can I help you to eat your food" Manav asked him

" Thank you so much" the boy nodded

Manav helped the boy to have his food .

Bodhi was looking at this scene standing a few metres away.

He came to Manav" We will stay here for a few more days"

Manav did not say anything.

Then Bodhi went to Sudama" Sudama ji, we would like to stay here for a few days. I would like to train your students"

Sudama looked at him " This will be a matter of great pleasure and honour"

"I won't let you do this all alone" Manav gave a pat to Bodhi

Over the next few days Bodhi trained the boys on how they can become stronger and fight off attackers. He trained them with basic weapon use. The two boys who had lost their arms he trained them on how they can do their work and even fight by using their legs.

"You have come like a blessing for the boys, especially for Ajay and Prakash, they will no longer depend on others for their day to day things and can live while keeping their heads high."

"Our mission is not going anywhere. The lead has gone cold. We may as well help the world in whatever way that we can" he told the Old man.

"Ohh. why? What happened? Shahid did not know about the man you were looking for?

"He is not able to remember much, he might have read the details but it would have been a long time ago and then there are so many records that he would have come across that it is impossible to remember an information like this which seemed banal" Manav told Sudama.

"Well, then there is nothing to worry about" Sudama looked at him, " I have the solution to your problem."

Manav and Bodhi were puzzled. Sudama explained to them " By using my ability to hypnotise people I can also help them remember things they might have seen or heard a long time ago but have forgotten. I will try this with Shahid and if he ever knew about the person you were looking for he will be able to remember it."

"That is great news" Manav clenched his fist in excitement.

Three of them went to Shahid and told them about the solution. Shahid agreed to try this out. Over the next three days Sudama worked with Shahid to help him remember the details while putting him in a state of hypnosis. "This was such a minor information for him, hence it is hidden deep in his brain and it is taking a lot more time than expected" Sudama informed them.

Meanwhile Bodhi continued to train the boys and Manav helped in the day to day work of the school.

Finally Shahid was able to remember the details, he had seen it in a record which had the details of all the residents of Gurukul "His family lived in a land thousands of miles away from here. The name of that place is Haedong. You will have to cross the ocean which is on the west of the country to get to that place."

"Can you give some more details on how to get there?" Bodhi asked him

" Yes, along with the record the directions to his place were taken since he was from such a far away land."

Shahid took a piece of charcoal and started making a map on a piece of cloth. He pointed to a spot on the islands of the present day Japan "Here it would be . Ashmit was the name he was given, his real name was Ashamura. He had his family there, he had been travelling as a hermit for many years to learn more about the various natural phenomenon and he stumbled upon the Gurukul after years of travel.He looked tattered due to the extensive travel. He was interviewed by the Acharyas here and then was given chores to work on, when he continued to do his duties well he was made a student, later he became an assistant to Acharya Prajwal."

"Yes, I know that he was from some very faraway land like few other students too" Manav said

"But how do we know he told the truth about his hometown?" Bodhi asked the group.

"Most probably he would have, we don't take in strangers especially those from faraway lands easily in Gurukul else it would compromise our security . To check that they are not lying they are given a special medicinal juice during their interview. It was secretly mixed in their water.

The interviews were taken by the most senior faculties of the Gurukul and they would easily catch a lie under the influence of this medicine, since lying will increase their heartbeat and that would cause a reaction turning their skin red."

"Well this solves the problem but the next problem is that it could take us months to reach that place and do we even know that he will be there? Or he is alive." Bodhi asked .

" You did not give up on me my friend and now we won't give up on this mission" Manav looked into the eyes of Bodhi.

"Let's do this" he gave a fist bump to Manav.

——---

They took the piece of cloth which had the map , made a copy of it and marked the locations on their way to this place.

"I know you two are brave and can face any danger But you are going to some uncharted lands. He pointed to a region some 200 Kilometres from the place they were currently at. No one has been to this area and come back. This is called the Achitra Aranya, be extremely careful in this area" the old man Sudama informed them.

Bodhi had been on the sea once during a recon mission a long time ago. Manav had never seen the sea. This was the furthest they were going from the village where their Gurukul was.

*****

CHAPTER - 10
THE QUEST (2)

The two of them continued their journey towards the destination, there were some villages on the way and one walled city. They avoided these to not get involved in any sort of trouble and delay. Few days later they reached the forest about which Sudama had warned them.

It was more beautiful than any other forest they had seen, the trees were much bigger and greener and there were streams of clean water at every few steps, and the rocks were full of shiny crystals. It was drizzling slightly and the sun was about to set, the last setting rays of the sun while falling on the crystals made the forest dance in various colours of light.

"I think the reason why people get lost in this forest is because of its beauty. It is surreal" Manav said to Bodhi. " Prettier than your girl in the city?" Bodhi teased Manav.

" Rubbing my wounds?" Manav looked with a straight face at Bodhi, Bodhi thought that the banter might have angered his friend and he too became serious and was about to apologise but before that Manav started laughing.

There was a large tree with a dense canopy, so they decided to make it their stop for the night. "The forest is an unknown territory so we should make this place our night stop and then start moving at dawn" Bodhi told Manav.

"Yes, and let us forage for some food here, I am starving" Manav replied.

They started looking around for trees with fruits and edible roots, and within a minute Manav exclaimed " Look at this tree and its fruit." The tree had a fruit which looked like a grape but was the size of a jackfruit.

Manav took the fruit, but Bodhi stopped him from eating it. " Just a minute", he took a small piece of it and put some powder on it that he was carrying. He examined the colour change and said" It's good to eat" .

" The testing kit, you still carry it all the time" Manav asked him.

"Yup, absolute must for a recon mission, now let's dig into the fruit." Bodhi replied.

They ate and went to sleep. The forest was shining brightly and a cool breeze was flowing. The breeze seemed to get stronger and stronger and both of them realised that they were flying high over the trees. The nectar of the fruit had some intoxication and that along with the tiresome journey made them fall into a deep sleep and they did not realise what had happened with them.

They looked up, both of them were in the clutches of two giant bat-like animals, one holding each of them. Due to the strong winds they were not able to talk to each other.

The animals were more than 20 feet tall and had a wingspan of more than 30 feet which were webbed like that of bats. Their skin had a bluish tint and they had deep red eyes.

Both the boys were more than 300 feet up in the sky and they understood that this situation means trouble for them and perhaps they will be the dinner of this strange creature. The two creatures kept on flying together but after a few minutes they changed their direction and Manav and Bodhi were separated.

The creature carrying Bodhi kept on going on its way for another few minutes, the topography beneath him changed. He could see a huge nest faraway; he knew this is the time to act, else it could get too late for him. He started swinging his legs front and back and gathered enough momentum to hit the claws of the creature over his shoulder. The force was strong enough that the grip weakened for a fraction of a second and he immediately gave a strong twist to his body, further weakening the grip and getting free from the clutches and he fell down from a great height. While falling he was able to glide and direct his falling body on the top of a tree with dense canopy, he was preparing for the impact of the fall but before he could actually fall off the creature swooped down to catch his prey back. The flight of the creature created a strong blow of air using which Bodhi changed his direction and used a tree branch to swing away some distance and hide in the canopy of a tree.

The creature flew around and started hitting the trees with its claws to shake them and make his prey fall in whichever tree he was hiding. It finally came over the tree which Bodhi was using to cover him, the claws came at great speed and were about to hit the tree but Bodhi leapt out a greater speed towards the creature and he struck the wings of the creature with his sword and grabbed the branch of another tree before falling. The creature let out a loud shriek and blood came out like a jet fountain. It turned back again in anger towards Bodhi. This time Bodhi was standing firmly on the tree branches, the creature came close and Bodhi jumped on its wings and used it as a trampoline to jump higher and stabbed the eye of the creature. He pulled out the sword and did a backflip to land back on the tree top. The creature was too injured to bother about hunting him; it flew away shrieking in pain and leaving a trail of blood on the trees behind it.

Bodhi let out a breath of relief and stayed on the tree top for a few moments to calm himself post this encounter. "Where is Manav, the other creature took him in some other direction. He is still not his old self and I am not sure how he would defend himself". He started looking around from the tree but he could not see much, it was still dark and all he could see were glistening trees all around him. " I should wait here only on the tree top till it gets brighter and then start looking out for him"

So he waited there till he saw a large shadow flying towards him from a distance.

A few minutes ago…

The second creature was carrying away Manav towards its nest. The nest was perched atop a rocky cliff. Manav kept on trying to break free from the clutches of its captor but the harder he tried the creature would hold him tighter. He soon came near the nest, which was made of large leaves and branches. There were bones of other animals that could be seen around the nest, it was obvious if something is not done quickly enough he too will become part of the carcass. As he came closer he could see the hatchlings of this creature in the nest, the two of them were looking at their mother as she was bringing them food "so today you are going to eat a human for dinner?" he said looking at them. Suddenly the speed of the creature increased and it started shrieking loudly, Bodhi saw that a huge snake was climbing up the rocks towards the hatchlings. The snake was much bigger than this creature, it was dark yellow in colour with red stripes. The moonlight was making its skin shine and its eyes were green and glowing. "This is the stuff of nightmares." he spoke to himself

The flying creature tossed Manav away and it fled towards its babies. Manav got air bound but he held the branches of the nest and landed on the cushion of the leaves near the nest. The snake raised its head to devour the hatchlings, but the creature attacked it with its claws. The snake and the creatures fought for a few minutes but the snake was able to grab the feet of the creature with its mouth and it threw it away and its head hit the cliff and it fell down.

Manav was watching this while remaining hidden and was looking for an opportunity to run away from this scene. He was slipping away, he lifted his head and he could see the huge serpent looming over him and the hatchlings, " What would it eat first? Human meat or bird meat?" The snake came down but before it could reach him Manav went into his siddhi state, this time he was lesser in trance than when he had gone into this state the previous time.

Now he could anticipate or rather see the move of the snake in advance. He grabbed a bone which was lying there, it seemed to be a femur bone of a big animal and while avoiding the fangs he put it vertically inside the mouth of the snake. The snake struggled for a minute to get it out of his mouth and while doing this Manav was able to notice that there was a deep scar on the right side of the snake, he pulled out his sword and using his entire strength he stabbed the scar with it and was able to tear through its thick skin. The injured snake got furious and turned around and tried to eat Manav who was standing close to the middle of the snake's body and its head wasn't able to reach him. So the snake tried to coil around him but Manav dodged it by jumping to the other side of the coil. When the snake again tried to attack, Manav got an unexpected help. The giant flying creature came back and attacked the snake by inserting its claw at the point where it was bleeding due to the sword stab. The snake could not bear the pain and tried to break free, the bird tore open the skin and created a bigger wound, the claw came out of the snake skin and the snake immediately crawled away from the scene. The flying creature did not try to pursue it.

Manav was preparing for an attack by the bird but he could anticipate its movement and he snapped out of his siddhi state. The creature instead of attacking him bowed its head in a gesture of admiration of saving its kids. "This is not a mindless creature, it possesses considerable intelligence" he realised.

Manav went ahead and patted its head and the creature seemed happy enough to allow Manav to do it. Manav thought for a few seconds and gently stepped on its wings and then on its neck. He patted it and the creature obliged by taking him on a ride. He started looking around when he heard the shrieks and when he followed the direction of the sound he saw the other creature flying away, he noticed that it was injured and traced the trajectory of its flight to the point where Bodhi was standing with swords in his hands.

Bodhi noticed the large flying figure and also saw a human on it, he was ready to attack on it but when it came closer he saw his friend riding the giant beast. Manav descended down and told the entire incident that had just happened to him.

The beast let out a call, which the two of them could not hear and soon one more flying giant came near to them. They got worried that this was a trap by the creature and got ready in an offensive position and Manav was about to go in his siddhi state but the other creature too came down in a position to let them climb it, Manav signalled Bodhi to go for it. He climbed the beast.

It seemed that the creature Manav was riding on signalled for its friend to come there and help it in carrying the two humans to their destination.

Manav guided the one he was riding and the other one which was carrying Bodhi followed it. First they went back to the tree where they were taking rest and grabbed the stuff they were carrying for the journey and then they flew away towards the ocean. Now even Bodhi got confident in steering his vehicle , Manav gestured him to take the lead and he started navigating their way through the compass being used by Bodhi. The two creatures flew at a great speed soaring above the jungle.

Below them, Manav and Bodhi could see the vast forests. They crossed a huge river which descended into a waterfall. Soon they flew over a hill range and kept on flying till morning, Manav did his Surya Namaskar while still flying. In the sunlight they could clearly see the land below them. The trees seemed like bushes , there was a herd of elephants and some other animals which they had never seen before.

After a couple of more hours they could see the vast blue sea at a distance. The creatures got down a few hundred metres from the sea. " I think that these creatures have never seen the sea, they would not fly beyond this point" Manav said to Bodhi.

"Then it's the two of us to the journey beyond these shores" Bodhi replied.

CHAPTER - 11
QUEST (3)

Bodhi recalled his first recon mission of crossing the waters. Manav remembered the things he had learnt about it. After many attempts they were finally able to build a raft using the woods from the trees near the shore which seemed strong enough to survive the waters. It took them almost the entire afternoon to build the raft and evening was falling so they decided to wait till next day and set sail in the sunlight.

They made a bonfire and ate coconuts from the coconut trees lining the shore. The sky was full of stars. Both of them lay down gazing at the stars. Manav asked Bodhi" When was the last time when you had watched the sky in such peace". Bodhi tried hard to remember, but he could not. " I don't know. Seems like it must have been ages."

"Yup it was, remember the night after the first day training of jungle survival. When both of us got separated from the group and after trying to find others we decided to take a rest. The night sky looked something like this." Manav narrated the incident.

"Yes, now I remember that night. Since then we have gazed at these stars so many times during our teenage years, thinking what lies beyond them, are there any other worlds like ours? " Bodhi had a smile remembering those days he paused and grew solemn and continued, "and now here we are trying to chase a ghost."

They continued talking about their old days and remembered their old friends and fell asleep in the middle of their talks, the next morning they set out for the journey. They took some food and fresh water for the journey and a desalination device they made using bottles to help them last the journey. They had made a map of the route and they decided to take the route which had more islands in the path so they could take breaks for restocking the supplies and to repair or remake the raft.

The point where they were currently at was the shore of Myanmar, the islands would start about 50 kms into the sea, but the island where Ashmit might be was hundreds of km away.

The sea was peaceful, the blue water initially thrilled them. They saw dolphins and many other marine animals on their way, some they could identify from the pictures they had seen and most others were unknown to them. By sunset they were able to reach the first island.

The island had a dense jungle." The night is near, we must tread carefully. We don't know what awaits us in the jungle. Better to remain on the beach." Bodhi warned Manav

"Yes I agree. Will get some coconuts for our meal and water." He picked up a stone and used it as a slingshot to bring down a coconut, it was an easy hit. Manav ran to catch it but before he could it landed on the ground and there was a strong blast which threw him back by a few feet.

" This island is laden with bombs," Bodhi screamed while running towards Manav. " Let us get away from here immediately" Manav screamed back while picking himself up. They immediately rushed towards the raft and started rowing away from the island but even before then could go beyond a hundred metres a heavy net dropped upon them and they saw that metal barriers rising on all sides of them making it impossible for them to run away.

They heard a loud roar in the sky, they looked up thinking it might be another flying beast but it seemed something else. It was a flying vehicle, a drone, which had dropped the net on them and then it dropped a cover to seal them inside the metal cage.

"We are badly trapped, they whispered to each other" Manav activated his siddhi state to predict the next move. He could sense that their cage would be tugged away by a ship but he could not do anything about it.

While they were being towed away, both of them tried to break the metal rods of the cage but whenever they touched it, it gave them a shock so they could do nothing but wait.

Few minutes later they saw another island. This island had large buildings on it.

Finally they saw some humans, four men who seemed like guards came to them. They were completely covered in light blue armour and were wearing helmets which had glass visors which were a darker shade of blue and their faces were not visible and they were carrying guns. The drones, the guns, all this they had learnt about in their subject about lost technologies but here they were seeing all of it for the first time.

One of the guards took out a remote and pressed a button, the metal bars got lowered on one side of the cage. " Come out and don't try anything funny, otherwise you will be dead even before you know it."

They came out silently and the guards led them to the island. One was walking ahead of them and the other three were walking behind with guns pointed to Manav and Bodhi. Bodhi gestured to Manav by slightly raising his head up to ask him to get in his siddhi state. Manav did that but came back to his normal state within a few seconds, he foresaw the action of his adversaries, the guards. He saw that as soon as he turned around to attack the guards they started shooting at both of them. Since Manav foresaw the move he could avoid the trajectory of their bullets but Bodhi despite his agility would not be able to dodge the bullets due to the small distance they are being fired from and his first time encountering a gunned opponent.

Manav slightly shook his head indicating to his friend that this was not a good time to go on offensive, Bodhi trusted the judgement of his friend so they continued to go along with the guards.

They came near a big gate, which opened when they came near when the guard leading them looked at a small device which emitted light on him.

Inside the compound they could see many other guards, some of them had a different shade of dress and were without armour. They did not see prisoners since it was night time. They were brought to a jail cell, the doors opened when the guard swiped a card on a reading device placed on the wall of the gate and both the friends were put inside it. The guard pressed a button, the gate closed. The stuff that both of them were carrying was taken away from them.

Finally the guard spoke, you will stay here for a couple of days after that the judge will decide on your case and you will get the appropriate punishment for illegally entering the country of AkhandaDweep Rashtra.

" It seems we have entered a new world. All these things are from the age before the great war" Manav expressed his disbelief. Bodhi too was in a similar state " Yes, it seems we are moving from one universe to another. Seeing strange creatures to encountering things which were told to us no longer existed"

"So what do you think we should do next?"he said after pausing for half a minute.

"I think we should wait and look for the right opportunity to get out. It will not be easy to fight their guns. The speed of a bullet makes it impossible to dodge, so we have to be careful."

They were given stale food to eat the next morning, it was given to them through a slot in the door.

After some time the gate was opened and they were taken to another building within the same compound. There was a huge line of men and women who were tied with chains and guards overlooking them. After waiting for some time, they were pushed inside. A judge was sitting on a high chair. One guard narrated the event of how they were caught, he was the same guard who had captured and brought them inside the prison.

"To be sentenced to imprisonment for five years with hard labour for the crime of illegally entering the country, next case" the judge pronounced.

"Well this won't be the first time that I have been pronounced guilty of a crime," Manav joked while they were being carried back to the prison "and won't be the first time when you will make a jail break" Bodhi continued the joke.

"You two will be soon assigned to a taskmaster, so go and enjoy your days with the hospitality of our prison" they were informed by a guard while being pushed inside.

Over the next few days, they were supposed to do hard labour along with other prisoners. They were sent to a factory which was adjoining the prison compound and along with over a hundred prisoners they were assigned different tasks in the factory where various equipment were being manufactured.

Both of them were assigned on two different assembly lines. The supervisor gave them a demo of how to do their job, the machine parts kept on coming on the line and they had to fix one part to it and it would move ahead to the next bay.

They were not informed what it was they were working on, both of them tried to ask from their fellow workers about it but they got the same response " just do as you told and don't think too much". The taskmaster was the one who overlooked the entire factory floor. Anyone slacking off or talking to the other prisoners would get greeted by the whiplash of the taskmaster.

Over the next two days they tried to understand the work and due to their years of training they started doing their work with more efficiency than their fellow workers. Manav had an old man who would find it difficult to complete his work so Manav helped him while Bodhi helped another man who was sick in his team. This helped them to gain the trust of their fellow workers very quickly and the two of them were accepted among the group of the prisoners.

During lunch hours when they again got stale bread Manav and Bodhi sat along with the old man.

"How long have you been here?"Manav asked him

"It has been more than five years" he told them

"And why did they imprison you?" Bodhi asked him

"My name is Brahmbhatt. I was a minister in the cabinet of this country before the coup. After the coup a rebel group took over the Government and established a dictatorship. Most of the ministers and government officials were killed. Some like me who did not seem to possess a threat were put behind bars."

"What about the two of you?" the old man asked them

"We were on our journey to a faraway land, we decided to take a break on the island before continuing ahead into the sea. But we were held captive by the guards. " Manav told him.

"We were not even given a fair trial and were sentenced to imprisonment with hard labour" Bodhi completed the story.

"Our country has remained hidden from the outside world, and we have done our best to protect the secrecy. Although before the coup the trial used to be fair and only the suspected spies or pirates were prosecuted. Innocent travellers were not harmed. But all this has changed. The current Government needs more labour to build weapons and buildings so they capture anyone they can to ensure the supply of labour." the old man grew sad.

"And what happens after they complete the sentence?" Manav asked him

"Well, no one ever has. They either die due to the hard labour or the sentence gets extended on any flimsy ground" old man looked straight in his eyes

" Our mission is important and whatever happens we need to come out of this shithole.We are new to this world, if you help us we promise we will help you to escape" Manav requested the old man.

"My dear friends, you cannot escape or fight against so many guards," Brahmbhatt told them.

" We are trained warriors and we have fought many soldiers at once. If you can help us more about the prison, the country and how to protect from bullets we can defeat the entire army" Manav tried to convince the old man, but he just smiled and patted Manav's shoulder and walked away dismissing the talk as the irrationality of youth.

Bodhi gestured at Manav to not talk too much, he was sceptical as the old man may not be who is telling himself to be or may rat them out. Manav later told him it is okay, what worst can happen to them anyways.

Later that day, when prisoners were going back home they saw a major commotion. A gang war had broken out among the prisoners, one prisoner informed them. " The guards will be coming here soon to stop them?" Bodhi asked him. " Seems you are new here. The guards don't come to stop it. Instead they bet on these fights on who will win, how many will have their legs or arms broken. It's a game for them. The only thing they ensure is that prisoners don't die. Manpower has been a shortage for the country and the prisoners can't be allowed to die in such fights."

What started as a fight between ten men became bigger and soon almost everyone got involved in it. Some of them grabbed the tools from the factory and started using them as melee weapons. Bodhi walked up to the old man to see that he was unharmed. Manav too stood near them. Bodhi told him " Don't go into the siddhi state unless absolutely necessary. It may land us in more trouble and will rob away our chance to take them by surprise" Manav gave him a nod.

Now the trouble seemed to go out of hand as the factory property was also being destroyed by the third group which was not involved in fighting the other two factions. Some tried to take advantage of this and attack the guards too but were shot. Finally one of the guards sounded an alarm and many guards came to the scene armed with batons in their hands.

As was expected the two friends too got caught up in the crossfire of this. Three guards and a dozen prisoners came towards them, all of them seemed intent to cause them harm.

Manav and Bodhi took their positions and covered the old man from both sides. Manav did not use his siddhi state as the guards were not armed with guns. He lifted the guard nearest to him and threw him at the two behind him and they fell down. Bodhi was attacked by two prisoners; he punched their necks simultaneously using both his hands; both men went unconscious immediately. Then four men attacked him, Bodhi did a roundhouse kick and all of them were brought down with it. The last two prisoners decided to run away from Bodhi for their safety. On the other side the guards had gathered back and charged Manav but before they could move ahead Manav ran at a greater speed towards them and he punched and broke the visor of the helmet and the nose of one of the guards. Another one tried to attack him from the back but Manav kicked him in the gut and the third one threw his baton at Manav. He ducked and kicked the ankle of the guard, he lost his balance and before he landed on ground Manav jumped on him and hit his chest with such a force that despite armour on his chest the blow sucked out the air out of his chest and he went unconscious.

Neither the guards nor the prisoners were any match for them and all of them were on the ground within seconds, this was so quick that other guards who were busy controlling the riot could not pay attention to the beating of their comrades. Bodhi signalled Manav to get out of this and they along with the old man came out of the riot scene while punching and kicking anyone who came in their way.

After they came to a relatively quiet area, Brahmbhatt said" I am sorry to have taken your talks of jail break as hollow enthusiasm. I realise that you guys are special. I will help you, but you have to promise to help me and this country."

"Yes Sir. We will do whatever it takes" Manav responded.

"You have to help to overthrow the current dictator," he asked.

" We will see to it that this is done" the two friends said in unison.

*****

Chapter - 12
RECOUP

Brahmbhatt looked back, he saw that the guards and prisoners were still fighting and more and more guards were rushing to the area; some of them had even opened fire. He could hear the sound of approaching ambulances, "this is our chance" he told the boys.

The ambulance picked up the injured guards and soldiers, and the riot was finally brought under control.

Ambulance was the size of a bus, and could carry many patients at once. Some young doctors were attending the patients. One ambulance had all the injured guards, there were more than a dozen injured guards. Other one had injured prisoners, one ambulance wasn't enough to carry them all

A doctor was attending to the guards, some others were attending to the prisoners. Morgue vehicles too came at the scene to pick up the dead. The guards were moved to a hospital, two of those injured guards were Manav and Bodhi, they took the clothes of the guards they had injured. Brahmbhatt disguised a guard who was overlooking the transfer of the injured. All three were out of the prison. In the next one hour, Brahmbhatt had taken a tour of the hospital and he came to the boys and gestured them to come with him. The ward which had the prisoners was heavily guarded but not the one which had the guards.

It was late in the night and the other patients in the ward were asleep, so they went up the stairs to the second floor. Bodhi broke the window in a single punch and jumped out. Manav followed him. Brahmbhatt hesitated but the boys asked him to jump quickly, he jumped and the boys caught him before he fell to the ground.

They ran on their all fours to avoid being seen and reached the wall of the hospital compound. Brahmbhatt warned them " The wires carry current , do not touch them". "Thanks for the heads up" Bodhi said and he took two quick steps towards the wall, and jumped over it straight. Manav lifted the old man and threw him over the wall and Bodhi caught him and finally Manav jumped over it.

Brahmbhatt took them to an abandoned house which was about an hour's walk from the hospital, they had to go from one island to another which was connected by a bridge.

The house was locked up, Bodhi broke the locks and three of them went inside. Brahm lit a lamp, "this was the house of a friend of mine" he told the boys. He too stood against the current Government so he had to leave the country to save his life. This house has been abandoned for the last few months, but let me see if there is some rice which I can cook for you."

He came back after about half an hour, during which Manav and Bodhi took a quick nap " here is some food" Brahm woke them up. The three of them ate and went to sleep.

Next morning, Brahm sat with them to chalk out the plan.

Step one was to make Manav and Bodhi aware of the things and especially the dangers of this world. The basic functioning of guns, the speed of bullets, bombs, vehicles and drones. The next step was explaining the layout of the city and the palace where the dictator lived.

"Changez was the leader of the rebel group, they had been planning the coup for many years. They did not believe in democracy and wanted to strengthen the country by conquering nearby areas and getting prisoners as slaves. They infiltrated the government machinery and then the army and finally overthrew the democratically elected government. The factory you were working in is being used to mass produce weapons and soon they will start attacking every other city and country. With their technological superiority it will be almost impossible for any other country to stop them and yes their policies have been subjecting the citizens to a lot of torture."

We will need a vehicle to reach the capital city, now most of the larger islands are connected by bridges or by land reclamation, earlier the country was actually a group of many islands hence it got the name of the AkhandaDweep Rashtra." Fortunately, they could see an old car in the garage of the house " lady luck is on our side" Brahm exclaimed. The three of them went on their way. They had changed into civilian clothes but had kept the guard uniforms hidden in the car. On the way Brahm gave them some information on many things which were new to the two of them.

They reached the capital city, Mahangar, late at night, Brahm had some friends who were against the dictator, they took shelter at their place. It was a flat in an old building, there were few other people waiting there for them. Brahm introduced them to his friends " Meet the guest of honour Bodhi and Manav, the two brave warriors from a far off land who rescued me from the prison". The curtains were drawn to ensure no one sees inside, the city was full of spies.

Everyone present there clapped on the return of Brahm and the bravery of the two warriors without raising too much noise. "Hi , I am Mark. I got the message of Brahm and so I gathered this entire team." A tall fair man introduced himself and shook hands of Manav and Bodhi and hugged Brahmbhatt. He continued " I am a writer and an engineer" then the others introduced themselves.

Arshad a former spy of the government. Rana, ex army major who left the army after seeing the atrocities done on civilians by the Government and Kylie who was a refugee from another country but was held as a prisoner but managed to escape."

Mark then continued" All of us are members of the Order of Humanity, a society which talks about human rights and also voiced its opinion against the Government. It was established more than a decade back when the country was still a democracy. We would write journals, hold meetings and peaceful processions. But all changed after the fall of democracy. Our voices were quelled, one of the meetings was attacked by the army and members were shot at point blank range without any warning or reason" he stopped, his voice trembling remembering the incident.

" I was there, on that day. Leading the men who were fired on the meeting" Rana continued his sentence" and that was the day I decided to leave the army and was declared a runaway."

"But he saved my life by hiding me under a dead body and then taking me away from there" Mark regained his composure .

"It was you who saved me that day, you saved my soul" Rana looked at Mark and then at everyone present there.

" Later on Rana, my old friend from the military training days, introduced me to Mark after he knew that I was tired of spying on the civilians " Arshad said " and we met Kylie who was lucky to escape when the truck carrying prisoners met with an accident and she was able to run away from there"

"And I knew Mark from the days I was still in Government. He was an Engineer and his company took many projects from the Government." Brahmbhatt informed Manav and Bodhi. "Later on entire contracts were taken over by the mafias and Mark became a part of the Order of Humanity. So I informed Mark and asked him to get his most trusted people for this meeting. He narrated his story to the two boys and then he addressed the group present there " All of us are wanted and fugitives and it is only a matter of time before we are caught or at best we can continue to live like rats and see our friends, family and fellow citizens suffer or we can take the last stand and give all that we have to fight against the tyranny of Changez"

Manav and Bodhi did not say anything, they had given their word to Brahmbhatt, others were at loss of words on hearing this impossible idea " We are talking about taking down a man who has an army of thousands and hundreds of spies all around the country" Rana finally broke the silence.

I know this is not easy, in fact this is close to impossible but then Changez, how powerful he may be, he is still a man and a man can be killed. If we are able to kill him and his top lieutenants we will be able to overthrow the entire regime. What we are forgetting is that he too had taken control of the country by a coup."

"Yes he took the power by violence, but he had many people who were supporting him and he had planted his men in all the important positions" finally Kylie too expressed her views.

"Yes he had support and we can also get it if we use our resources smartly. There is a lot of angst against Changez" Brahmbhatt tried to push the case

"Yes , there is. I think if we are smart and plan well we can at least make a dent. It is better to go down in a blaze of glory than living like rats" there was a voice in support of Brahm and it was of Arshad.

Finally Mark budged from his earlier stand and said " Okay my old friend, you have had a long career as a minister and a civil servant before that. You know about people in power more than us. So help us out with a plan, even if there is a 1% chance then I will give my all in."

Brahm took some steps and came in the centre of the room and addressed everyone "I have spent countless hours in the prison thinking of the day when I could get a chance to fight against Changez, I made many plans to defeat him and even tried to run away from the prison but I failed and when I had given up hope I met these two brave men who could fight and defeat a hundred men. Give me a pen and a paper and I will discuss all my plans with you folks and now with all your expertise I am sure I can make the plan more robust."

Mark got him stuff to write- a pen, a diary and some large sheets to draw. Rana and Arshad brought some snacks and drinks from the kitchen while Kylie chatted with Manav and Bodhi. "It is after a long time that I am meeting people who are not from this country. The last time I saw foreigners was when I was in prison."

" We can understand, it must be difficult to be so far away from your homeland and not able to contact your family" Manav said

"Yes, it is. I hope that we succeed in this mission and I can go back to my home. I was the daughter of the chieftain of a tribe, we lived on islands which are thousands of miles away from this country. I was caught in a tornado while on the sea and landed up here and was caught by the guards. I wish I could tell my people, they would do anything to help us"

"Don't worry we will do something about it" Manav consoled her.

Over the next two days many iterations of the plan to overthrow Changez were built till the final version of the plan was frozen which most of the people present in the room agreed upon

and then came the time to execute it.

Three days later, Nirjan Island, a small island about fifty kilometres from the capital city. The island is barely inhabited and hence was not connected by a bridge but the major reason for that was that it has been a hub of illegal arms and drugs trade from which even the current ruler of the country made a lot of money. Arms were supplied to the pirates who raided the nearby areas and countries and brought the share of loot and prisoners for the Government. The drug trading happened between the manufacturers and the suppliers which too was under the protection of the Government, they even had licences for it under the garb of special medicine manufacturer and supplier, but anyone doing these trades without the approvals was given harshest of punishment. The gang members who supplied drugs too bought guns from the army at high rates. The rampant drug abuse and street violence made life easy for Changez as the youth of the country was trapped in drugs in violence and he was safe from any kind of major uprising against him. Rana had known all about it since the time he was in the army but could never do anything about it, the officers who wanted to do the right thing were too few and they knew they would face court martial and a certain death if they stood against it.

It was the dark of the night, there were boats all around the island. The market of drugs and arms was getting ready. The island was surrounded by the army and the patrol ships and drones to ensure no one could get inside without permission. The buyers and sellers were busy negotiating the prices of the goods. Three men wearing oxygen tanks emerged from the water, one of them slowly climbed a patrol boat and made the guard on it unconscious by a blow to his neck, the other man climbed up and they went to the room of the captain, the other two guards were taken out in a similar fashion. The captain was hit by a dart laced with sedatives before he could see who was entering the quarterdeck. The man then removed his mask. It was Arshad, Bodhi was following him.

They steered the boat away from the island towards a row boat where the others were waiting for them. Arshad through his spy network had managed to get licences for Rana and Kylie and they came on the island as gangsters and went on to the area where guns were being sold, they picked machine guns and went to the side of the island which acted as the testing range. They were accompanied by guards who were armed and were wearing armour. The guns were loaded with rubber bullets so that the buyers could test them but not try to do anything funky. Kylie and Arshad turned around and started firing at the guards accompanying them at point blank range before they could react. The rubber bullets did not kill them but the impact made them unconscious, no one suspected the gunshots coming from the practice range. They then picked up their actual guns and went towards the area where drugs were being sold. Rana hid behind a tree and he could see the stash of drugs from the binocular attached in the gun which he had taken from the guard. He fired shots at it and it went up in flames. There was a conundrum seeing this and many guards came at the scene, they started shooting towards the side where Rana was hiding but they were met with a volley of bullets from Kylie who had taken cover behind an empty shed.

Manav and Bodhi too had touched down on the island while in disguise of guards and they had planted a bomb near the area where arms trade was going on. It was a sonic bomb made by Mark and the blast resulted in knocking down everyone in the area unconscious due to extreme pain in the ears and those who were in the area where drugs trade was going were knocked down for a few seconds. All the intruders were wearing ear muzzles which were buzzing at a frequency to cancel out the sonic blast. The blast gave opportunity to Rana and Kylie to run away from the scene and they grouped with Manav and Bodhi and they picked up crates of arms and ran towards the patrol boat where Arshad was waiting.

They told the guards on the way that they are removing all the ammunition from the area as there has been a terrorist attack. The boat was loaded and off they went.

Stage one of the plan to procure weapons was completed, they even had a patrol ship now.

Two days before the attack on Nirjan Island , while the plan was still being made Brahm said " Changez lives in his fortified palace which was impenetrable. He travels in bulletproof armoured cars with a huge caravan of vehicles and it was difficult to know which was the vehicle in which he is travelling"

Arshad added " Next week he is travelling away from the capital city, Mahanagar to the second largest city Nayanagar to unveil a huge statue of himself. This city was recently rebuilt and his loyalists were given huge bungalows as a reward. He would have to come out of his car to unveil the statue, but the entire square will be manned by drones and snipers on the top of every building. The area will be thoroughly searched before the visit and no one was allowed to enter without being thoroughly searched for." Arshad had gathered all this information from his friends on the movement of Changez, these friends were the spies of the other nations and cities who were in threat of being invaded or had already been invaded by Changez's army. "His top lieutenants would also be travelling with him that day"

So Brahm figured out there was only one way to take him down. He reminded Mark that he was involved in the contract of one of the bridges which was to be used in this commute of Changez. Mark was a consultant on the project. " Yes I remember that," Mark replied. " Think my friend, you were the one who made it , can we use it to take down the dictator."

"I ensured all the projects I took or consulted for were perfect" Mark replied with a hint of irony.

"There must be something, anything that we can use?" Brahm pushed him to find the chink in the armour of his own project.

Mark took out a calculator and a piece of paper and did some calculations.

On the night before Changez' travel to Nayangar.The entire team was checking the ammunition and the other equipment that they had to use. Manav and Bodhi were given a quick training on the use of the guns, bombs and devices necessary for the plan. It did not take them long to figure it all out. " Where is Kylie?" asked Arshad. " She hasn't been around for more than 24 hours" he continued

"After we returned from Nirjan Island she said she will be going to the orphanage where she has been taking care of the kids. She said she wanted to meet the kids in case this might be our final mission" Brahm told the group.

"Let me check with the orphanage" Mark made a quick visit to the orphanage and returned. " She did come to the orphanage but has been missing since then, she also took some kids with her. I also saw on the way that our patrol boat which we had parked in the backwaters was missing." He informed the group after returning.

"I think she ran away to her country, " Bodhi said. "I too think so," Arshad added, " She was on this mission only to return to her country, she got the necessary things, a patrol boat, arms and guard uniforms. There was no reason to risk her life for trying to kill Changez"

"Well then, without her also the mission is still on" Brahmbhatt said in a voice of enthusiasm to lift the spirits of everyone. They packed their things and left.

They used a normal boat to get close to the bridge;the caravan of Changez was to cross in a few hours. Arshad, Rana, Manav and Bodhi all dived under the water and carried with them bombs to plant on the bridge.

Brahmbhatt and Mark were overlooking the entire thing using night vision binoculars.

"The bridge is sturdy" Mark had told them "but the caravan is too large and the armoured vehicles weigh many times more than a normal vehicle. That puts pressure on the bridge, if at the same time there is substantial structural damage the bridge may collapse."

" And since the cars they are travelling in cannot swim, Changez will need to come out of it and that will be our chance. A shot to his head and those of the other lieutenants." that was the plan

The dynamites were planted on the pillars of the bridge and all of them were connected by wires, they were planted just under the surface of water to avoid detection. The switch of the bombs was on the boat, all this was done before dawn.

Few hours later, guards came to the bridge before the caravan arrived and they stopped the traffic of the citizens on the bridge.

After 30 minutes the caravan arrived, the boat was covered with sea weeds and mud to remain inconspicuous in the vegetation of the sea. Rana and Arshad were having the sniper guns, Rana was on the boat and Arshad was hidden behind a tree which was on a swampy part of the Nayanagar island. Manav was manning a rocket launcher; he was also behind the same tree. Bodhi was on the boat and had a machine gun. Both of them carried swords too, ready to take on the enemies the way they knew best.

Mark was with the binoculars and was looking out for the right time to hit the switch of the bomb. The first vehicle of the caravan entered the bridge and then the next, now all the 13 vehicles were on the bridge. One of them was of Changez though it was impossible to know which one it was, the best guess was that it would be one of the three in between which were the heaviest vehicles. He was waiting for the right time, the load on the bridge should be maximum. There was a complete silence on the boat. The men on the island too were waiting for the moment. Mark placed his hand on the shoulder of Brahm, which was the sign to press the button. Brahm did the same and there were simultaneous blasts on the pillars on both sides of the bridge.

The bridge started shaking and all the 4 men with weapons got ready to fire at their targets. "The bridge would buckle in about five minutes, do not fire before that. Let the vehicles fall in water and wait for Changez and his men to come out. There would be too many men to take all of them down at once, so focus on the targets." Mark had told them when they were planning the attack.

There was panic among the bodyguards of Changez. It was evident that they had been ambushed and if the bridge were to fall it might mean the fall of the rule of Changez. Angar, the Chief of security and also the general of the army, was in the vehicle immediately ahead of Changez. He called Changez" Sir do not worry. I have informed the security forces in the capital. Soon we will have back up and you will be airlifted. The entire area will be covered by our patrol boats, drones and copters. Air-ambulance is also on its way. "

Changez shouted at him" You idiot, this is your security? I want to see the heads rolling of all those behind this attack."

More than five minutes had passed by and the bridge did not fall. The attackers were still awaiting the opportunity to open fire. Another 10 minutes had gone by and now they heard the sound of helicopters, " He is being airlifted and soon we will be surrounded. We are doomed" Arshad said in utter frustration.

The helicopter was in sight now, Rana decided to take matters in his hand " If he gets airlifted we are doomed and I not going down without shooting my shot" he changed his aim and shot at the pilot of the copter, the copter started swirling and fell down at the end of the bridge. This was the final impact and the bridge started giving way. After about another five minutes one vehicle fell down. Some patrol boats which were near the scene had arrived and they gathered near the bridge. Safety nets, divers and life jackets were ready to save their leader.

Soon drones started flying all over the area to locate the attackers and the soldiers on the patrol boats started shooting randomly in all directions away from the bridge. The team of Brahm was short of manpower to deal with this situation, they were not sure whether to attack or hide, but the intensity of shooting kept on increasing with more and more backup coming to protect Changez. Bodhi too decided, enough is enough and started firing his machine gun. Manav too followed him and fired a rocket launcher, his shot hit a boat and it went up in flames. Rana and Arshad started shooting down the drones. Mark too started firing from his rifle and finally Brahm who had never used a gun before joined them. Manav understood being the most trained warrior and bestowed with a special power he will have to do something here now if he has to save himself and the others. So he went into his siddhi state, took a deep breath and dived in the water and went towards the enemies. Bodhi swam in another direction and opened fire to draw the fire away from the boat to protect Mark and Brahm who were the most ill equipped to save themselves.

Changez's car was still stuck on the bridge and was swinging in the air. Copters were not brought to the scene to avoid another accident, the team below was ready to save their leader but they noticed a human emerging out from the water. With swords in both his hands, they fired at him but they could not because he easily avoided their gunshots and deflected the bullets using his swords to bring down the shooters. Using this pandemonium Bodhi went nearer and started shooting them and all the guards and drones were distracted by these two and Rana and Arshad kept on bringing them down one by one by their sniper shots. The boat of Brahm and Mark was no longer under fire and Manav was reaching near Changez but before he could reach the inner circle over a hundred soldiers on small boats came on both sides of the bridge. So now even with his siddhi it was getting difficult for Manav to dodge so many bullets being fired at him. Bodhi too was barely able to save himself by constantly ducking under water and changing his position and a few bullets whizzed past him. From a distance they could see more soldiers coming. The car finally fell down but it was not possible to take a shot as the view was completely blocked by patrol boats and soldiers and due to the heavy firing they could not get nearer to the boat.

The boat of Brahm and Mark too went up in flames. One bullet hit Bodhi on his arm. Rana was hit by a bullet from a drone and Arshad was hit by a splinter from a grenade which fell near him.

Manav decided to go on the defensive and he was now trying to reach Bodhi and take him to safety. Changez jumped out of his car and was safely caught in a net and he was coming and was being taken away in a boat. It seemed all lost for team Brahmbhatt.

Manav managed to come close to Bodhi and they started swimming away from the Bridge. The only thing which seemed most important at the moment to them was to somehow stay alive, he had been in his siddhi state for way too long, the use of it was draining him physically and mentally both.

They then saw in the sky an arrow and it hit one of the enemy boats and there was an explosion. A volley of arrows soon followed, arrows exploded after hitting the boats and the soldiers.Some arrows hit the soldiers who were on the island and there was a fresh round of panic in the ranks . The arrows were shot from another patrol boat which was approaching the bridge.

Bodhi saw a girl on the deck of the boat , "Look, a girl is leading them towards ", he pointed out to Manav." . Two other boats were following them and shooting arrows at the soldiers of Changez. The soldiers now started firing at these new entrants to the scene. The boat carrying changez was trying to manoeuvre away from the area but the captain was finding it hard to do so with all the fire they were taking and the burning boats around them blocking his path.

All this new commotion gave time to Manav and Bodhi to reach the shore. Manav saw Mark and Brahm trying to swim towards them; they had jumped out of the boat in time. He went up to them and brought them to the shore.

The boat helping them had come closer," It is Kylie with some people, who judging by their dress don't seem to be from this country" Mark said while lying injured on the shore. We need to get you both some medical help and we also need to locate Rana and Arshad. " Brahm told him "Rana was with us and he had jumped out of the boat earlier when he was hit by a bullet" Arshad was on the other side.

Rana, after being hit by a bullet, had decided to swim towards the boat carrying away Changez. The boat was also having General Angar who too had jumped out of his car.

He swam under the surface and was hit by many bullets. It slowed him down a lot but Kylie's entry helped him as Changez was not able to run away from the scene. He finally reached the boat and threw a smoke bomb on it. Before the smoke cleared he had shot the soldiers manning the boat.

Only Changez and Angar were left on the boat. Rana was covered in blood and was walking towards them with the last bit of life he had in him. " Angar you were the one who had made me fire on innocent civilians. More than Changez, I wanted to take revenge from you."

"You have a few seconds to live and your bullets will do us no harm," Angar said. Angar and Changez were covered in bullet proof armour from head to toe. Changez was standing behind Angar and was trying to hide himself.

"Yes you won't be killed by bullets, but by this " Rana said and ran towards both of them. He removed the jacket he was wearing and underneath there were explosives tied to his body. Angar emptied his revolver by continuously firing at Rana but Rana did not stop,he pressed the button to light up the bombs and grabbed Angar and Changez. The explosion completely blew up Rana. Changez and Angar did not blow up; but their armour was damaged and they were injured and badly fell out of the boat. Some soldiers saw this and jumped in the water and brought them on another boat . The armour meant to stop bullets could not save them from the explosion of the bomb from such a small distance damaging their internal organs and they were coughing up blood when their helmet was removed. A medic rushed up to them but before he could do anything much both of them breathed their last. A soldier on the boat saw this and started running away and shouted in utter panic. " The Supreme leader and General have died". His supervisor immediately shot him.Out of the three boats lead by Kylie one of them one was destroyed by the soldiers of Changez but the other two had come close to Changez's boat. The news of the death of Changez was heard by soldiers on a nearby boat. They threw their arms and raised their hands in surrender. The Captain raised a white flag and waved it towards the boat of Kylie. She signalled her men boat to immediately reach them and take them in custody. The other captains who had seen the burning of the boat of Changez, guessed what would have happened when they saw the surrender of some of the soldiers. They too shouted on his boat, " No point fighting for the dead dictator, surrender and save yourself" and raised white flags. The soldiers started throwing down their weapons immediately. An officer was enraged and he decided to shoot his men but his soldier put a hand on his gun " It's over, no point of further bloodshed". This officer too threw his weapon and raised his arms.

The entire armed force present on the scene followed the suit and Kylie's men took the weapons and tied their hands, most of them worked for Changez and Angar because of fear and no option to move out, deserters were always rewarded with death. Now it was clear to them it is better to surrender and hope for a better future than fight for the revenge of the dead dictator and general.

Next morning, Bodhi opened up his eyes. He saw he was in a building " Was I caught by the soldiers?" This was the first thought that came to his mind and he was about to jump and run. But he looked around and he was in a hospital. He took a deep breath and laid his head back, he saw a beautiful face with a gentle smile coming near him. It was Kylie. In this stillness of the moment and having returned from a certain death he noticed her face for the first time and realised that she is beautiful and also the woman who saved his life.

She came up to him and helped him to get up and sit and said " Don't worry, everything is fine. Changez's army has surrendered and his Government has fallen"

" How is Manav and how is everyone else?" he asked her

"Manav is well and getting some minor treatment, Arshad lost his leg. Mark and Brahm are still under observation and Rana…" she went quite

"What about Rana , what happened to him" He asked her

"He made the ultimate sacrifice, he blew himself up and took out Changez and Angar." she said with tears in her eyes.

"He was a soldier and a true warrior" and Bodhi whispered a silent prayer for the departed soul " May he get moksha"

"Take me to Manav," he asked her.

Manav was in the next ward. Bodhi hugged him with happiness.

" How did you manage to turn the tide in our favour and get all the supporting troops?" Manav asked Kylie.

She told them the entire story" After the success of our mission at Nirjan island, I went to the orphanage I have been taking care of to meet the children. I was not sure whether I will see them again or not. After meeting them I realised that I can rescue some of them and take them to safety away from this country since I had a patrol boat and this was an opportunity for me too to return to my country because that was my reason to come on board with the mission.

The boat was solar powered so it was easy for me to travel far without needing fuel. So I took off and I was able to establish contact with my tribe a day later. They were happy to see me and I thought of staying with them, but I remembered the sacrifice you all were making for the citizens of this country and also of those who will suffer the brutality of Changez once he conquers the neighbouring countries. So I informed my folks and we headed back. Our land has minerals to make gunpowder so we took a stock of it along with other weapons, captured a few more patrol boats on our way and came to the scene before Changez could get away."

" We were fortunate. Had you reached a few minutes late, none of us would be alive and Changez would have unleashed new terrors on the public after the attack on him" Bodhi told her.

"You guys were risking your lives for the word you gave to an old man whom you barely knew" I could not let you lose. She looked into his eyes and held his hand. She had narrow eyes and a broad smile. A long nose and brown skin of the colour of honey. Bodhi who had always maintained a distance from the other gender felt butterflies in his stomach and his eyes remained fixated on her. Manav was looking at him and was smiling but did not say anything.

Kylie shook Bodhi's hands and he realised he had been staring at her while holding her hands. He moved his hands away and blushed.

By evening Brahm and Mark too regained their consciousness. The army had captured all the high ranking officials of Changez's regime and his supporters and it was announced the elections will be held soon. An army man came to meet Brahm. He was with some other soldiers but they wore a dress different from what was worn by troops of Changez. This man was a colonel who had left the army and was leading a resistance group against Changez. Brahm was still being attended by nurses. The man came and sat near him " Congratulations Sir. Your group of rebels have ousted the forces of the Dictator and we are soon going to have elections.My name is Shashwat and I am the incharge of the army now"

Brahm smiled at him. " But before we can have the elections we will need to have an interim Government to oversee the affairs of this country because all the previous ministers and officials of Changez have either run away or been killed."

"Elections. That is great news." Brahm said to him

"But we need your help" Shashwat came closer to Brahm

" How can I help you?" he asked

" You are the only minister from the previous Government so we want you to run the interim Government till the time new Government is elected"

"This will be an honour. But I will only help to get elections done and step down after that. There are better people to lead the country" Brahm accepted with this condition.

Manav and Bodhi decided to wait for a few days to completely recuperate before heading towards their original mission. During this time Kylie showed them around the city while lending a hand in the rebuilding of the city and helping those who had suffered in the previous regime. Kylie and Bodhi had become good friends and had spent a considerable time together.

There was a huge gathering in the Capital Square when Brahm took the charge of the interim Government. He announced "Our country is free of tyranny and will usher in an era of peace and prosperity. Soon you will get to elect your representatives. I would also like to honour those who laid down their lives to help us get this freedom" He walked a few steps towards his right and unveiled a statue " This statue is of Major Rana who made the ultimate sacrifice and gave up his life to get rid of the Dictator and his General. May his sacrifice always inspire us to do what is right for the country." His words were met with thunderous applause from the crowd.

But all those who had fought alongside him were teary eyed.

After the event Manav and Bodhi met Brahm. They had managed to retrieve their old possessions which were taken away from them during the prison and they were carrying it in a new bag. " So we have fulfilled our promise. It's time for our farewell."

"I can understand. You have another mission awaiting. Just wait for a day more, today the entire country is celebrating, be a part of these celebrations"

"Ok, we will wait" Manav replied him and gave a slight nod to Bodhi

During the celebrations they had good food after so many days. Kylie met Bodhi and he told her about the plan to leave. She kept quite for sometime and finally spoke

" I wish you could stay here. Live in peace here or in my land" she stopped for a few seconds " or maybe take me with you to your land."

Bodhi fell silent. He gathered his thoughts and looked at her and said " You are the most extraordinary girl I have met. Beautiful, brave and kind. But I have a vow to uphold and I cannot settle down before completing it."

"I will wait for you then" she replied.

" My mission may even take years to complete. I don't know the dangers I will face or whether I will be alive to see you again. You must move on in your life" he tried to convince her.

" I know you will succeed and I will wait for you" she held his hands.

Next day, when the two warriors were ready to leave, Brahm and the new general met them. They accompanied them to the shore and presented a war boat. " This is a small gift from the people of this land for you to help you in your mission" The boat has everything you will need for your journey: food, water and ammunition and it will help to shorten your long journey to a few days. So the time you would have taken to reach your destination by your raft had you not stayed here, you will still reach there by that time " Then he also gave them a bag of silver and gold coins. " This will be useful if you move across the cities. Despite having different currencies around the world everyone appreciates silver and gold"

"That's very kind of you" Manav and Bodhi thanked Brahm and the General. A captain helped them with some training on how to use the equipment and gave them a manual. " If you ever get stuck, use this transmitter and you will be able to reach our headquarters. I have given them special instruction and they will guide you with anything that you would need" The captain told them while giving a demo.

After a few hours of training , off they went to find the nemesis they were searching for so long.

Chapter - 13
FINDING ASHMIT

"This boat is a thing of beauty and so easy to sail it" Bodhi said to Manav. A few hours had passed since the time they had taken their leave from the people of Akhand Deep Rashtra. Bodhi was sad because of parting with Kylie and Manav knew that so he had kept quiet while both of them tried to get familiar with the equipment of the war boat.

" Oh yes this is. Our struggle at the island resulted in something good for the mission. Who knows, using a wooden raft we would have even reached our destination or not" Manav said while having some fruits from the pantry.

The sea was calm and after three days they could see land, Manav rechecked the map which was given to them by the Captain and verified with the rough map they had taken from Shahid.

Bodhi, who was more adept at it, was steering the boat. "Look ahead, it seems that our destination is near" he pointed out to Bodhi.

"Yes it seems so. But we must be cautious. The last time we entered a country we had to undergo a lot of trouble." He slowed down the boat and instructed Manav " Man the gun on the boat. We must be ready for anything offensive coming our way."

Manav went to the large gun which was on the deck and kept an eye out for any potential attack.

Coming closer they saw many other boats and ships, none of them with a comparable technology though. It seemed that this place was more welcoming than the previous one.

They reached a harbour. The city around it seemed like a trading post. They saw people, they looked like they had come from different countries and belonged to different ethnicities. Although it seemed the native people looked fairly similar ,they were very fair, slightly short and had narrow eyes and worn gown like dress.

While they were parking the boat a man rushed to their boat and waved and spoke in a language they could not understand " Sorry I cannot understand your language". The man could not understand what Bodhi said and again spoke something unintelligible to both of them. Manav and Bodhi then tried a couple more languages. He could finally understand one of these language partially and said " I will get someone who speaks this tongue"

The man got a boy along with him. The boy was around 15, he looked different from the native population. He was wheatish and tall but had similar facial features like the others.

He introduced himself "My name is Moon Law and I help the visitors by providing my services as a guide and interpreter " and bowed to these two visitors.

"Thank God, we met you else we would have had a great trouble here. My name is Manav and this is my friend Bodhi" Manav told him.

" You can park your boat here but you will need to pay for it and you will need to pay for my services too" Moon smiled at them.

"Surely we will pay" Bodhi took out some coins and gave one to the man and one coin to Moon.

" What brings you here?Trade? Or something else?" Man asked them

"We are looking for someone who took something valuable from us" Bodhi told him

" I will help you to find him" Moon told him " as long as you keep on paying me"

Bodhi took out a silver coin and gave it to him and showed him a gold coin" This is once you help us find our guy"

"So what is his name, which city or village he lives in?" Moon asked them.

"His name is Ashmit" Bodhi said " Ashamura, his name is Ashamura" Manav told the real name of Ashmit and continued" we just know he lives in this part of the World. His city or village, we do not know"

"It will be difficult to find this guy, I will need 2 coins to find him" Moon told them.

" We will give you 2 coins, just help us find him as quickly as you can," Bodhi said to him.

"It will be done," the boy told them.

"Tell me more about him and I will think of how to begin our search", the boy asked them " But before that come have some tea. We always treat our visitors with a hot cup of tea" and he took them to an eatery near the harbour.

"He had come to our lands many years ago. He seemed like a hermit when he had come to the school, we call it Gurukul. Where many great minds taught us and our friends. He lived there for many years and I think he would have come back here, maybe a year back." Bodhi told him

" You said he was a hermit and had come to your land many years ago and I think you come from a far off country. So he must have taken a sturdy boat which would take him that far. We don't have boats like the one you had, a journey on a wooden boat in the water filled with dangerous creatures, not many have undertaken such a journey and survived. We should start by asking the boat owners and the boat crew if they know of such a person" Moon had the starting point to find Ashmit.

Moon helped Manav and Bodhi get a lodging near the harbour and the three of them spent the next two days asking everyone around to help them find Ashamura.

Moon would ask about this person from the boat crew and owners offering them silver coins if they are able to give the information. To cross check the information Manav and Bodhi would ask for the facial description, age and mannerism of this person but they did not find any luck in getting any information. The only information they got was from people who tried to fool them by giving fake stories to take the reward on offer.

"I think we must wander into the country and see if we stumble upon this guy," Bodhi suggested to Manav.

Moon was also with them" There are many city states here, they are ruled by Shoguns. You might not even get to enter them because only the harbour village is free to enter and leave as this is managed by 3 different Shogunates who make good money by allowing trade and travel here and taking a cut on all the transactions.

"So in that case are we stuck here?" Manav asked him and Bodhi

"We have come so far from our homeland, in this foreign country. We cannot give up after coming so close" Bodhi got up and sat near Manav. Moon was standing a few feet away from them. "We can still sneak into these cities. I have done many times earlier, it will be few more times and we keep looking for Ashmit till we find him"

"Finding him might take all our lives. We do not know with certainty that he is here, he might have run away to some other place or never came back or perhaps he is dead.." Manav replied to him in a pensive mood.

" You are right about this" Bodhi's enthusiasm reduced and he asked" so what do you suggest"

"We have to be a little more thoughtful instead of searching for him randomly." Manav suggested him.

"So let us narrow down the possibilities and then we start the search" Bodhi agreed to the idea.

"Ok, we first note down all that we know about him" Manav asked him

Both of them went quiet for a few minutes and then went into meditation and tried to remember everything about Ashmit.

"He was a hermit, he took many years of training at the Gurukul and was well versed in science" Bodhi started the character sketch of Ashmit after he came out of his meditation.

" and was also a good warrior, maybe better than we thought he was" Manav added to it.

"And may be a spy too" and Bodhi added a conjecture to the character sketch.

"So where do you think we can find such a person?" Manav asked Moon after he gave him the download of Ashmit.

"He may be a Shadow Warrior, a Ninja" Moon made a guess.

"Do you know more about them?" Bodhi asked him.

"I have heard a bit, they live in the mountains in the north and they take up missions on behalf of Shoguns or those who can pay them" Moon told them.

"We have a direction now. We should head out to the mountains and take this man down" Bodhi got up and picked his bag.

"I will take you close to the mountains but I won't go there. I have heard they kill anyone who tries to enter their area" Moon firmly said.

"It is fine, you just help us to reach close to that place and we will manage from thereon" Manav assured Moon.

"Okay so wait here for some time, I will get some preparations done for the journey and will come back soon. " Moon told them.

Bodhi and Manav too did their preparations, they got some food for the way and went back to the boat to get some essentials for travels and weapons to fight against the threat Moon was warning them about.

Moon came back in an hour and took out a map and showed the route to the two of them while placing it over a table. The map was hand made and it had the geographical details of the area and names of the rulers ruling over various areas. " This is the route we follow. This goes mostly through no man's land so will not be bothered by the Lords but we need to be extra careful of the bandits and wild animals. Manav and Bodhi smiled at each other, bandits and wild animals were of no concern to them.

Moon had arranged horses for the journey and they loaded their bags and went ahead. Manav mounted a tall white horse which had long hair and Bodhi mounted a grey horse and Moon was riding a brown horse which was the shortest of the three.

It was already getting dark when they had started but Bodhi insisted that they should not wait for morning and start the journey without any delay. They made a makeshift camp after midnight and continued their journey the next morning. By late afternoon the outlines of the mountains were visible to them.The forest cover had become thicker and their speed of travel had reduced

" We have reached the edge of the mountains before dusk. I will return from this point." Moon told them. Moon took his fees and before he returned he gave them a souvenir, a wooden knife which had a shining stone on it. "This is for good luck, and now I will take the leave of you two gentlemen. Since the mountains might have foes it will be better that you travel when there is light" He bowed to them , mounted his horse and galloped away.

"We should wait and move ahead in the morning "Manav suggested Bodhi, who agreed with the idea. They ate the bread they were carrying, Bodhi got water for them and Manav gathered some grass and leaves for the horses and they went to sleep. The two of them woke up with heavy heads and masked men overlooking them and their hands and legs tied up with thick ropes. "Here we go again," Manav whispered to Bodhi thinking that they had been caught by the bandits

There were about twenty men and one of the men removed his mask. He seemed to be the leader of this group, it was a familiar face. It was the face of the man they had been looking for, Ashmit. Both of them were taken aback by surprise. "You were looking for me, so here I am."

They had been looking for him for such a long time and were not even sure if they would find him but once they did they had no idea what to ask him and they were still in shock.

"In case you are wondering how I knew about the two of you, I got this information from the very guide you had hired" Ashmit told them and then he picked up the souvenir that Moon had given them "this is a beacon, I tracked the two of you using this" he bought a device near it and the jewel in the knife shone brightly "and this emitted a gas which put you in deep sleep. I know you are the warriors of Gurukul so I would not take any chances with you"

Manav and Bodhi knew that this is the most formidable foe that they have ever encountered, the one who knows their strengths and now has them tied up.

He took them to their place of hiding. There were more men" I have my spies all over and they always keep an eye out. Moon had initially tried to stall your search and had sent me the information about it, I asked him to bring the two of you to me. I wanted to know who was looking for me. No one else apart from the two of you could have managed to do this"

"Why did you not kill us?" Manav questioned him.

" Yes, I could have done that very easily and I can still do that but I have my reasons. The first is the guilt that I had in my heart for killing the people who had trained and given me knowledge but more important was the second reason" Ashmit said calmly.

"And what is the reason?" Manav again asked him while Bodhi was quiet and was observing the place. It was a large cave which was lit by fire torches. There were more than fifty men and all were armed with many weapons, the weapons of Manav and Bodhi had been taken away from them.

"We have met after such a long time and you keep on asking questions. Take some time to enjoy my hospitality. " Two men came with some food and drinks. "Have it, I insist". The two men tried to feed Manav and Bodhi but they moved their faces to the other side. "Don't worry this is not poisonous. As I told you I can kill you whenever I want I do not need to mix poison in food for that" Ashmit laughed.

Bodhi finally spoke, "Stop all this facade. You killed our teachers, the ones who took you in and taught you. You killed them. You killed almost every student of the Gurukul. Why? Why did you commit this treacherous act? Who asked you to do that?" He was full of rage but could not do anything about it.

"If you insist so much I will tell you all about it… " Ashmit smiled " but before that let me tell you something that had happened thousands of years ago"

Ashmit narrated them a story.

The Mandala was taken away to a safe place when its place of hiding was first attacked, this is said to be more than thousands of years ago. But it was too big to move so it was broken into two parts and quietly taken away through an underground tunnel. The two parts remained in their respective places for many years because its guardians feared that the foreigners then ruling over your country could use the power of Mandala for their evil deeds and with time the idea to join the Mandala was dropped . These two parts of it were kept hidden over the years and were just an object of worship and meditation. It survived the great war but its power was forgotten.

One of the parts, the bigger one was at your Gurukul and the other part was at a temple which was in another part of the country". " he paused and took a sip of wine and continued again"

Few years before you two had graduated, Acharya Prajwal came across some ancient texts about the power of Mandala and because of that he had been conducting extensive study to understand its origin and how to harness it. The piece at your Gurukul was also powerful but it was not easy to use its power. It was till the day you were able to tap into its power" He told it to Manav

"I tapped into it? So you mean to say my Siddhi is due to the power of Mandala?" Manav asked with wonder.

"Yes, you had some powers in you from right from your birth and it got increased due to the training and Yoga at Gurukul. You had developed an extremely strong sixth sense because of this. In fact you might not know this , it was because of your sixth sense that you were able to reach the Gurukul when your family was attacked, the compass your father gave was just a small tool to give you confidence. Over the years many students were given tests but finally it was you who was able to develop this ability to look into the immediate future and know the moves of your enemies. This convinced Acharya of the mythical stories they had heard about the Mandala"

Manav and Bodhi were listening to it in complete silence

" Acharya believed that if the two pieces of Mandala are brought together its power will amplify and he convinced Pracharya to join the pieces together. Thus the other piece was brought together. He was working on how to join it and put some amplifying structures at right distances just the way the Iron pillar was used by King Vikram. Everything was done and your training was also about to complete. But before that it was attacked by my men"

"What was it that you wanted from the Mandala?" Bodhi finally asked

" I was told about the Mandala many years ago by my Master. He talked about a thing which gave the power to see beyond time. One who could see beyond time will be able to rule over the World. He told me he had encountered an old man when he was passing close to the village of mystics. That village is a forbidden place and the master went to that part of the world because he was being chased by his enemies. The enemies entered the city and were killed by the mystics but mastered was richer due the knowledge about the Mandala. So once he came back he decided he would find the Mandala. But he did not know the exact location of it so he asked his best students to find it. So I killed your master to keep the promise I had made to my master."

"I managed to convince everyone and get an entry into the Gurukul after clearing the test. I had to tell them about my real place of origin else I would have been caught lying in the interview by the experts but I never told them my reason to come there, I just manipulated the truth that I came there in the search of truth which was not a lie." he paused and his face turned meaner.

I spent more than four years to know the truth and when I knew that the power of the Mandala was about to be unveiled I managed to get mercenaries and bandits from the towns surrounding the Gurukul. I had learnt every security hack and weakness of every member of the Gurukul. The surprise attack took out most of the people and I ran away with the blue prints and took away the Mandala in a wagon with me. Your so called intelligent teachers could never fathom my plan and your bravest fell down like a pack of cards.

Manav and Bodhi were getting furious and finally Manav lost his cool and started hurling abuses" You filthy bastard, may you get the worst punishment for your treachery"

But Ashamura just laughed over their anger and continue" You two and a few others were lucky to survive." He pointed at Manav using his index finger. I saw you falling down in a river, I thought you would either die or even if you were to live you would never know what happened so I did not bother finding you. I got what I had come for in the Gurukul."

"After getting the job done I gathered all the mercenaries in a secluded house for their payment and burned them to death. I waited outside the house and shot with arrows whoever escaped. So I ensured that there is no trace left of what I have done. But you two got lucky and managed to find me on the other side of the world"

"God and truth are on our side and we will destroy you and whatever you plan to do with the powers of the Mandala. Just untie me and see it for yourself" Manav challenged Ashamura.

" You think I am stupid that I will do that?" He again laughed and said" and with regards to your point of God being on your side I think you are wrong about that too "Ashamura stopped laughing and said in a serious voice" Actually… I wanted you to be here."

Manav and Bodhi looked at each other and were confused now, why would he want them to be here

"After I had got the two parts of the Mandala and did all the reconstruction from the blue prints I showed it to my master to test and experience its power but when he started his meditation with the Mandala he could not come out of it and lost his consciousness and died a few days later. My clan is also aware of the power of meditation but somehow we could not use this. Either it did not work or people ended up dying or becoming mad, even I could not use it despite my years of training at the Gurukul. So I remembered the boy who was believed to be the one who can explore the power of the Mandala" he paused, looked at Manav" and here he is."

So now Manav and Bodhi understood that he doesn't intend to kill them but wants to use them as a tool so that he can use the power of the Mandala for his nefarious plans.

"And why do you think I will even try to use the power for you?" Manav questioned him. "Because if you don't then you will lose the only person you have in the world " one of Ashamura's men put a sword on the neck of Bodhi.

"Even with all your powers you will not be able to save your friend, who despite being the best warrior will not be able to fight so many men of mine. So do not try anything fancy here" Ashmaura warned them.

Manav and Bodhi looked around, there were archers with their arrows pointed at Bodhi, Ashamura was speaking the truth.

Manav looked at Bodhi and gave a slight nod, suggesting that they will have to comply with the plan of their foe.

Soon it was morning and Manav took his bath and did SuryaNamaskar and prepared to meditate while focusing on the Mandala. Bodhi was now put inside a prison and two guards kept an eye on him continuously. As he sat down he could feel his siddhi state getting triggered without being under attack. He went into deep meditation but all he could feel was nothingness, he came out of the meditation after fifteen minutes.

"What did you experience ?" Ashamura who was standing near him all this while immediately asked as Manav opened his eyes.

"What did you expect me to see?" Manav replied him sarcastically

" Don't act smart with me." He tied an equipment to Manav's arm. " This is the equipment they used in the Gurukul to know if someone is lying. It will measure your pulse and any change will tell that you were lying"

"So tell me" he again asked

" I did not see anything, it was completely blank" , there was no change in the heart beat.

" Try again. I want to know" he ordered.

"I can try again after sometime only. I am feeling drained" and Manav fell and became unconscious.

Ashamura rushed towards him and picked him up, he immediately called his men and sprinkled water on his face but Manav did not get up. " No no no, not again. If you die then I will never be able to uncover the power of the Mandala."

"Take him to the healing room, and get a doctor here immediately. Do whatever it takes to get him back up" Ashamura ordered his men.

They took Manav to another room and made him lie on a bed made of wooden logs. The room was lit up by candles and there were medicinal incense sticks around. A doctor soon came to attend him and treated him with herbal medicines. Manav finally woke up after many hours.

The moment he opened his eyes, a boy who was attending him immediately ran to call Ashamura, who was delighted to know this and came rushing to see him.

"Wake up. Your long sleep had given me jitters, I thought another one has gone down in trying to use the powers of the Mandala. But you were not chosen without a reason."

Manav did not feel like talking to Ashamura and asked the doctor" For how long was I unconscious?"

"More than 12 hours," the doctor told him " You passed out because of extreme physical and mental stress. But do not worry, you are completely fine."

" Take some more rest and enjoy my hospitality, I will see you tomorrow. You have to start the unfinished business again" Ashamura told him and turned back.

"Where is my friend?"Manav asked him.

"He is completely fine. I won't let any harm come to him too, after all he is my bait" Ashamura said while walking away from the room.

During the time he was unconscious, Manav had visions and it seemed to him as real as he was seeing them physically, but he kept this to himself.

*****

Chapter - 14
VIKRAM'S 9

Pataliputra, India, 405 AD

The most majestic city on Earth

King Vikramaditya, the third ruler of Gupta Dynasty, was pacing up and down in his room in the palace. His queen Anantadevi was asleep. Ever since the battle of Udaygiri he has been uneasy and hasn't been able to sleep. His biggest victory had brought him no joy, over a million men had perished in the battle and the land of central India had gone red and the stench of rotten bodies filled the air. The war with the Kingdom of Shakas was fought for over 10 years, and while the entire country had bent on its knees in front of the might of Vikramaditya, the men of Udaygiri refused to give up. This was the final frontier for Vikramaditya, the pinnacle of his victories but it did not give his heart the happiness it sought. Soon after this victory he did an Ashwamedha Yagya to prove that he is the Emperor of the land of Bharat and there is no one to stand against him.

Whenever he slept he felt someone calling him in his dream. The dream seemed more real than reality itself. The queen got up from her sleep and asked him about his worries, he assured her it's nothing and he forced himself to sleep.

But tonight when he went to sleep he could see the images in his dream, he saw himself trapped in complete darkness and it was so dark that he could barely see his own hands. He tried to run but ended up hitting a wall, he turned and ran on the other side but again the same result and he fell down. He felt there was someone around him and calling his name softly, he called out" Who are you?" but the other person did not say anything. He tried to move around to reach the person but the voice kept on changing directions. Then he heard something more, the sound of the guards from outside shouting at a prisoner, he realised that he was in a prison. Slowly he felt he was drifting out of it and was now outside the cell.

The prison cell seemed familiar, it was the *Kaalkothri* he had built to break his strongest enemies where they would be kept in the dark for days till the time they would be ready to do whatever Vikramaditya would ask them to.

Next morning Vikramaditya called for his minister and advisor Yashas. Vikramaditya knew he could trust this one person who also happened to be an accomplished scholar and astrologer and told him about the dreams he was having. The old minister did the calculations and saw the planetary charts.

"Maharaj, I believe that destiny has something more in store for you. Something more than the conquests awaits you. I would suggest that you go to the *Kaalkothari* by yourself to see what is troubling you. You might find some answers to your trouble."

"I think you are correct *Mahamantri Ji*. I must go there and see it"

King Vikram immediately proceeded towards the prison cells which were built towards the South of the city. He mounted his white horse Pawan and went there alone without any guard accompanying him. The guards at the gate of the prison complex were perplexed to see the King coming alone and un-announced. They all got alert and saluted the king. " Take me to the *Kaalkothari*"

Immediately the head of security of the prison came and accompanied the King to the Kaalkothari.

He went to the cell, the guard outside was half asleep of boredom. The head of security tapped his baton on the ground to alert the guard. The guard got in the attention position.

"Who is currently in this prison?", King Vikram asked him.

"Maharaj, it has been empty for a long time now" the guard told him.

"Who was here for the last time?" King asked.

Security head said " I will have to check the records, I will ask someone to fetch it"

"I want to go inside it , dont disturb me till I come out."

The security head and the guards were perplexed hearing this but they could not say anything much about it.

The door opened with a creak.

King Vikram went inside, it was dark but not as dark as the dream that he saw. He sat there for a few minutes and tried to remember the dream he had last night. While sitting he felt that there was something on the floor. It felt like someone had made an etching on the floor , which was deep enough to be felt by the foot. Vikram asked the guard to open the door and bring a torch , under the light of the fire Vikram could clearly see the etching, these were mantras written in Sanskrit and a circular shape which resembled a Mandala.

The security head had also returned by then with his records." Leader of a rebel group, he was an eccentric man. They had attacked our soldiers who were patrolling around the forests of the Karakati region. He was strange, did not talk but kept on mumbling something all the time. The other members of his group died when they attacked our soldiers.

"How long was he here?"

"For about 13 days"

" And what happened to him afterwards? Was he killed? Released?"

"He took *samadhi*, died while meditating"

King Vikram knew that this had something to do with the dreams that he was having.

He went back to his palace and called for his general Ugrasen " *Senapati. A few* months back our soldiers were attacked by a rebel group in the forests of Karakati. Are you aware of it?"

"Yes Maharaj, there were some 10 men who attacked the soldiers"

"Can you tell me more about it?"

The soldiers were driving out the *Dasyus,* dacoits, who had attacked a nearby village and while chasing them they ventured deep into the forest. It had gotten really dark so they decided to camp in the forest itself. They saw an old temple and they thought they could stay there , but when they tried to enter the temple some men attacked them. The soldiers were alert and they killed these men except one who was their leader. We think these were dasyus"

"And the leader was brought to Kaalkothari?"

"Yes Maharaj"

"Were these men armed?" King asked him.

"They had tridents," the General replied.

" And were any of our soldiers killed by them?"

" No one of our soldiers was killed," the General told him.

" Did the soldiers enter the temple afterwards? What was in it?" The King had many questions.

The soldiers did go inside, there was nothing much in it. There were some old paintings on the walls , even the sanctum sanctorum did not have any idol, only a shape like Mandala which did not resemble any God. It seemed related to some occult. This spooked all of them and they decided to leave that place. This was an unusual thing and so all this came to my knowledge.

King Vikram was a wise man, judging by the course of events which had happened he realised that these men were not rebels or dacoits , the soldiers had mistaken their identity and these men were just trying to stop the soldiers from going to enter the temple. The prisoner could not have been an ordinary person. There was something else to this entire episode, perhaps something about the temple.

He knew that he must visit it to find out about it so he consulted with his minister who agreed that this was the right decision. The king asked his minister to prepare a small entourage as he will be going to see this place. Some of the soldiers who were part of the troop which had gone to the Karakati forest were also in the entourage.

Next day the entire group left from the capital city of Pataliputra towards the forest of Karakati. The Emperor was sitting on an elephant, his minister Yashas , the general Ugrasen and about 20 soldiers and 15 personal attendants of Vikramaditya accompanied him. They left before sunrise and were able to reach the destination before evening .

He saw the temple, it was an old building with moss and plants covering most of the outer walls. It seemed to have been built by cutting a large single rock. It wasn't a huge building, single storeyed and about one fourth of an acre at max. He came down from his elephant.

Minister Yashas went to the king and said " Maharaj, the answer to your dreams lies here. You must face the mystery and seek the answers ".

"We are going to stay here for sometime, I am going inside the temple and I am going alone" Vikram told his men

"But it might be dangerous to go inside," General Ugrasen lightly warned the king.

The King smiled and placed his hands on his sword, King Vikram was not only the ruler of the Entire country but also the bravest warrior of the land.

While stepping inside the temple premise he felt a strange energy. The walls inside the temple had paintings which seemed hundreds of years old and there were carvings too. These depicted scenes of war and some unexplainable things. The biggest painting seemed like that of a Crow with big eyes. King Vikram went closer to it. He removed the dirt and moss around it. He could see a large crow and under him a battle was going on, he looked closely at it and it seemed like a Knight was shooting an arrow.

There was another sculpture of the crow. It seemed strange since crows are not worshipped except for the time of *Shraadh,* the time to pay respect to the departed elders of the family.

He went inside the sanctum sanctorum and just as Ugrasen had told him, there was only one Mandala which seemed to be made of some crystal. It had multiple shapes woven into a circle and was dark in colour and had a radius of about 3 feet.

Vikram bowed to the Mandala and sat down near it. He started meditating and remembered the events of the last few days and recalled the writing from the Kaalkothari and slowly chanted it, *Manavnetrat pare kim vartate iti darshayatu* : Show me what lies beyond the human eye.

It grew dark and quiet around the temple immediately. He continued chanting it. The darkness grew more and more and the Mandala seemed to shine now. Vikram continued the chants while looking at the Mandala and it felt the light from the Mandala had covered everything around him now. He looked around and all he saw was light and suddenly he felt movement and he could sense as if he was being pulled ahead with a great force by an unknown object.

He saw the picture of the crow and battle and it started coming to life. The Crow was Kaagbhusundi, the one who stands beyond the realm of time and watches everything. He has seen the birth and death of the universe hundreds of times. King Vikram could see the beginning of the Universe with the Big Bang and the collapse of it.

He could see the battle of Lanka Between Shri Ram and Ravana through the eyes of Kaagbhusundi and that of Mahabharat, these battles took place hundreds of times whenever the new universe was created after the destruction of the old universe. He saw Arjuna raising his *gandiva* to shoot an arrow at Karna, the most powerful weapon the *Pashupati Ashtra*. But Shri Krishna forbade him to use it" Parth this weapon could destroy the entire Earth, the impact of it is immeasurable.

" Keshav, but I have evoked the celestial weapon , now I cannot take it back."

" Shoot it in the emptiness of space" Shri Krishna told him.

Arjuna shot it in the sky, Kaagbhusundi had seen the battle many times and this was the one time he did not pay enough attention to it. The arrow went beyond the boundaries of universe and time itself and hit the eye of Kaagbhusundi and it started bleeding. Kaag released its mistake, as the keeper of time he cannot overlook. He asked for forgiveness.

" You must protect the Universe from a great evil that will fall on it" , he saw Krishna in his majestic form.

"But I can only see and not intervene," Kaag replied.

" You will guide the men. Through this" he said pointing to the blood coming out of the eyes of Kaag.

Kaagbhusundi threw the blood droplets on Earth in the shape of this Mandala. Some other drops of blood had got scattered across the universe , these became the worm holes which were the passage between time , space and parallel universes.

Over the years people noticed that it had magical properties and those with the strength of heart could get the power of clairvoyance through it. The temple was made to worship the Mandala and the leader of the supposed rebel was actually a priest of the temple. This was always a carefully guarded secret and therefore they tried to stop the soldiers from coming into it.

And then King Vikram could see things that would lay beyond in the future, millennia ahead because seeing this was his destiny as only the most powerful and wise emperor could have the power to use the full potential of the Mandala.

Finally King Vikram came back to reality, everything was still around him. There was moonlight around him and the Mandala was no longer shining. It seemed to him that many years would have passed but when he came out he realised that it had been only a few minutes.

"Ugrasen keep some soldiers to guard the temple. No one should come inside it" he instructed his general. On his way back he asked his minister to assemble the finest scholars of all the fields- science, literature, warfare, arts, astrology, medicine, philosophy, politics and religion.

Over the next few days the Minister and the other advisors of the King discussed who are the most suitable people for this. After over two months of discussions the candidates were selected and were given special invitation to come to the court of the king.

One of these men was the great poet and Saint Kalidas himself, others included Amarasimha, Dhanvantari, Ghatakarapara, Kshapanaka, Shanku, Varahamihira, Vararuchi, and Vetala Bhatta.

These were later known as the Navratnas of King Vikramaditya.

"I am humbled by the presence of such an elite company in my court today. You are the finest men of this generation and I have asked you all for a very important task. Something that will shape the future generations"

During the last few days

Vikramaditya had extensive discussions with his minister Yashas that he has to preserve the knowledge that humanity has gathered and continue to do so, though there will be multiple hiccups over the years but this should keep on going unbroken, no matter what. Also the temple has to be kept hidden from everyone as it possesses great secrets which can be misutilised by evil men.

"Might I suggest something maharaj?" the minister said

"Please go ahead mantri Ji".

" You should create a *maha gurukul,* a mega university, and a library at the place where this temple is situated. You can hide the temple in the vicinity and the gurukul will ensure knowledge creation and preservation both happen simultaneously."

" I can protect it now but centuries later…. Kingdoms rise and fall… however this treasure must be protected. You are right, the temple can remain hidden in the Gurukul compound and will be easier to hide."

In the court of King Vikramaditya...

The King announced " I will create the biggest university that the world has seen , the one which will bring together those thirsty of knowledge and those ready to spread it together. It will house the collection of all the important books and manuscripts that have ever been written in the world and you are the ones who will lead this."

The court sang the praise in unison" Jai ho"

I have identified an ideal place that is not far from Pataliputra. There is a small village in the jungles, the place is called Nalanda.

And then the construction of the university and library began. Students from across the globe tried to become scholars here and the best teachers were recruited under the guidance of the Navratnas.

But the duties of Navratnas were more than this, they had to ensure that they select worthy successors who would continue their work before they retire and no matter what the legacy has to continue, Manav's father was part of this legacy and he was one of the Navratnas. They also had to protect the secret of the temple and the Mandala, though only the head of the Navratnas would know how to partially use its power. The first Navratna to use it was Kalidas. The temple hidden within the massive University.

King Vikram continued to visit the temple, to increase the strength of the Mandala both mental and physical prowess were needed, but to increase it further he created an iron pillar which would act as an amplifier for the waves of the Mandala and when used correctly would unlock the complete potential of the power of the Mandala. The amplifier had to be at the correct latitude and longitude and was made of an alloy which would never rust. The water used to quench the iron was the one which had flown over the Mandala and granted powers to the alloy.

The university and library continued to grow in the reign of King Kumaragupta, the son of King Vikramaditya and reached its heights of glory; he constructed another University in the memory of his father by the name of Vikramshila which was not very far away from Nalanda. It was a peaceful era , the time when Bharat was called as the Golden bird. But the future was not so bright. King Vikram had seen glimpses of it.

*****

CHAPTER - 15
WHEN THE LIBRARIES WEPT

'The most potent way to destroy a civilization is to kill its knowledge.'

A hundred and fifty years after the death of King Vikram, the empire started to disintegrate. Many parts of the country now had their own kings and there was no ruler who was regarded as the Emperor of the country. Pataliputra was losing its glory.

Few centuries later Bharatvarsh was now known as Hindustan, over the last five hundred years there have been constant attacks to loot the country and destroy its heritage.

The iron pillar which was made in the holy caves of Udaygiri was taken away to Delhi.

Invaders from the western lands defeated the kings of the country and were now ruling over the Northern part of the country. Delhi was now the seat of power. The Sultanate wanted to not only rule over the entire country but also break the thread of heritage and culture which had made the country so great.

Many centres of learning were destroyed and temples were razed, and one day the army of Bakhtiyar Khilji, the general of Qutub-Ud-Din Aibak, came to know about the biggest centre of learning in the world. Qutub-ud-din was a slave who ascended the throne after the death of Mohammad Ghori who had defeated PrithviRaj Chauhan and had instructed his men to spread a reign of terror and destroy everything in their path.

It was the year 1197 AD, the ruler of the state of Bihar and Bengal Lakshman Sen had fought valiantly but he could not stand against the might of the army of the Sultanate.

Everyone at the University was worried about what may happen if the army decided to attack the university. There were not enough guards to protect it.

When the army reached the gates, the sentry at the gate tried to divert them.

There was no King living in it, no riches to plunder " This is a university, there is nothing of value to your army Huzoor" he pleaded with a commander"

The commander laughed " It has nothing to plunder but a lot to destroy, he took out his sword and struck down the guard"

There were 2 more guards at the entrance, they met the same fate.

A night before the *Pracharya*, the principal of the University called up all the students and teachers" The teachers and the students will have to take up arms to fight the invaders to protect the University. The warfare and martial arts department will take the charge of becoming the first line of defence along with the few guards who were posted there. The other students and teachers will support them.

There were only four in the current navratnas, who were in Nalanda. The other five were present in various other parts of the countries. The identity of Navratnas was a secret since the decline of Gupta empire and no-one outside this group knew about their existence. The secret of the temple was also well kept.

" We were told about such a thing happening many years ago, now is the time to work out the contingency plan. The secrets of the temple or this group cannot be known to these marauders", the chief of the group Pushpakumar told the other tree. The five who were outside were part of this plan.

The Sultanate army did not expect any resistance on their way, they expected to see crying people running for cover. The soldiers marched in.

Thirty students and teachers from the warfare department waited some distance beyond the entrance, in a *Veeragrandh*a, a straight line formation to block the enemy with their spears and shields. On the walls of the university the other students and teachers had lined up to fire projectiles of burning logs, rocks and hot oil. There were also some explosives which were developed in the University. The archers were ready with poison tipped arrows.

The soldiers were greeted by the projectiles and arrows, the university wall allowed only 20 soldiers to enter at once and the entire first line was annihilated. But the soldiers kept on rushing in, and falling. Some of them were able to move ahead but there were traps laid out on the path, and another 30 were killed. Those who crossed the traps were killed by the warfare students. Within minutes a hundred soldiers died. But the hordes of soldiers kept on coming in. The Nalanda men and boys kept on fighting and falling. They were too few to protect the university.

Khilji was waiting outside the gates of University, after an hour the resistance had fallen. Khilji ordered his men to kill anyone they saw inside and burn everything.

The library had over a million books. It was set to fire , the fire kept on burning for 90 days. All the wealth of knowledge , the ancient arts were lost.

CHAPTER - 16
THE PORTAL

Manav had seen the origins of the Mandala, he knew that the power was infinite. By tapping into this power one can see beyond time and become omniscient. This was the reason why the Navratnas did their best to hide the Mandala, using this power one can easily destroy or uplift humanity. King Vikram was the first one to be able to tap partly into the magic of Mandala and he used to usher the country into its brightest century the time when Bharat was named as the Golden Bird. But he also knew that his kingdom would not last forever and he made sure that the Mandala remained safe. He knew of the great war that would befall on mankind and he nominated the Navratnas to protect not only the Mandala but also all the knowledge that humans have acquired and will acquire over the years.

After the Great war of the 21st Century the nine masters were split and they moved to various parts of the country but then slowly they regrouped and established the Gurukul and trained Bodhi who rescued Manav who in turn unlocked the secret of Mandala. But the Mandala was not only the portal to view beyond time, it could unlock something more than that.

Next morning Ashamura again asked Manav to start his meditation. So Manav sat down and started his meditation, soon he again drifted into nothingness and he felt that his soul had moved out of his body and that he was travelling to a place far far away. He saw himself in a strange place, it was eerie with darkness all around. The entire place was covered with swamps and had a foul smell like rotten flesh. It was dark because the trees that grew from the swamps made a permanent canopy and the gases rising from the swamp made a cloud cover completely hiding the sun. He saw a shadow walking towards him and it came close to him and now he saw its face, it was decaying and horrifying . This made him snap out of the meditation.

Manav had sweat beads on his forehead." What did you see, what did you experience?" Ashamura immediately asked him.

"I think.... I saw a ghost" Manav said while collecting himself and getting back his senses as he himself was not sure of what he saw but he told Ashamura about the place he saw.

"Maybe you are just hallucinating" Ashamura dismissed what he was told and asked Manav to try harder.

Manav had no option but to do as was told by Ashamura. He again tried to meditate and now he did not see visions but he could hear voices he felt that he could hear the chirping of birds which were far away from them. Then he again seemed to drift away and he was dragged into the sky and he floated far away and he was sucked into darkness which seemed like a tunnel. On the other end of the tunnel he saw there were many other tunnels from which he could see different scenes of separate places simultan

He again came out of the meditation and like earlier he had to tell Ashamura about the things he saw. Ashamura did not say much but he smiled and went away, he sensed that his prisoner was now making progress in the assigned task. Manav again started to fatigue and told the men around that he wanted to go and rest but before that he just wanted to see his friend to make sure he was safe. Ashamura allowed this since he knew Manav would not do anything stupid to risk the life of his friend. Two guards accompanied Manav to the cell where Bodhi was held prisoner. He was inside a room, the door had a transparent window to look inside and monitor the prisoner. The walls were solid brick and the door was made of steel. He saw in the room many spears which were protruding from the ceiling and the walls. He asked " what are these spears?" The guard pointed to a lever " If I pull this lever then all the spears are shot at once and it will be impossible for anyone to escape. This is the mechanism to ensure that your dear friend will not try anything smart" he continued after a pause " and if you too try to play any tricks using your powers your friend will become a dead body"

Bodhi saw him and gently waved at him and asked how Manav was doing. Manav gestured that he is fine and asked about Bodhi who too said he is fine. They looked at each other with sadness and helplessness for a few seconds and then Manav felt he could hear Bodhi say "I am fine, you take care of yourself. Soon we will find a way to deal with this situation"

"These voices must be my emotions overpowering me on seeing my friend caged like this" He again looked at Bodhi who looked a bit puzzled.

He then heard the voice of Bodhi again " Was I hearing Manav's voice?"

They looked at each other and now understood, they were able to establish telepathy with each other " they talked, this could be due to the meditation " Bodhi said. "Yes, I too think that" Manav replied in his head. Then he quickly told him all that had happened since the time Bodhi was taken away and that he has discovered the origins of the Mandala but he will have to help Ashamura in his nefarious plans else he will kill Bodhi.

"I think I should head back. The guards are getting suspicious" Manav said in his mind, " You must" Bodhi agreed and Manav said to the guards to take him back. He was taken to another cell, which was not as fortified and decked with spears but still had guards outside.

While moving him inside the cell the guard said" You had enough rest in the healing room. Now get used to this cell" Manav did not respond and simply went inside the cell. Once he went inside he again tried to talk to Bodhi but he could not " I can talk to him only when we are near each other, perhaps the power of telepathy is not yet strong enough so I must meditate over the Mandala more"

Next morning he was again taken to the Mandala, this time while he was in his meditation.For few seconds he saw complete darkness and then he felt he is running and then he could see inside the cell where Bodhi was held and it appeared that he was seeing it through Bodhi's eyes, his psychic connection with his friend was now complete. He gave a message through telepathy to Bodhi, "I am now connected with you and I can see through your eyes". "So what's the plan now?" Bodhi asked him. " You are trapped inside this cell. If you even try to run, the guard will press the lever and all the spears will be released and few of them will hit you for sure, but if you come out of it I don't think they will be able to stop the two of us, " Manav told him via telepathy.

The two of them took a pause and thought of the possibilities, Manav suddenly had an idea. He went into his siddhi state while still being telepathically connected with Bodhi. Now he could not only see the things that Bodhi was seeing, he could see the dangers that could fall on Bodhi and keep on telling him to avoid. Through his siddhi he saw that the guard will push the lever when Bodhi tries to escape and he saw all the spears that will hit Bodhi. Bodhi asked him "Have you thought of something? I am in my siddhi state and I can see that once the guard pulls the lever at least 2 spears will hit you in the vital organs and will kill you" he told in a grim voice. "

Whatever it is I cannot remain stuck here and you won't be able to hide this power of yours from Ashamura's lie detecting device and if he is able to use the powers of Mandala everything will be destroyed. Now is the time , now is the Manav. I am going to take my chance. Avenge me if I fail to make it out"

Bodhi took a couple of steps back and jumped, the guard looked inside and he saw that the fire torch had been put out, he shouted out " what the hell is going on?" he repeated but there was no response. He looked at the other guard and asked " should I pull the lever?" The other guard nodded, and he pressed the lever, it was too dangerous to open the door and look inside.

They heard a loud cry from inside and they opened the door after about a minute. One had his loaded crossbow and the other had swords in both his hands, they were one of the most trained men of Ashmura. It was dark inside, they waited for a few more seconds till the eyes would adapt to the dark and then they stepped in, in the dark cell they saw pieces of spears spread across the room, they stepped on a liquid. It looked like blood. " Is he dead?" the guard with the crossbow asked the other one with swords. The guard with swords replied " I think.... " He could not complete his sentence because a spear was hurled in his mouth. The guard with the crossbow shot the arrow in the dark and immediately turned back to lock the door but a hand grabbed his neck and twisted it, before he died the guard could only see the eyes which had had no pupil.

When Bodhi had said that he was making his move, Manav knew he could not talk him out of it. Bodhi leapt up and in a powerful kick broke the fire torch but Manav could still see due to his siddhi state and he knew which spears would hit Bodhi and in the next 2 seconds Bodhi broke those spears before the guard pressed the lever. Some of the spears did injure him and blood was flowing from his shoulder and thigh but these were minor injuries for a warrior like him. He rushed out of the room and picked the swords of the dead guard, though the power of telepathy and his siddhi Manav was able to warn Bodhi about all the dangers that were there in his path.

He moved forward and a volley of arrows came his way, he cut through the arrows by using his swords like a windmill and moved forward. The six guards at the corridor who were shooting the arrows did not get time to reload and Bodhi slit their necks using the two swords in each of his hands. All the guards fell on his either side and he walked through the middle of this mess. One guard saw this and instead of trying to fight decided to sound the warning horn he had put the horn on his mouth but before he could blow it Bodhi threw the sword in his right hand at him and it went inside his chest he died immediately.The super strength and fighting skill of Bodhi combined with the power of Manav was now impossible to stop.

Bodhi ran towards the central room where Manav was in his meditation. He entered the room and he saw Manav sitting there in front of the Mandala and some of Ashamura's men surrounding him. These men saw Bodhi and three of them rushed at him, one with sword, one with spear and the third who was the largest of them all had a spiked club.

Bodhi was holding a sword in his right hand and in the blink of an eye he threw a knife at the fighter with a spear who could not dodge it and it hit him in his eye and he went down. This distracted the other two for a second and this gave Bodhi enough time to leap and tackle the sword fighter. The sword fight went for about 10 seconds and Bodhi severed the head of his opponent. Which fell at the feet of the third fighter who was slow to come near Bodhi. The fighter with the club swung it at Bodhi with all his might but Bodhi ducked and rolled to the other side. Meanwhile two other men who had entered the room were taking aim at Bodhi using their crossbows. One of them shot an arrow at Bodhi. Bodhi was skillful enough to dodge or divert an arrow fired at him but when combined with the siddhi of Manav he was capable of doing that even with an arrow shot by a hiding enemy. Bodhi diverted the arrow and it hit the arm of the man with the club, he dropped his club and Bodhi went on his knees skidding and holding his sword in both his hands above his head he thrust it inside the stomach of his opponent.

The arrow of the other shooter was loaded and shot but it missed Bodhi by a whisker because Manav had come out of Meditation and he punched the guts of the shooter, who had made the shot while falling down. Before he fell down Manav kicked his temple and the shooter was dead even before hitting the ground. Since he came out of the meditation he could not transmit the power of siddhi state to Bodhi now.

All this while Ashamura was doing his weapons training. Two of his personal body guards both heavily built and over seven feet tall and looked like they belonged to a different country, were standing a few feet behind him. A servant of his came rushing and shouted" Boss the prisoner has got out and is wreaking havoc."

"Which one?" he asked without looking at the servant and continuing his practice " The one in the maximum security cell."

Ashamura was about to stab a dummy while practising but his hand froze and his brows tightened and he threw the knife at the servant who wasn't able to dodge it and took it on his shoulder. The servant went down and grimaced in pain while Ashamura quickly dressed and took his gear and ran out towards the scene of the fi

He reached the central room where all this was going and he saw Bodhi stabbing his men. He was the most skillful fighter and had become the leader of the Shadow Ninjas because of that, Manav's sixth sense had tingled by then and he knew that Ashamura was about to attack, Ashamura threw a bomb which when fell started releasing a thick smoke. Manav through the telepathy informed Bodhi that this is the same gas which had knocked them unconscious earlier. There was a water jug near the mandala, Manav grabbed it and used it to wet his shirt and then threw it at Bodhi who caught it and did the same. Both of them tore a piece of their shirt and tied it on their face covering their mouth and nose.

The thick green smoke coming out of the bomb filled the room. Ashamura and his bodyguards wore masks which helped them to breathe without trouble, the smoke had reduced the visibility and the effect of gas was making Manav slow though he could still predict the movement of enemies easily. The two body guards went ahead to fight with their swords, each to take on Bodhi and Manav who were diagonally opposite of each other about 50 feet apart. Manav knew that the visibility would be a challenge for Bodhi while the bodyguards had practice of fighting in this gas and would be able to move more easily than Bodhi so he quickly ran close to the other bodyguard to tackle both of them at once.

The bodyguards were extremely skilled in sword fighting and used their size to good effect to block Manav's attack. The two of them started with a mirror image attack, both moved in a perfect sync which would have made it difficult for any other opponent to predict the attack but Manav had predicted it a few minutes back. Then they attacked from both sides, moving their swords like a whirlwind and attacking Manav from both sides. The sword fight went on for a few minutes, Manav struggled due to the effect of gas but the two men were not able to land a single strike on him, he blocked all their strikes with his sword.

Bodhi was lying down and just trying to look at the fight that was going on. He knew that the two fighters will not be able to defeat Manav and he can fight them blindfolded but what he had not expected was the fight going on for so long and perhaps the fighters are not trying to defeat Manav but were only trying to tire him out. Manav had been in the siddhi state for a long time and had used up a lot of energy in establishing the telepathy with Bodhi. The gas too was having its effect and even after covering the mouth some amount was getting slowly inhaled, he came out of the siddhi state and continued fighting the two, he knew he had only the last ounce of energy left in him and that his opponents were trying their best to tire him out. So he outmanoeuvred them, he did a black flip and jumped over the fighter who was standing behind him, slid towards his left now both of the opponents were in front of him but instead of attacking them he dropped his sword. The two of them went still for a second, they were instructed not to kill him, they then went ahead and he tried to hold Manav who used this opportunity to tackle the one who was on his left and kicked his shin and he lost his balance, he collided with the other one. Manav used this to grab back his sword and in a single strike cut through their guts and then he fell unconscious but he was able to fatally injure both of the bodyguards. Ashamura was watching this from a distance, and once Manav fell he decided to make his move. He walked towards him, he threw a knife at Manav to check if he was actually unconscious. The knife whisked past his ear but Manav did not move. Ashamura was sure, Bodhi too was unconscious about five feet away from Manav and the two body guards were taking their last breath half conscious and blood flowing out of their mouths.

He took out a chain to tie up Bodhi, "I still can't figure out how you managed to escape from that cell but this time I am not going to take any chances". He tied up Bodhi's hands with the chain. He then took out a syringe and filled it with a dark coloured liquid from a small bottle he took out from his tool belt. "This venom will keep you in permanent sleep, you will never be able to run and I will use you as my bait forever ". He bent to give the injection on the neck of Bodhi. The syringe reached his skin but before he could do so Bodhi slipped aside and caught hold of Ashamura's hand and twisted it and made him inject himself with the venom on his neck. All this was so quick that it did not give Ashamura a chance to act " How did you? " Bodhi had broken his thumb to loosen the chain while Ashmura was filling the syringe, the green gas around helped to reduce the visibility. Ashamura was so sure that Bodhi was unconscious that he had lowered his guard and that split second was enough for Bodhi to act.

Ashamura repeated his question and Bodhi answered him " Manav had seen your move when you had come. He asked me not to fight so I would not need to inhale too much and I slowed my breathing so I did not go unconscious under the effect of your gas. Just before he went unconscious he told me what would happen. I was ready. You could defeat the others at Gurukul using your bag of tricks but not us." Ashamura went into a permanent sleep after hearing this. Bodhi took a sword and beheaded Ashamura, "This is for all those who died because of you."

Bodhi took Manav to the healing room, the healer was still there. He ordered him to bandage his wounds and tend to Manav and he would spare the life of the healer. The healer obliged, and after an hour Manav got up. " We have taken the revenge of our Gurukul. Ashamura is dead" Bodhi told him. Manav got up. " So now our mission is complete we should head back" Bodhi said. "But where do we go ? Gurukul was our home" Manav asked him.

"Gurukul is still our home" We take back the Mandala to the place where it should be and we re-establish the Gurukul in the memory of our teachers and friends.

They carried the Mandala over a horse wagon which was stationed in the stable of Ashamura and released the other horses to run away. The two of them then doused the entire den of Ashamura in flammable oil and put it on fire and went back to the shores where they had parked their boat.

Chapter - 17
THE JOURNEY TO HOME

Manav and Bodhi reached the shores in two days. They did come across bandits who were attracted by the wagon and were expecting a bounty in it but all they got was death. With Mandala by his side, Manav's siddhi powers had become much stronger and he was able to predict the attack in advance and he decided to test the telepathy and Bodhi with the help of telepathy guidance defeated the entire group of ten bandits.

On the way Bodhi asked Manav "I was thinking, can you establish telepathy with anyone?"

"I do not know, I did try to see in the minds of the men of Ashamura but I could not. I think I was able to establish telepathy with you because of the bond that we share but I do not know what the possibilities are. I saw visions of strange places, there is much more to know from the Mandala"

On the shore they saw a huge crowd around the area where their boat was harboured and it appeared that one man was auctioning off the boat. The boat was a novelty and many buyers had come there. They saw Moon at a distance, " he must have informed the harbour guys to sell the boat expecting we will not return" Bodhi laughed and said to Manav.

Manav too laughed at him" They are about to see ghosts"

They got down from the wagon and had swords in their hands "This boat is ours and anybody who dares to take it will have to go through us" they proclaimed. Two strongmen attacked them with swords but were disarmed in a moment. " We do not want any blood shed, it is better you let us pass through without any trouble" Bodhi told. Moon saw them and told the men not to mess with them, he understood that they would have killed Ashamura, the most feared man on this land.

They loaded up the Mandala on the boat. They saw a huge army had gathered by then, there were over a 100 men and then many locals too were with them . They were all armed and ready to attack the boat with spears and arrows. " I think it's the shogun's men," Bodhi said.

"No problem" I was expecting them Manav said and then he reached the big gun on the boat" Time to put it to use" He started shooting and killed a dozen men and destroyed the boats which were there on the shore. The harbour was destroyed in minutes and everyone ran off.

And then off went the two friends. This time Manav was at the helm and he asked Bodhi " Should we stop at AkhandDeep Rashtra and return their boat?" He knew that Bodhi liked Kylie and he wanted him to meet her again. " I could not get the love of my love, she betrayed me but the girl he likes is honest and loves him" he thought. Bodhi gave it a long thought "Yes, we should return it, our mission is over and the journey on sea from that country back home is not long. We won't need this boat" Manav could not gauge what Bodhi was thinking because they were not connected with telepathy at that time,also he was happy to let Bodhi have his personal thoughts to himself.

Next morning after his daily ritual of Suryanamaskar Manav started meditating with the Mandala, now he had already established the connection with it so he knew it would be easier to do it again without the elaborate set up.He remained in meditation for more than three hours , Bodhi saw him sweating and growing uneasy but he did not disturb him. He finally came out of meditation. Bodhi got him some water and fruits and then asked " What was it that made you sweat?"

" Remember I told you about seeing ghost-like figures in a strange place. I saw them again" Manav told him while having the fruits .

"So what was it ?" Bodhi sat near him and asked

" I saw that place again. I felt that i was flying over the oceans and reached a place where I saw walking corpses and spirits which were without bodies and then it seemed I was suddenly transported to another place , as if it was beyond starts and I saw something I don't know what it was but it seemed that I could hear crying voices from inside it. This is all that could remember" Manav told him

"Take rest" Bodhi comforted Manav

Some time later Manav had more visions and he told Bodhi " We have to change the course, I felt that the Mandala is guiding us to a different direction in the sea which is away from the initial destination. The Mission is not yet complete"

*****

CHAPTER - 18
THE TRAINING GROUND

A few days had passed since Jose had won the HRP competition, he was now a celebrity. Getting interviewed by TV channels. The TV channels were for all types, the 2D and 3D for those who still liked it retro and in Hyper Reality for those who liked to view things closely.

It was another interview that Jose had been called for, of course he was giving it from the comfort of his home while being connected with the HRP box. The interviewer named Catherina greeted him. The Interview was atop a mountain which had a waterfall. The stream passed beneath the stage that was made for Jose and Catherina.

Catherina was a bright reporter who had recently become an interviewer, she was a major in anthropology and had travelled to various parts of the World physically. She had actually seen the beauty of the world, the deep oceans which covered most of the globe. She had dived into them and had seen the lost cities which were now Underwater.

The initial questions were about his life and how he had prepared for the contest. But soon she moved to something more meaningful. "Due to the extremely sedentary lifestyle driven by bots and HRP most people suffer from obesity and diseases associated with it but then to dull the pain of reality HRP is always around. For someone who has been in Hyper reality so much dont you think this could lead to another wave of mass extinction for us?"

Jose too was severely overweight and barely walked. He would often think if he could in the real world only be a fraction of what he is in the hyper reality. He made girlfriends in the Hyper reality but never in real life. Those girlfriends were sometimes both and sometimes the avatars of real girls who always refused to take things ahead with him when they met in person.

" Yes, I agree that people should pay enough attention to the physical aspect of their life. HRP has made life easy but one can have a truly happy life if he is physically fit also."

The audience had mixed reactions, some were really impressed by this candid talk and others said this is nothing but flowery talk by a new celebrity who would soon be forgotten.

There was a particular man who got deeply interested in Jose and Catherina after listening to their views, he was Dr. Ozkhaman . He was a senior scientist with HRP Corp who had been instrumental in merging the various servers of HPR , so that people can move from world to another without any need to logout of the server. This was the most important breakthrough in HRP in the last 2 decades. It was like moving from one slide of a presentation to another, earlier it was like moving from movie to another by changing the disk. This breakthrough was creating a parallel world and everyday it was getting more and more enhanced. It got him promoted to the designation of Deputy Director.

A senior scientist for the HRP corp like Oz was akin to being a high ranking government official. He met Catherina and Jose' after the interview was done and congratulated them for raising this important issue" I am truly impressed by this dialogue today, not young people have been raising the right issues"

"But sir", Catherina said after looking at his badge" you are a senior scientist at the corporation, this is something that goes against what HRP is doing. Making the virtual world and relations replace the real world."

"I completely agree with you Miss Catherine, and in-fact I have been a chief architect of doing this when I merged the servers. I have realised my mistake, but the realisation was too late. My young son died because of obesity and depression" , he paused for a few seconds" I want to make amends so that I can save the other young people."

Oz was into his late 50s, he looked like a normal scientist, he was thin and had grey unkempt hair. His eyes were deep and they showed the resolve that he had.

" This is great," Jose chipped in, "but how do you plan to do tha

" Well the path to move out of the addiction is within the addiction itself. I have added a new server for this. But I need help from people like you to be the promoters for this. As the Deputy Director I cannot officially be a part of a project which would reduce the timeshare of HRP corp."

" We can very well understand your predicament here Sir" Catherina assured her

" The developers of my team were not aware of the project that they were working on, they just knew the bits and pieces which were relevant to them and I have managed to hide the codes from being viewed by anyone to know the source." Oz informed them.

Jose smiled in appreciation.

" Mr. Martinez you will have to project yourself as the one who has conceived this project but you can't advertise this openly to avoid risk of being unplugged by the surveillance. You are champion of this year so the youth are going to follow you. Once you have enough members signed up in the program we will let them know what this is about and Miss Catherina you will be the voice behind it. Your research and knowledge will go a long distance in convincing them to stay in"

"Why don't we all meet face to face. Here is my address" Oz said, sharing his visiting card " and here is my secretary. He will help you in your travel arrangements " The secretary was a bot who took the details from them for the meeting.

A week later, the meeting was fixed. Jose air travelled to the Orca city. The bot driven taxi took him to the home cum lab of Dr. Oz. Catherina was living in the Orca city itself. They reached at the designated time 9 Pm. It was summer in Antarctica so the sun was still shining brightly even at night.

Both Catherina and Jose arrived at the same time, the huge metal door unlocked itself after doing their facial recognition. A small bot guided them through the stoned pathway which was built though a small garden.

The door opened and Dr. Oz greeted them " What would you like to have?" he asked them while pointing out to his bar "I have the finest collection of drinks from the round the globe"

"Would try out anything that you suggest, " Catherina said.

"Jose, I will go with my regular whiskey" Jose replied

A bot brought the drinks for the guests

"I have developed a program where if the participants follow a certain regime the brain waves will impact their physical conditions too. As I told you, the cure lies within the problem. I have not yet made this live on the main server. " He paused and continued" Mr. Martinez, why don't you give it a try. I think you will be able to perform better in this simulation owing to your abilities in the hyper reality."

" Sure, let me try" he enthusiastically replied and he plugged himself into the program.

" Miss Catherina please observe and share your views"

Stepping inside the HRP program feels like waking up from a dream. People can choose their avatar which would be like a display picture of a social media account. They can change it any time. But the avatar of one person can interact with the avatar of another person just like a human. In case of violation of law even in this virtual world people would face fines and ban.

This place seemed like a village and seemingly devoid of any modern amenities. When he went ahead he saw some people busy doing their chores. No one was talking to him. Jose went ahead in the village and soon saw a castle across a valley. The valley had multiple obstacles such as a raging river, treacherous rocks and wild animals but Jose was able to cross all that and reached the castle. Having played so many games he knew the castle is where the main battle would be, it would either have a treasure guarded by powerful entities or some innocent people trapped it.

He went to the door and it opened quite easily with a single push.

As expected he was attacked by a demon inside, then he moved further inside and saw a maze, it was again not very hard for him to come out. Outside the maze he saw a ghostly figure. The figure said" I am The Phantom of the castle, the protector of this place, to go ahead you must tell me about yourself, answer my question honestly and do not lie, if you lie your head will burst into a hundred pieces. The Phantom asked him about his life, the sad part of his life and the happy parts, the things he would like to change in his life. He said "I would want to be more confident in my real life "

" You have spoken the truth, now go ahead and change it as per your wish, remember those times where you think you could have made a difference"

He remembered the time when he was bullied at school but could not stand up. He could see the school and the boys bullying the teenage Jose. The adult Jose in his avatar went up to the boys and beat the hell out of them. He then picks up the young Jose and tells him "Listen kid, next time I might not be around to help you but you need to stand up for yourself and for that you need to be fit and confident."

He leaves smiling and next moment he sees himself back in front of the Phantom" You have done well , you can now proceed ahead"

After that he encounters hurdles and monsters, many of these monsters seem to have the faces of people he had known and those who had hurt him in the past.Finally he reaches the treasure , the treasure case when he opened had a heart, one which was beating and a happy music was coming out of it, it jumps up and goes inside Jose and the level was complete.

After coming out of it Jose said " I can feel as if I have worked out. But how did the simulation have faces of the people I knew of"

"It was your own imagination, this is known as Neuro Linguistic Programming. By training your brain you can impact many things in your life." the scientist explained

Catherina too was out of the Hyper reality " that's great Dr Oz, it really works The future has hope"

" Yes it does. I had tried it on a few test subjects but the time taken for them to experience this was much more since they were not pro in HRP gaming like Mr Martincz. Now since you have experienced you would need to pull in more people in this. I will integrate this with the main server of the HRP"

Since he was the Deputy Director it was easy for Dr Oz to add this to the main server, he was able to get the necessary clearances but none of those quality controllers knew that the impact of this will be on the physical self t

Soon more people started joining this only to experience a new world because of the influence of Jose and Catherina but were not aware of the other impacts. Jose told them that this was the training ground to improve performance in any hyper reality game.

Catherina now had a show dedicated to improvement in performance in Hyper reality games and she often talked about the training ground in it. Many participants too were interviewed who expressed their happiness on finding something like this "Well this is how sports have evolved, back in the early 20th century when Olympics started athletes entered as amateurs and rarely had coaches to help them train but soon the games became huge in popularity and then came the coaches , government backing and what not . Despite being big in terms of popularity and prizes the hyper reality games too have started to enter this second stage of professional training"

Seeing the shift of the time share to this new World the auditors did their routine check, but they too got the same info that this is something developed by Jose to train more people to perform better in games.

The next year's contest too was won by Jose which further stressed the point that the training ground was working fine and more people joined it. Dr. Oz saw Jose being crowned the champion again, he went inside one of his rooms. The room was well decorated and had various pictures and artefacts related to science on the walls and the shelf but it was freezing cold. There was a glass box kept in the middle of the room, it was attached with various machines which were pumping some liquid in it and had monitors attached. Oz looked at it. He could see an old man lying in a state of deep sleep, he looked just like him but a few years older.

Dr Oz then pressed a button , and his eyes started glowing and near the button there was a monitor which was showing the battery being charged, he wasn't a human but a bot.

The actual Dr Oz was a child prodigy. He majored in robotics, neuro linguistic programming and hyper reality. He believed that through HRP the real world can be changed and humans can live forever. HRP could save their consciousness and the consciousness when connected to a robot can make them live forever. The robot can be replaced as many times as possible. He did extensive research on this but there were some issues with it. The amount of server space it needed was too huge as per the analysis and the energy generated could disrupt other programs and secondly to prove the validity it was important to have a human test subject and it was too dangerous to try this. It never got passed by the Ethical Committee of the corporation.

But Dr. Oz continued working on it, till the day he got to know he is suffering from Muscular dystrophy. It would mean he would end up being paralyzed and would meet his untimely death before completing his dream projects. So he knew he had the subject to test his project out, himself.

So he went ahead and gave his voice and face to a bot, which was fairly easy to do. Artificial Intelligence was quite developed; it had still not replaced humans because it was not unable to think independently or have emotions and hence it still depended on human instructions.

He connected the bot with the program that he had created and he let his consciousness get captured in the Training Ground program. To do this he first used neuro linguistic programming to make the body feel actual sensations within the program and this made the consciousness believe that this is reality, the castle was the mind palace which would store the memories of the person. Final step was to stop the exit of the consciousness to go back to the actual reality. To do this, slowly the consciousness would build things in the ground for itself which are related to the life of the individual. Every few days the program will make the individual forget the things he had built earlier and finally after completing the last maze of the training the consciousness would forget that this was the world it had built for itself and thus remain there forever.

But for himself Dr Oz had built a special library which told him all about all that had happened so it can work out the future plans even while staying in the hyper reality. This consciousness was the lifeline for the physical bot which was the guide of its action.

Once the Training Ground program was linked with the Hyper reality server the consciousness of Dr Oz could freely move around in the Hyper reality world. Also remaining in the cryo chamber slowed his ageing and death and to avoid any chance of consciousness getting back into his body he had sedated the nervous system of his body completely using neural anaesthetic chemicals . With further advancements in medicine probably his body too could live forever.

The bot Dr. Oz had spent time at HPR Corp and it had noticed that the system had glitches in it. He did well to hide them, not because he wanted to save the reputation of the company but because he knew the glitches meant possibilities for the evolution of Hyper reality.

A very important protocol was to ensure the ability of the individual to logout out of the Hyper reality and get back in his world without any problem. Even if there is a glitch in the server or any of the programs this protocol would take over and the participant would get pulled out of the hyper reality.

The Training Ground had a lot of facilities such as obstacle courses, fight simulations, and athletics. It actually helped the participants to perform better in the Hyper reality games and now it had the pull with so many people coming in.

When one World of Hyper reality would get too much of the time share it would create a gravitational pull which can cause the programs and worlds in the vicinity to malfunction but this has never happened since beyond a point entry of participants would be stopped, if this phenomenon is coupled with extensive physical activity then the gravity would become stronger.

Dr Oz knew of this and he knew by creating the Training Ground he could generate enough force so that it can impact other programs. He on purpose uploaded the Training Ground program on the server which was close to the safety protocol server.

A month after the second championship had completed, Dr Oz checked the load on the server on which the Training Ground program was uploaded, it wasn't much to raise any suspicion of the corporation engineers but it was the right threshold to upload the final maze for all the participants.

Catherina and Jose too were part of this and Dr Oz had told that today he will open up a new maze which will enhance the physical abilities of the participants even more.

There were ten thousand participants that day whose consciousness had created enough memories for a parallel reality, the Oz bot sent out a radio wave to the program, and the final maze was activated.

Suddenly a lot of glitches started coming in various programs of the hyper reality. Some Worlds in the hyper reality started facing distortions. The helpline chats were getting SOS messages. The load on the server was reaching the max capacity the timeshare of one program had increased too much. " Sir the issue is coming from the Training Ground Program" said one the analysts"

His manager replied" but why is it not shutting down automatically?"

"Sir the safety protocol has failed"

There was panic in the headquarters of the HRP Corp due to this.. The entire top cadre was present and were trying to debug the issue, the bot of Dr Oz was also present there pretending to help.

" We have to disconnect the server, it will impact other things in the hype reality but anyways things have gone astray" Dr Bhaskar said.

This had never been done before, but this seemed the only way to address this. The server was disconnected but nothing happened.

" They got a message from the one of the chat operator bot"

The people who were in the corrupted programs are not able to return to the real world, they are stuck.

"What the …." fear had frozen everyone present there.

One by one the consciousness of the participants had kept on getting sucked and before the alarms could go off the load on the server had become so much that it corrupted the safety protocol. The gravitational pull became like a typhoon which started sucking everthing around it. The programs and the Hyper reality worlds around it started to malfunction and they too became the part of the Training Ground, due to extreme high pull even without the use of the mazes the consciousness of these people too got sucked in.

The Training ground was now running on its own without being connected to the Hyper reality server, this meant there was no one to control it or even see what was happening inside it, it was a black box.

"Send out the communication to every living soul on the planet, Do not login into the Hyper reality" the CEO of the corporation Samarth Narayan who was now an old man shouted in agony. Communication was sent out to every government, to every authority and broadcasted over every medium which was not connected with Hyper reality but the unfortunate part was that these media were now too rarely used by the common people.

All the heads of states were on a video call with The CEO Dr. Samarth and other chief scientists and Engineers.

"Should we destroy the server so that the people can come out of the Hyper reality" Head of the Antarctica country Peter Santiorini asked Samarth and Bhaskar.

We have done our calculations, now hyper reality is running without any external power supply as it is now generating its own power , the activity inside the server is creating enough kinetic energy which is getting converted to electricity. If we try to destroy it using a bomb the impact could be very dangerous, this can cause an explosion like a nuclear blast. We are not even able to go near the server as it is generating powerful shocks and two of our engineers have died because of this.

While all of them continued finding solutions working 24x7 for the next few days, the people whose kin have been trapped in the Hyper reality started agitation. The offices of HRP Corporation across the world were pelted by stones. Even Government offices were vandalised in many cities. The police were trying to ensure that riots don't happen.

The people who were trapped inside were still lying in their homes and offices for the last 7 days, some of them had been put on drip to ensure that they don't die in this vegetative state that they had gone into. Many others did not have anyone to help them out.

The worst was yet to come. Inside the training ground the people were getting increasingly confused, they kept on asking from Jose about what was happening since the landscape of the Training Ground had changed a lot and why they were not able to come out of the Hyper reality, but he had no answers. All that he said was that this was the last maze to complete the training. Catherina was trying to placate the people who had got sucked in from the other programs that this might be a glitch and it will get back to normal very soon and they should not lose patience.

Although they kept on forgetting what they did the last day and so Jose had to answer them with the same thing again.

The electric surge around the server kept on increasing and now it had started affecting other electrical and electronic devices. Half of the city had to be evacuated because it was too risky for the lives of residents.

The physical bodies of people who were stuck in the hyper-reality started dying one by one, the doctors tried their best to save these people but they were not able to do anything and soon the problem became so huge that there were no doctors to save them. Mankind was nearing another mass extinction, no one had answers.

Once these people died then it was not just the minds or consciousness of the participants but their souls which were getting trapped inside the hyper reality. The soul, being much more powerful than the mind, could remember that they had been stuck in the Training ground for a very long time, they could see that their avatar had changed a lot and it did not resemble the human version now , they were like shadows, this had increased the strength of the electrical discharges to an extreme.

Dr Oz all this while was in the Training Ground, he had created a special lab for himself by which he was still controlling the hyper reality. He could do this only once the Hyper reality was disconnected from the main server, knowing how the people and systems work at the corporation he knew that this will be done sooner or later. Everything was falling into place.

He had made his calculations, what would happen if the bodies die, will the minds remain inside or will that too die. There was about a 10% chance that he would be able to trap the minds inside, but a success meant a world where he would be the God of this World , since only he knew all the rules of this world. He had an entire library of programs which were yet to be made live, these were made for various situations that he could face in this world.

He no longer needed the bot version of himself in the outside world once he knew that his prisoners can survive in the Training ground even without their physical self. And since the physical bot of Dr Oz is the last remaining link between hyper reality and the physical world and a possible clue to let the Corp know about what has happened. He set the self destruct mode of the bot and he sent out a communication to the people in the corporation that he is committing suicide as he considers himself as a culprit behind the fiasco and he cannot bear the guilt of it . He also burnt his lab and all the research work he had done for the Training ground project.

The entire building which was housing the server had now become a hazard , all the electrical and electromagnetic devices which were coming in contact with these discharges were becoming a part of it and were sending out shocks and whoever were getting hit by them would go into a state of comma similar to what had happened to the participants of the Training ground and would die in sometime and their souls getting trapped in the Training Ground.

The electric lines were getting caught in it and the electricity for the entire city had to be cut down. This was like a volcano whose lava was flowing around and destroying everything in its path.

Ten days had gone by and this threat was enough to wipe out the entire mankind. Orca City was almost deserted by now.

The top brains and administrators had put forward all the ideas, all of them had an element of uncertainty because they were dealing with something no one could have predicted and no one knew how to handle. So after multiple deliberations and proposals finally the last resort solution was decided. It was clear to Samarth and others that those stuck in Hyper reality and not dead yet will not come back, this meant almost a tenth of the population will be lost, it was important to save the rest of mankind.

"This is the most painful call we will have to take", The Prime Minister announced.

For the next steps the help of the ISVO, International Space Voyage organisation was taken. The Director of the organisation was called up and it was decided that the entire corrupted unit has to be transported out of Earth' atmosphere so that it can do no more damage to the World and there was only one organisation capable of executing such a huge task. All the employees of ISVO who were still alive got into action without any delay, although only a handful knew what was going to happen.

The core of the contaminated area was covered with a gigantic magnetic dome which was tied with the biggest spaceship of the planet. The dome was strong enough to withstand the friction while crossing the atmosphere and it could survive the discharges from the contaminated area for a few days before it would break.

The spaceship VXM 3 of ISVO was a cruise ship, large enough to carry over two hundred passengers and a hundred crew for a luxurious space cruise to Mars. It had done two trips earlier with the richest people of Earth onboard, many of them were employees of the HRP corporation. Underground blasts were to be deployed simultaneously along with the rocket launches so that the entire contaminated mass can be lifted.

There was one problem though, the spaceship could not be controlled via automation. It needed at least six pilots to control it. Many brave spaceship pilots responded to the call, fully aware that they would be carrying the most dangerous thing on the planet and they might never return back to Earth. Those with the most impeccable records and experience of piloting huge ships were selected and immediately flown to the palace which would be the launch site. After a brief training they were ready.

That evening every person on Earth prayed just for the success of this mission. The prayers were answered, the spaceship was able to lift the entire mass and off it went out of the atmosphere of the Earth never to be seen again

The plan was to release the entire mass out in space and the six pilots to come back using a smaller detachable ship back to Earth while the contaminated mass would continue its journey and would keep on going away from Earth.

CHAPTER - 19
WELCOME TO HELL

When the spaceship was launched along with the contaminated servers and other devices, things went on well for the next five days. The entire team had a small celebration the day before, they called themselves The Saviours of the Earth, the superheroes who had saved Earth from a certain doom. The Magnetic dome could survive for a maximum of ten days and by the sixth day the distance of the spaceship would be large enough to let it drift away from Earth in any direction. So the sixth day was deemed right for evacuation

On the designated day, at 12:00 hours they got into the detachable ship. The command station from Earth was online. "We are in position" the Captain told the command centre. "Here we go, 3…2..1… Go" . He pressed the evacuate button but nothing happened. " It did not work" he told

Command Center" Try it again"

He tried again and again " it is stuck, it is not working"

The command centre tried to guide them, the engineers looked at the design and what could have gone wrong and the possible solutions.

Everything was tried but nothing worked, after 3 days of trying and failure the saviours had realised that they will not be able to return back. They sent their last messages and on the 10th day, the dome collapsed and all the devices in the spaceship stopped working. The six brave pilots laid down their lives to save Earth.

A memorial was created for these bravehearts on Earth. Meanwhile Hyper reality Corporation was shut down, the biggest economic entity on Earth, and with that all the other companies which relied on Hyper reality went bankrupt.

Economy collapsed and along with it the society too. A tenth of the population was killed in the HyperReality and many others died in the events post that.

When the spaceship was realised the magnetic domes prevented the electric discharges from the server but a small amount of current kept on seeping through it, before the evacuation of the pilots the devices in the spaceship had got attached to the servers and the evacuation switch failed because of that. The pilots remained stuck in the cockpit and continued to guide the ship , their minds and souls were now in Hyper reality and were being controlled by Dr Oz.

The souls inside the server were continually tortured by their master. *This place where the souls were trapped is not a Training ground, this is HELL! And the Devil was running it.*

This ensured that they are continuously frightened and it created entropy to give energy to the hell. For torturing he used his earlier hidden programs and using that he would show them their worst fears. Sometimes it would project the souls as hungry monsters trying to eat each other and they would start fighting to protect themselves. These were endless loops which ensured infinite torment of the trapped souls, sometimes they felt as if they were being burnt in pots.

For many years the spaceship went on drifting in the vast emptiness of the universe, it had gone beyond the solar system. The Devil was able to navigate around, by controlling the souls of the pilots which helped the spaceship to stay away from potential threats of asteroids and gravitational pulls of stars and planets which would have destroyed the ship.

After endless drifting of more than a hundred years, he sensed some strong signal in the open space, he could feel that he was able to see things which were happening far away on Earth, he got glimpses of things that happened millions of years ago like the forming of stars and the creation of life. This kept on getting stronger and he felt more powerful to make changes in the hyper reality.

These signals were coming from a wormhole, the portal which was a gateway to a different time and different dimensions. It was circling around a nebula and was slowly sucking its mass inside.

The energy within the spaceship which was carrying millions of souls in it activated the wormhole, it needed metaphysical energy to activate it and open the infinite gateways inside it. The wormhole was barely a metre in width and was shaped like an oval but inside it lay the great power to travel across time and universes. But it is not possible for a living creature to pass through it and access the gateways because the body will not be able to bear the gravitational pressure that will be applied to it. The pressure inside it was like that of a blackhole.

The speed of the spaceship kept on getting increased and due to pressure its shape kept on getting changed as it approached the wormhole ultimately getting sucked inside it. It crossed one of the gateways and ended up on the moon of Saturn in a time when humans were yet to appear on Earth. After coming out of the wormhole the entire mass of the server, spaceship and the other contaminated devices expanded again and later crystallised along with the minerals on the surface of Caliban.

Mankind has always talked about hell and the eternal suffering of the souls trapped in it, hell finds mention in the religious literature of most of the religions. But no one in the modern world knew if it really existed or it was just a tale because it was impossible to come back from it.

But the proverbial hell which was created through the server of HRP became the real hell once it went back in time. Over the years it was able to attract and trap the lost souls of those who after their death got neither reincarnation nor moksha and they got trapped in this hell for eternity.

The enlightened men, saints and prophets could sense this though never they saw it and it became part of every lore.

After lakhs of years of the hell being stationed at the Caliban, these crystals of Hell were seen by Dr Sullivan who in an ill fated decision proposed to bring a part of it to Earth. Who thought that these have the power to change the fate of mankind, he was right but the change came not in the manner that he had imagined but in the worst possible way. During all this while the controller of Hell, the Devil, had forgotten much about the past life.

A piece of the crystal was enough to control the mind of Omar and made him plan the biggest destruction on Earth. He got the piece on the island and the souls trapped on it communicated with him through whispers and planted ideas in his head. Unfortunately the souls inside the crystal which was with Omar were evil who were trapped in hell and it had made them yearn for control and unleash destruction on the planet they had been a part of.

Chapter - 20
THE TWO OF MANY WORLDS

When the first universe was created it was a singular entity but every major event in the universe has created branches in the timeline and every branch corresponds to a different parallel universe. When the first universe was about to collapse into nothingness the sudden implosion caused another big bang and a mini universe was created which continued to grow on its own. Thus two parallel universes were created, this happened again and again and many other parallel universes co-existed each at a different life stage and time, some threads and connections remained between the Universe which were part of each other.

Kaagbhusundi was outside these Universes and time and he could see all of the universes together but Arjuna's arrow was powerful enough that it was able to cross the boundary of space, matter and time and hit the only creature beyond it.

When Kaagbhusundi's eye was injured the blood droplets created wormholes. These wormholes were the interconnected portals and they could transcend the boundaries of time, space and even parallel Universes. Whenever an object crossed them it often resulted in timeline fissures which would create parallel timelines. The meteor which had hit Earth and caused the extinction of dinosaurs was one of them but in a parallel universe dinosaurs continued to exist and the ape which became the ruler of the planet on this Earth could never reach that position in the parallel timeline.

The Mandala was also made from the blood drops falling from the eye of Kaagbhusundi and it was connected with all the wormholes made from the same blood. Since it fell on Earth its powers increased and it allowed the one who could master it to see the past or future and even the parallel universes and timelines through the wormholes.

When the spaceship carrying the contaminated server of HRP passed through the wormhole it went back in the time of its universe and thus two parallel universes and timelines were created connected by a time thread which had kept their individual timelines the same till the 21st century.

Both the worlds had faced a disaster in the 21st century, one World faced massive global warming and its aftermath resulting in complete change of the face of Earth, the other one went through World War III which almost finished humanity. Earth 1, the one which faced global warming and flooding, rebuilt itself till the time it was again crippled by the HRP debacle. Earth 2, the one which faced World War III, went into the middle ages and lost most of what mankind had invented in the twentieth and twenty-first century.

Earth 1 was undergoing a crisis which was about to explode to further unmanageable proportions and death knell for those who were still alive and Earth 2 which was already living in a dark age was about to be plunged into further darkness, which might wipe out every last living human from the face of it.

After getting directions from the Mandala to move away from their earlier route Manav and Bodhi went further into the ocean instead of going towards land. They stopped at a small sparingly inhabited island after two days on water to restock the supply of food and water and went back on the course of their new journey.

On Earth 1, a few days after the launch of VXM 3, the entire population got to know that those trapped in HRP will never get up. All of them started dying. The Governments knew that this would happen and were making a plan to deal with this situation but it led to mass rioting which became impossible to control. With most of the services connected with HRP, its absence was causing major disruption and Governments were facing problems in ensuring law and order. Soon many rebel groups sprang up all over the major cities in the World and then civil war broke out all over the World.

One month had passed since VXM3 took its last flight.

One of the rebel groups was headed by a man called Carlos Sifer, who was a former scientist with HRP and a former associate of Dr Oz. He had gathered a group of civilians who were agitated due to the deaths of their loved ones and had been facing problems in managing the basic necessities of life in the Green City, which was fifty miles from the Orca City- which had no citizens left in it. Some had lost jobs because their company was based on the applications of HRP because most commerce based companies had HRP features where buyers can select products from the HRP interface and place orders, others were the various ancillary industries such as supplying hardware or manpower for HRP projects. The group was founded by a few friends and soon more people joined. Once

Carlos joined he further radicalised them by telling them truths and lies about HRP and the stories of Government involvement in the project and how many of the risks related to the project were ignored by the officials in lieu of heavy kickbacks from HRP. This fuel helped to increase the size of the group and soon the group was the biggest rebel group in the entire country. Carlos helped them by providing them with weapons using his contacts in the military. The armed members attacked a police station and gained control of a small area of the city and then continued to spread by attacking police stations and looting the armouries.

" We have to gain control of Orca City. The city has very few commoners left but it is the safe haven for the officials of HRP, IVRO, the Government and the military. They are the ones whose negligence caused us so much pain. If we take control of the city we can rebuild everything, we will have honest men running the country and such incidence of negligence will not happen again" Carlos roused the mob and it supported his ideas and they marched towards the Orca city in their trucks and cars carrying all the looted arms they had. Orca city was completely barricaded as the radiation which had spread after the contamination was dangerous and only the authorised people were allowed to enter the city. " There are more secrets buried in the heart of the city and the building of HRP. They are only hiding it from us" Carlos 's voice buzzed on the radio frequency which the group was using to communicate. " We have to break the barricade. Our numbers are more than the army and we can go through". The number had swelled up after their attacks on the police stations, and more and more locals joined them. Other rebel groups from nearby cities too joined forces with them. The army was spread thin, they too had lost many men in the HRP mishap and a lot of men were spread across the country in relief operations and riot control.

This rebel group calling themselves 'The Voice' attacked the barricades from the Southern side of the city, Colonel Majid was incharge of the post at this side of the city. One of the men from the watchtower sent a message to him "More than two hundred vehicles with over a thousand men are on their way. They looked armed"

This was the first time Colonel was about to face something like this, there was no major war in the last 3 decades since he had joined the army and only minor riots and scattered separatist activities that he had to deal with during his tenure. He ordered his men to hold fire and use non lethal methods. The army used water cannons first. But the mob responded by firing at the men. Majid asked to respond by rubber bullets and gas bombs which would knock the mob unconscious. Carlos knew that this would be the first plan of the army so he had made all the men wear light armour made of easily available things like fibre, chain mail, wood and the ones leading the attack wore gas masks to negate the effects of gas bombs. " Stop this nonsense and go back. We do not want to kill our fellow citizens" Majid made a stern announcement on the speaker, some of the rebels heard it but they continued moving ahead firing at the soldiers.

Seeing that the mob had no intention of stopping, Majid had no option but to open fire. The hundred soldiers barricading the entrance took their aim. The guns had laser guided bullets and had more than 90% accuracy of hitting the target. The first round was shot, the bullets penetrated the vehicles of the rebels, the drivers and the passengers were hit. Some of them got off-road, others stopped in the middle and many rolled over. Two vehicles collided and a bullet hit the gas tank which led to an explosion. All the rebels stopped in their tracks as vehicles and dead bodies piled on in the middle of the road. There were mountains on the other two sides of the city so this road was the only way to enter into the city. Voice of Carlos again came on the radio, " Take cover behind these vehicles and take aim and shoot". The rebels did the same and started shooting from behind this cover. The snipers in the group took down some soldiers but this group was not a match against the weapons and armours of the army.

Both the groups continued exchanging fires and then a rocket was launched at the barricades by the rebels, it was taken from an illegal weapons dealer. The barricade fell and many soldiers were blown to pieces, the rebels taking advantage of the moments rushed towards the city. The soldiers who were alive kept on shooting but the rebels kept on advancing and some of the vehicles managed to go past the check post , but they had hardly managed to cover a few hundred metres when they all were blown to pieces by rockets and artillery. Majid had requested for air support and before it was too late the support arrived. A second rocket was fired and it took down a helicopter too which went down and collided with the barricades. The other three copters opened fire on every vehicle on the road. The armoured vehicles and tanks of Majid's troop came out on the road and rolled over anyone who came in the way.

The fighting was soon over; most of the rebels had been killed , others ran away and their plot to take over the Orca City was foiled.

All this while someone else was carefully going about his business, Carlos along with his two trusted men had managed to get inside the sewer, the sewer lines were connected with a small stream which flowed from the mountains. Carlos had quietly slipped away while the fighting and using the sewer lines he had entered the city, this was the backup he had come up with when he realised that his civilians will not be able to overcome the army. It was serendipity that noticed the sewer and took two men and got the job done while no one realised it.

The three of them came out from the sewer in a desolate part of the city. While at the city entrance those who were still alive were treated in a makeshift hospital just outside the city limits and the repairs of the barricade were going on. Colonel Majid was actively involved in overseeing the operations.

The two men who accompanied Carlos, Vinod and Asif, were followers of Carlos from the time he became part of the rebel group but their main reason was to collect pieces from the destroyed server from the contaminated area . The debris from the HRP server was in extremely high demand which would fetch them a fortune in the black market as souvenir for the super rich collectors or in the weapons market where the smugglers would try to build weapons from it. Carlos too wanted to get the debris because he wanted to understand what had really happened to the server that led to this catastrophe and he wanted to avenge his failure of being ousted from HRP by making this public and make a better virtual reality world.

It was night time and the city which till a few days back was buzzing with the sound of music coming from pubs and horns of vehicles was silent as death. The three of them silently moved towards the HRP building using the navigation app. The building was under heavy surveillance and there were soldiers , patrol cars and helicopters going around the building to avoid anyone going inside it. Carlos noticed it from a distance, " we must wait for the right time to get inside. It is too risky now" he told his men. "What do we do till then ?" his men asked him. " We must blend in with the population of the city". They entered an abandoned house and started living there for the next few days and would daily go around the HRP building to look for any possible opening to get in.

They waited for months for this and finally when the commotion around the event settled a bit , the patrol around the HRP building was reduced. It was planned to demolish the entire building, the three of them entered the area disguised as engineers who would do the survey of the building. They entered the area which was condoned off and managed to reach the debris which once belonged to the server. " This could be the most valuable thing on Earth" Carlos said to his associates and they hid it inside their clothes and equipment and took off.

They came out of the city via the same sewer they had once used to enter it. After coming out of it they looked back at the checkpost, it was all calm now unlike the day when thousands had decided to take over the city and the roads were littered with dead bodies and burning cars.

On Earth 2, Manav and Bodhi had been going towards the direction when their boat hit something and was about to tumble, Bodhi steered it and prevented it from capsizing. The Mandala started glowing. It was a sign, Manav closed his eyes and saw something and then rushed towards the Mandala. The Mandala was engraved in stone and weighed over 300 kgs and only men like Manav and Bodhi could lift it. Manav took it out of the boat and gently dropped it in the water and did a Pranam to it. Bodhi was not able to make any sense of what was going on and he could not ask Manav what he was doing. A few seconds after the incident he went near Manav who was standing silently and looking at the water, he held his arm and asked " What did you do? You threw the very thing for which there was so much bloodshed and that one thing which was guiding us? "

Carlos, Vinod and Asif went to their old place. The very place where the plan for the mob rousing was laid out. Calos set out on his experiments to test the material they had obtained in the lab in the basement of the house. Vinod and Asif took their leave from him by saying they now want to return to their home but went out to contact the buyers for the stuff they had obtained.

The two men contacted all the leads they had and there was a bidding war for the forbidden material which had decimated a huge chunk of population within a very short span, which no other weapon could do in the history. Some more enhancements to it would mean making it a weapon to wipe out the entire planet, someone knowing how to do it could wield the power to bend the world. " We are going to be billionaires, " the two of them said to each other but both of them were also planning to take out the other one to get the entire money for themselves. It was a secret web where anonymous bidders could place their bets, but to get access into the portal required many elaborate steps which ensured no one from any of the law enforcement agencies could get an entry either as a buyer or a seller. The winning bet was 10 billion, which was more than the economy of some of the smaller countries on Earth 1.

After the entire details of the transfer and details were sent to the buyer the two of them again took each other's leave and decided to meet after three days at Carlos's place. During these three days they made grand plans of how they will spend the money. Vinod decided to move out of the Antarctic land and had plans of buying an entire island far away from this place, " I might as well declare myself as the King of that place" he thought and chuckled.

Asif too thought of running away to some other country and he was making plans for a safe escape. "I will get married, I will marry a rich woman. Rich, yes, but she should be very beautiful. I might as well marry a famous celebrity now that I am this rich " he was lost in his thoughts.

The advance of 10% reached them in their cryptic account, an account which cannot be traced by anyone nor can anyone trace who deposited money to the account. Rest of the 90% would be delivered once they would supply the material to the buyer. The two of them went back to the house of Carlos, they both were armed with laser guns and ready to kill Carlos and take away the prized possession. They disabled the alarm and broke in the door. They expected Carlos to be still busy in his work, killing him and taking away the bounty would not be very difficult to do.

They entered with laser guns in their hands, but before they could say or do anything they were shot with a single bullet from a sniper who was looking at the house from some distance. The bullet pierced their temples and they fell dead dropping their guns.

Ever since the time the two of them had auctioned off the material someone was following them. The bidding portal was secure but these two had started looking for super expensive stuff and had withdrawn all their money. They were also looking around for super high speed jets and boats which clearly meant they were planning to run away. This raised the suspicion of a hacker, he tracked their other activities and he was also aware that recently auction of the infected material of the HRP server was done. Lastly these two were missing for many months. Connecting the dots he knew that this was his jackpot and he reached out to his network to steal away the material and sell it themself. He managed a team of a sharp shooter, an expert burglar and a scientist to pull this off.

Step one was to chase the two guys Asif and Vinod. Once they reached Carlos's place the shooter took both of them out in a single shot. He got up and put his gun inside the case, got on his bike and drove to the house where already one more man had reached, it was the burglar. The watch of the burglar beeped. A camera flashed, there was CCTV around. He took out a gadget from his utility belt. It was a round object with a button at the centre, he pressed the button and dropped it on the ground. It sent out strong waves which disabled all the CCTV cameras but they would continue showing the same picture which they last captured before being disabled so anyone looking at it wont get to know that camera has been tampered with. Soon the third guy, a scientist, joined them.

The three of them went inside the house. The burglar had a three dimensional sensor device which was giving them direction where to walk, it was tracking radiation from the infected material. He was having a large backpack which had a container to secure the material and take it away. They walked in the direction of the sensor. It was pointing down, they looked for the stairs to the basement. There was no sound in the house. Either Carlos was busy working or was outside. They carefully walked ahead, the burglar kept on looking at this watch to see if there was an alarm for hidden booby traps but there were none. They came to the door, it had a password which would need a retina scan but the burglar attached another of his device to the lock, the screen had calculations running and various shaped and sizes of eyeballs kept coming and going till it stopped at one, the device hacked the shape of the retina which was the key to open the lock . The burglar and shooter went down the stairs, the scientist followed them but remained few metres behind to avoid any danger, there were many gadgets and screens in the room and at the centre of the room the scientist was doing his work unaware of what is about to happen, the two of them were few metres away from him facing his back. The shooter took out a laser pistol and aimed at the head, and he pressed the trigger. The gunshot created the head to explode, the two men let out a laugh seeing the blood come out of it. And walked towards the table which had the booty they were looking for but before they could take a step they were met with a volley of gunshots. The burglar took a hit and fell down with blood coming from his hand and stomach, the sharp shooter took a hit on his hand and his gun fell down. He survived the hits on his body due to the armour he was wearing. Carlos was wielding his gun and was shooting like a maniac.

"You kids thought that you could steal from me. You can kill idiots like Vinod and Asif but not me. Entire army could not stop me from getting what I wanted and just you two could stop me?" Carlos gave a chilling laughter and shouted at them at the top of your voice.

"But how did you…" the burglar asked him grimacing in pain but could not complete his sentence due to pain

" I knew something was off right from the time my two associates went away, seeing no movement on CCTV I felt tampering had been done. So I placed this dummy and waited for whoever was trying to get in. Though I was expecting my two former associates, I got to see two unknown faces."

He walked towards them and asked while pointing his gun at them" who are you?" Tell me and I might let you live"

"We were tracking your associates who were trying to sell off the contaminated HRP server that you guys have got. We killed them both and were planning to do the same to you to take this away from you" the shooter told Carlos with the gun placed on his forehead.

Unknown to all these three , the hacker who was the mastermind behind this heist was watching this through a small camera he had fitted on the clothes of these men. He had not interfered with the work of these two so far as he knew they are the best people for the job, but now was the time to take things in control. The scientist was his plan B who though not expert with weapons or burglary was skillful enough if given the right resources. Scientist had a small chip on his temple for the hacker to communicate, the hacker said " The other two are down, it is up to you now because if we miss this chance now the bounty will be gone. I can see everything that is happening, our target does not suspect that there is anyone else. It is your chance, kill him or injure him and run away with the package."

"But I don't have any weapons" the scientist replied

" Use the tools you are carrying, you are a scientist just improvise. I will be your eyes." the hacker told him. The scientist looked in his bag for something he could use. Meanwhile Carlos was dealing with the two men who tried to kill him. The burglar was dead, Carlos double checked his body and he tied up the shooter.

Scientist took out a radio wave gun which he used for experiments to test the properties of stones and crystals " It may not kill the target immediately but the waves will certainly knock him out" he slowly walked down, lifted up the gun with trembling hands and fired it.

The waves were strong but due to trembling hands the waves did not hit the doctor directly but a partial impact gave him a strong pain in ears and he lost his balance and fell down. But the impact of the waves was felt on the desk where the HRP material was kept. It was surrounded by some other crystals and many other chemicals, some of which Carlos was using to analyse the material and others which were just there in the lab for other experiments. The impact of the radio waves caused the bottles holding these chemicals to break and they all fell on the desk. The waves also changed the properties of the chemicals and crystals when they all got mixed together.

Carlos again got up and saw the man who had attacked him, he picked up his gun and fired, the scientist again pressed his gun and this time the waves hit Carlos he got disbalanced and fired his gun and fell down unconscious. The gun shot hit the light which was at the centre of the room. It crashed and hit the desk where the HRP material was getting mixed with all the chemicals. This provided the final catalyst to the reaction and there was a huge blast. Some souls were still trapped in the contaminated material and the concoction of chemical and catalyst of radio waves and electricity released their energy resulting in such a powerful blast that the entire house was blown away in a single second. The blast was so powerful that it resulted in the creation of a pocket sized worm hole where the material was placed some seconds ago.

The Crystals in Caliban on Earth 2 had passed through a wormhole on Earth 1 via a blackhole which was formed from the blood drops of eyes of Kaagbhusundi hence it was connected with all wormholes and acted as portal to the multiverse and points in time in the past and future.

This all was happening at the same time when Manav and Bodhi were on the boat with the Mandala.

CHAPTER - 21
THE CITY OF GHOULS

Manav and Bodhi once they landed, looked around. There were some trees lining the coast, they walked past the trees and they saw a huge stretch of desert in front of them. " We are in for a long journey it seems" Bodhi said to Manav. They went back and picked some stuff and parked their boat at the coast, "hope to see you again" Manav said to the boat not knowing if they would return or not.

They saw a swirl of wind and sand, often known as a "sand devil" but is a common natural phenomenon in the deserts . But this one was something different as it grew and became bigger as it collected dust and it moved towards them , inside it they could see shapes which looked like distorted human faces. Manav said to Bodhi," This looks strange and the problematic thing is that it is coming towards us, we should run.

Manav and Bodhi tried to run away from it but the small typhoon followed them." Use your powers to see what direction it will go" Bodhi asked Manav while still on the run " I can't see anything. My powers are not working on this thing. We have to defend ourselves without the powers" Manav told him while trying to keep up the pace with him. " We should split up" Bodhi told him and started running at a 45 degree angle, Manav did the same. The typhoon too split into two but it again started gathering air and sand and its size kept on increasing till it came very near to both of them, the typhoons were as high as a three storeyed building and it was only due to their superhuman strength that Bodhi and Manav had been able to outrun it for so long, they saw a small oasis and jumped in the water . The typhoon kept on blowing and a lot of water was taken away by it, the two of them stayed at the bottom of the pond till they felt that the turbulence had gone down. They came to the surface , the sand storm had passed , it had picked up so much water that the sand became heavy and started settling down and it lost its strength." We were saved by a stroke of luck, else we would have been blown away" Manav said while regaining his breath. "Yes we were lucky that we could save ourselves by hiding inside this water body but that was something dangerous and unlike any man or animal we cannot fight such things" Bodhi expressed his thoughts on the grim situation at hand. " None of the powers or the training will help us here, it's just us and the wish of God it seems" Manav concurred with him.

Three days of walking across the desert the landscape changed again. It soon became marshy and the air was getting filled with the stench of decay, dark clouds gathered and there seemed to be mist all around. "

A Few hundred miles away

Surrounded by a huge and deep moat filled with aquatic carnivores there was a city which had half dead men and spirits all around the place. Some were screaming and running around aimlessly, some were tied up to trees and poles and were being beaten by others. And then in some distance many others seemed to be building something.

At the centre of all of it was a strange looking creature, the hair was all gone and the skin was completely pale. The eyes were devoid of pupils and he looked a bit like a zombie or ghost but still had a face which resembled a human, a human male. Someone who had lived hundreds of years ago, the one who had caused the biggest massacre on Earth and wiped off more than 90% of the human race, the face was of Omar.

Few hundred years ago

After he triggered the great war he too took part in it and was believed to be dead by all. But he had run away. He had got the pieces of crystal from the moon Caliban when he had gone on the trip with his friend. These were the crystals which were brought to Earth by Dr Sullivan's mission, they did not know that the lightning they saw and the energy they believed residing in these crystals was of souls which were being tortured or were getting captured from the multitudes of planets in multiverse harbouring human like sentient beings . When the craft of NASA landed on the moon these souls were selected by their master. They came back on Earth and to complete the task assigned by the Devil - To start his empire on Earth. These malicious spirits started whispering to Omar. They had the power to see things around them and possessed some precognition when they landed on this Earth due to the time they had spent on Earth as a human.

Through their whisperings they guided Omar to rise up the hierarchy of the army, capture the Government and then lead the world into the last World War. These spirits when they came on the Earth after millions of years of torture at the hands of Devil got an opportunity to wreak havoc on men and rule them in the name of Devil but in a few years they realised that whatever they try to do it will not be possible to rule mankind in its current form because of the presence of so many countries and the pawn they had chosen will never be able to control the other nations. So instead they decided that they could rule over the dead. All this took hundreds of years but this was like a minute to the one who had spent millions of years since he was a human on Earth 1, the Devil.

Omar, now called himself the Khadim of Shaitan, was the Governor of the Devil's empire here on Earth 2, in this city of Ghouls. Few years before the the great war Omar gathered most of the other crystals which had scattered across the Globe after the explosion of Cal E. Soon the spirits taught him dark magic and gave him the ability to live forever although he would not live completely like a human but half dead like a zombie because using the powers given by these spirits his soul will not leave his body. He would repair any damage to his body by replacing them with the bodies of the other dead humans and therefore he continued living. Using this dark magic Omar went around and recruited many followers, soldiers injured in battles or civilians dying who were ready to do anything to live. Although most of them later realised later that they have been trapped in a cycle which they cannot break, their spirit cannot leave the body and they are bound to serve Omar to help them get new body parts. He then along with his followers, which numbered a few hundred, moved away and he found a secluded place in the Jungles of Amazon where he established the city of Ghouls as his Capital. The dark magic did not work on everyone, the ones with pure souls would not come under it and the timing of the magic had to be perfect; it had to be just seconds away from death. Doing it early or late would not make it work. Hence increasing the followers was slow and Omar continually had to get new bodies to keep up this undead army. Over the next few decades his army would raid the villages and cities around them and bring humans to harvest their bodies and would get back to the city.

Many civilian warriors fought battles with them but lost. One of them followed the undead army to their city and he came back and revealed it to his village. They relayed the message and more than ten thousand men armed with weapons, fire and holy symbols went to destroy this city of evil. They were commanded by Shamans and Priests of the different religions the people of the followed and they wore the holy symbols so that their bodies wont get possessed by the evil spirits. The humans attacked the City of Ghouls and using the holy powers they were able to kill some of the Ghouls and burn much of their establishment. It seemed that the humans would win when the spirits came out of the bodies of the Ghouls and created illusions. The leaders of men fell in hallucination and turned against their own kind and they all killed each other.

The Khadim knew that he would have to better prepare himself to counter such a situation, so he asked his undead army to kill every human in the hundred mile radius. The undead and the spirits went on a killing spree and they killed everything they saw, humans or animals. This place turned into a desert a few years later.

Khadim fortified his city. The high levels of nuclear radiation and the supernatural influence on the planet had modified many species and had speeded up the rate of evolution many million times over the natural speed. This had resulted in creation of many new animal and plant species , some of them harmless but most were nightmarish for any human encountering them.

Khadim decided to use it to his advantage by creating another army, over the next few hundred years, of such creatures to help him fight off any attack and hunt humans for him. The city of Ghouls was now impenetrable even for an army of ten thousand men. The Khadim continued to rule over his Kingdom of death and destruction.

A few years before the day Manav and Bodhi encountered the sand Devil

All these hundreds of years as they went by were nothing but a fraction of a second for the Devil who was still ruling over hell for millions of years. The souls which were doomed owing to their poor karma were often captured in hell and were tortured for eternity. When the number of his prisoners increased he needed some assistants to help manage the cycle of torture and ensure that the souls dont get free so those who after bearing years of infliction of pain were able to pass the loyalty tests of the Devil were made his assistants. The loyalty tests were simulations where he would make the souls believe that they can get free from the hold of their master and then he would try to see who would be ready to betray him to do so, a very few made through and others who failed were given inflicted upon more torture forever. These assistants would help capture other souls, some would act as the guards to ensure no soul can break free and would give torture to these and the most trusted assistants were the record keepers.

His chief record keeper, the most loyal servant, informed him that the new souls which they have been capturing has reduced over the past few years. " One of my messengers told me that the population of humans on this Earth has gone down."

"Yes my Sire. You are right at the time of the great war on Earth, which was enabled by your servants , we had captured a lot many souls and after that human population has gone down but it seems there is some other reason behind this. If it pleases you my Lord, you could send some hunters to see what is going on"

The Devil sent some of the hunter souls to Earth whose task is to capture the souls which did not get reincarnation or liberation. They soared over the Earth, one of them felt something" There is something on the western hemisphere of the planet. I can smell evil souls and some familiar odours" he told his mate. They went towards the direction of this smell and they saw a spectacle which made them happy when they saw so many souls and undead humans.

The two of them descended on the city of the Ghouls. The spirits in the city surrounded them and tried to hold them using their magic but none of it worked on these two who in turn captured these spirits using their magic. Some of the undead too rushed towards this commotion but they too met the same fate. Omar got to know of this and he came out of his castle. He was accompanied by the controlling spirits who immediately recognised the hunters from hell.

" So this is done by you all. But you were supposed to establish domination over the mankind" the alpha hunter asked them

" Yes, we tried that but we failed. The chosen human was not powerful enough to help us do that but we did supply many cursed souls to our Lord in Hell when we had started the great war on this planet" the spirits replied in unison which resulted in resonance across the area but only the hunter and controlling spirits could know the meaning of the sounds.

" So you decided to play the Devil yourself and rule over the spirits and undead using your magic and the Khadim?" a gush of wind came as the hunter shouted in anger at them and everything around them trembled.

The controlling spirits trembled, they knew they might be able to defeat the hunter even by using the magic they have acquired over many years or with the help of their army but doing that will result in getting in conflict with the Devil who will send many more hunters from his army to defeat them. Wisdom was to make peace.

" You are getting us wrong, we serve the same Lord, the Devil" the controlling spirits immediately tried to placate the situation

"Then what is all this? You have made your own mini version of Hell, your own empire? "

" This is the dominion of the Devil. The human we chose to help us in our mission calls himself the Khadim, the servant of the Devil. Our plan has gone differently and we have not harvested the souls for Hell but we are here working to make it work." the spirits replied

"Come here and meet our friends from Hell itself, the soul hunters" the controlling spirits introduced Omar aka Khadim to the hunters.

Khadim bowed in front of them " If you help us we can make this entire planet serve our Lord" he said.

"Okay, we will report this entire thing to the Lord and let him decide the future" the hunters told the spirits and Omar and vanished to go back to Hell.

CHAPTER - 22
HELL COMING

In the Hell

The Hell was not visible to the human eyes or to any of the inventions of humans, it existed in a different realm which was impossible for any living being to see or enter. Only energy in the form of souls could come and go. To the human eye and instruments all that was visible was the moon of Saturn, Caliban and the crystals which had a light blue shine on them. But inside them was the prison for souls and at the centre most part of the moon was the Palace of the ruler of this place. It now had many million souls captured over the entirety of human existence.

The Devil could choose any appearance that he would want because he controlled the reality of the entire realm. The palace he chose for himself when viewed from the vision of a soul was single storeyed but very high . It was black from outside and inside it shone in dark pink light which seemed like the diluted colour of blood. The Devil sat on his throne made of human skulls and bones and wore a crown of human ribs which looked like horns. He was tall, over 9 feet and had the face of a dragon and wings like that of an angel. His eyes were glowing and blood was flowing from them in the direction away from his face. He wore gold armour which had a diamond skull at his chest. He held a tall black metal staff with a shining globe on this head and wore a golden cape.

The hunters who looked like flying skeletons with wings and black cloak came to the palace and seeked and audience with their King " My Lord we have news for you from Earth"

"What is that ?" the Devil asked them.

 "The spirits you had sent to Earth to unleash destruction and bring your reign have been up to something which has reduced the soul harvesting" the alpha hunter told him

"What are they doing now?" Devil frowned

" They have established city where they are trapping some of the evil spirits and have been raising an army of the undead" hunter narrated the entire incident

" Are they planning a rebellion? If so I shall crush them immediately" the Devil was getting angry

" I am not sure but they said they are just serving you and would want to establish your empire on Earth," Hunter replied calmly.

"Very well then. I shall like to know more and understand how they can serve their purpose" The devil calmed down and relaxed in his throne.

Hunter told him everything in detail and the Devil thought about it long and hard

" Very well then, If I have an army on Earth which are not just shadowy souls but are half humans then I can put them to good use. I would bestow them with more power so that they can help me extend my control on the entire planet just the way I have captured and devoured souls on countless other planets but nothing compares to the human souls" He said to the hunters " Human that I once was before I became an all powerful God. " he spoke to himself.

He pondered over the thought for a few days on how he could do that. Before the server got contaminated and was transported it was connected with the Infonet. It had all the knowledge known to man and was used to create Hyper Reality. After becoming the ruler of Hell, Dr Oz Aka Devil made it look like a library where he would spend some of his time when he was no longer torturing souls to plan ways to acquire souls from other planets which would often result in the complete annihilation of the planets.

Back on Earth 2, the wormhole was very slowly increasing in size and sucking up things and throwing them off into different universes and time. The souls of Carlos and the three men who had come to steal the contaminated material too got trapped in the wormhole and they got transported to Hell due to the gravitational pull from hell which was made of HRP material and the HRP material present in Carlos's lab.

The souls of the four men who died in the explosion arrived in hell and they saw that they were in the middle of a small courtyard of a building with high walls and there were some doors around the place but they could not see anyone. The four of them could not fathom what place it was. "What is this place and how did we come here? All I remember is the blast" the scientist asked his two partners. Carlos was standing some yards away from them trying to figure out all that was around him. " My father was a priest and he often told me about the afterlife, it seems this is it" the shooter told the other men. He was correct and the others soon believed it once they saw demonic creatures who were floating a few feet over the floor coming towards them. They all were gripped with fear, but they realised they could not feel their heartbeat, at that moment all of them understood that they were dead and were probably in hell.

The demons took them to the area where the new souls were initiated into their afterlife, their entire previous life history was viewed by a warden who would be one of the assistants of the Devil. Using this they would torture the souls after putting them in one of the prisons which would be a simulation of the events of the life of the souls and they would be made to visit their nightmares.

When these new souls arrived in Hell and the Devil felt that these souls had a different energy frequency in them. He asked one of his minions , a messenger, to bring them to his court. " Get me the souls who have recently arrived" he ordered. " A few hundred souls have come in the last few hours my Lord, which ones do you want to come here?" the minion responded.

"Check with the wardens, some souls have come from a different place. They would understand once they will be checking the life history"

While checking the life history , the warden realised that something is different about these four. They seem to have come from Earth but everything about the Earth seems so different that they had never seen this in the story of any other soul. The warden decided to report this to the Devil but before he could the messenger arrived. " Have some souls recently arrived who seem to be different?" he asked ." Yes these four, they are from Earth but the things I have seen in their life history are very different from the souls we have got in the last many thousand years" warden told him. " The master had sensed something about such souls arriving in hell and he had ordered me to bring them to him".

"Yes, take them immediately. I was also thinking of conveying this information to our Lord. These demon guards will accompany you so that these new arrived souls don't cause any trouble for you" The demon guards tied them in chains and brought them to the Devil's court.

The Devil looked at them. One of the faces seemed familiar, he pointed at him and asked " Who are you?" The man replied" I am Carlos, I was a scientist at the HRP"

"Carlos.. HRP…" It had been billions of years since Dr Oz had become the ruler of hell so it took him a few seconds to recollect his time as human on Earth and he remembered the former colleague of his. He asked a minion to fetch some things for him, it looked like a clock with gears and dials and a book. He went through the pages of the book and did some calculations on the clock-like device. "HRP existed in the 32nd century AD on Earth, it already is 32nd century on Earth and they are far away from building such a technology then how is this possible" he pondered about it. He again started questioning the four men and what had happened in the moments just before they died the more he became sure that this is the old Earth "The spaceship in which they took the entire HRP building which passed through a blackhole and it went back in a time when there was no human life on Earth. All this while I thought the time between the period when the crystals of hell first came on Caliban till today was being rewritten, but I was wrong. The timeline had split when I went back in time and there are at least two Earths which exist in different Universes. The one Earth where I was a human and the other other Earth where I rule over the cursed souls."He figured this all out in a few minutes while the four souls from Earth 1 were standing in the court worried and thinking of what would happen to them.

"Keep them in the special cells near to the palace.I want to keep an eye on them" Devil ordered the demon guards and they duly complied. These four were put in cells where the prisoners were not tortured. The Devil used these cells to observe the souls who had a different vibration frequency in them to use that energy for his benefit and make them his soldiers. He also used these cells to observe the ones which were caught from different planets to understand them and plan how he could send his army of hunters to capture more souls or use the whispering souls to create chaos and deaths to get more souls.

This was now a delightful situation for the Devil. While he was planning to bring his empire on Earth he realised that there is one more Earth to conquer, which is an even more prized possession because it's the one where he lived. " I will conquer them both and even if there are any more Earths in any other universes. I will conquer them all, I will rule them all" he clenched his fists and let out a roar of laughter.

It was not possible for the Devil to leave the Hell, in the current state if he would leave Hell the entire simulation for souls that he had built from the time it was a part to HRP till date would collapse. So over the next few weeks he got his messengers spread all over and he studied the books of his library to find a way to satisfy his ambition.

Meanwhile in the city of ghouls the undead army was tasked with a way to bring their master the Devil to rule over Earth. They increased the intensity of their operations and attacked more human settlements to increase their strength. To this end the undead army started making a navy and the workers of the army, the ones who were the least competent in fighting or not committed to the cause, were put to task of building the boats and the equipment. Khadim had declared " We will not remain hidden far away and carry out small attacks on villages. We will go out and make the World tremble". The army let out a roar of war cry and shouted " Blood, blood, blood".

Some more whispering souls came to help the undead army. They created bloodlust in the hearts of men and the World which was already in darkness started plunging further more into. In the next few months many more villages and city states were annihilated. They soon reached the island where Ashamura lived, it was just a few days after Manav and Bodhi had left the island. The undead army started looking for new scouts and they found one of the men of Ashamura who was on the verge of dying and he took up the offer of selling his soul to the Devil for immortality. His name was Yomasaki, one of the men who had fought Bodhi when he had got the siddhi of Manav. His head was severed and was also burnt but he kept on holding his head and managed to survive and in his last breath he was found by the undead army.

He got to live with body parts of other men and while he was being inducted in this group he was asked by his captain on how did he meet his fate and whose army had burnt down this place, he thought that this army would be a good addition to his own army but to his shock he got to know it was just two boys. " Just two of them?" he asked again. " Yes my Lord. I won't dare lie to you. But they were not ordinary humans they had super powers" Yomasaki told him

"Superpowers, interesting" the captain wanted to know more" Where did they come from'

They came from thousands of miles away. To avenge their friends and teachers who were killed by my Master who stole a powerful artefact from them. These boys killed the master and his men and took the artefact, which could give mysterious powers to the one who can unlock into it"

"You said the boys had powers, what were they and what was the power of this artefact?" He asked"

"One of the boys could see the moves of his enemies even before they did it, he called it a siddhi, and the other was an expert in martial arts and had superhuman strength. They were unstoppable. My master tried to use the boy with siddhi to tap into the powers of the artefact called the Mandala but it made the boy even stronger and he could transfer his power to the other boy. The Mandala I overhead is a portal of sorts to know the past and future and maybe something even more which even my master did not know."

Why did he need the boy to get these powers?" Captain asked him

"Not everyone can use the powers of the Mandala, it was very dangerous. Many had tried and failed and they died." Yomasaki told him

"An artefact which created bloodshed in places separated by thousands of miles, it must be something very powerful. I better report it to the Lord, " the captain thought. "Also if I can capture these boys and make them part of my unit then my unit will be the most powerful unit of the army and I will become the commander of the entire army. So I will just inform the Lord about the artefact and try to find these boys by myself"

"This is good information Yomasaki, your new master will be pleased by it and you will be rewarded by healthy human bodies.

The captain sent this information out to Khadim. He was delighted to know about it. He asked the whispering souls," Can you get more intel on this artefact and where is it? I must get this power."

The undead army and whispering souls now along with the destruction they were creating also started searching for the artefact.They tortured every human they met or any human spirit they caught hold of.

It was at this moment that the Mandala guided Manav to drop it in the Ocean to keep it away from the hands of darkness.

For a human it was difficult to tap into the power of the Mandala, only the extremely powerful humans like King Vikram or ones blessed with superpowers like Manav could use the Mandala. But for an entity like Omar who was only partially and had magical powers, using the Mandala was very easy.

Khadim informed the Devil of this artefact, he told that the army is trying to find it and using this his powers would magnify and he will build the Devil's empire. Devil after knowing this scourged through the entire library but he could not find any mention of the Mandala, "If this Mandala is so powerful why is there nothing ever written about it?"

He pondered hard " there are millions of souls captured in Hell since the eternity of times. Someone must know about this Mandala. Some one must know. I should find it out" It was not difficult for Devil to make all his prisoners do exactly as he wanted. He ran a simulation where the prisoners had to answer about the powerful artefacts and portals they knew of. It took him few days of simulation and torture to extract all the information that any of his imprisoned souls had. One of the old trapped souls from the time before King Vikram was even born was the one who knew about it. He was a member of the clan which had made the temple on the Mandala. He was the head of the clan and had tried to use the power of Mandala. He was initially successful as he was able to see many events of the past and was able to predict the future. He was even able to transport his soul to different parts of the world and inform his clan about what was happening in the world while they lived in the deep forest. But the more he tried to dig into the power of the Mandala he was not able to control it. His soul was transported far away from Earth and while it was wandering in the endless universe until it got trapped in Hell. From that day the new head of the clan decreed that the clan will protect the Mandala till the last man lived. If it fell into the wrong hands it could spell disaster for humanity. Hundreds of years later the last leader of the clan was captured by the army of King Vikram. He had some power of clairvoyance and telepathy from the Mandala and when he was captured the Mandala informed him that the work of the clan was now done and the responsibility of the Mandala was to be passed on to King Vikram.

The Portal to transmit minds and souls to different dimensions, If Khadim and his army can get hold of it I can use it as a portal to open a path to go to different universes and travel to Earth and back. I can rule over the Entire Universe not by planning their destruction by my whispering souls but by directly controlling their destiny using my powers.

*****

PART - 2

THE UNDEAD ARMY

Manav and Bodhi walked ahead in the mist. They saw many dead bodies which were torn in pieces. The stench forced them to cover their nose and mouth with a kerchief. "Seeing these mutilated bodies. I think something really unholy and strange has happened here" Manav said.

Bodhi seconded his thought " This does not seem to be the result of war or pillage. Neither seems like an attack by a horde of wild animals. This seems something else" , he bent down and looked at a mutilated body. It was cut open and some internal organs had been taken out. Bodhi pointed it at Manav. " Look here, some internal organs have been taken out from this body in a surgical manner" Manav went closer and took a look. " Yes, something is extremely fishy here. Encountering the sand storm which had evil spirits in it. This too seems work related to dark magic. "

Walking ahead Bodhi heard something and his steps went slow and he put his right hand on his ear to hear the sound carefully. He signalled Manav to walk slowly and follow him and Bodhi walked towards the direction of the sound. He stopped at a dense bush and slowly removed a branch, a loud shriek accompanied. There were three children hidden in the bush, one was about 3, one 5 and the oldest one was about 10. The children were weeping, and Bodhi had followed the sound. The kids were terrified, but Bodhi gently put a hand on the head of the youngest one. Manav gestured to the kids to not be afraid. Manav and Bodhi took the kids in their arms and got them out of the bush and gave some food and water to the kids which they had carried with them. Once the kids calmed down a bit they asked them what had happened but the kids spoke a language which they were not able to understand. So Manav gestured towards the entire destruction and asked how, he gave the oldest kid a small stick to draw in the mud to explain what happened, while the smaller kid sat in the laps of the two of them.

The older kid drew, fortunately he drew well. He drew people in the village , then he drew some ghosts and demons like people coming to the village. He then drew that people were cut and their body parts taken out while they were alive. He also drew some people and added horns and big teeth to them depicting how they too became ghosts. Manav and Bodhi looked at each other with sad eyes and held the kids tightly. They understood what would have happened to the villagers.

They looked around the village and found a hut which was intact, most other huts were burnt or torn down. It was getting late in the night and the kids fell asleep." What do we do now?" Bodhi asked Manav

" The Mandala had guided me to this place. I think it wanted us to warn of what is happening in the world and perhaps save these kids. " Manav thought deeply and replied with calm, tears filling up his eyes.

"What do we do next? What did the Mandala tell you? Bodhi asked him, he tried to hide his worry but was failing to do so.

"Nothing, it just guided me in this direction. I think we should keep moving ahead." he told Bodhi

"But the kids. How will we …" Bodhi himself stopped in the middle of the sentence while looking at Manav because he knew Manav did not have an answer. Neither of them had any answer.

It was getting dark, a small lamp was lighting up the hut. They too went to sleep.

Manav woke up the next morning early to do his surya namaskar and got some more water from the well. The five of them stayed in the hut, Manav and Bodhi still contemplating what to do and finally had come to a conclusion. " We will go back along with the kids. Find some safe place for them and in the meanwhile figure out a way to deal with this ghostly menace." Both completed each other's sentences. They took some food and water for the return journey and packed their stuff to make a move.

They walked for a few minutes and Bodhi heard a rumbling. He asked Manav did you hear it, Manav heard it too and his siddhi state got active. " They are coming in this direction again. We must run and hide" . They lifted the kids in their arms and ran towards the other direction of the voice. But the rumbling kept on coming nearer. Soon they could hear sinister laughters and wailings. They again changed direction and went at 90 degrees to the sound. " Why are we not able to outrun them?" Bodhi asked Manav while still running with the kids. Manav's siddhi worked only on the living, it worked partly on the undead army but it did not work on the spirits which were accompanying the army. They could sense humans from a great distance and they guided the army towards it. The kids had escaped due to the stench of death all around the village , the spirits could not trace them but now Manav Bodhi and the kids had crossed the village so their electromagnetic signals were felt by the spirits and the army followed to harvest the bodies or make them a part of it.

" I think it's the spirits who had chased us earlier. I can't see their next move. I can see some glimpses of some strange ghostly men coming towards us but it's more dreamy than the clear visions I usually get" Manav told him, his brow tight with tension

"Let us get to some place of safety, the kids should be kept safe at all cost" Bodhi was ready to go the distance to ensure this.

"Yes, the kids must be kept safe but the way they are coming. I don't think we can find a place to keep the kids safe" Manav said with desperation in his voice.

Knowing that outrunning their foes was impossible, both of them thought hard till the time they reached a cliff. There was nowhere to go now. Both Bodhi and Manav took out the amulets and lockets which had images and symbols of God and tied it on the hands of the kids. "The Gods shall protect you" They made a circle on the ground around the kids and wrote sacred inscriptions and Mantras on it to protect the children from the evil powers. They moved away and gestured to the kids to remain inside the circle.

They took out their sword and waited for the attack. Cloud of dust started coming towards them accompanied by noises of running and laughing. What they saw was terrifying, humans with pale skins and stone cold eyes with disproportionate body parts, covered with blood and laughing maniacally. In the air they could see floating shadows similar to the ones who had attacked them a few days ago. Manav was trying to use his siddhi but the visions kept on blinking.

The first four undead men came close, they had swords and spears in their hands. Bodhi took a few steps and severed their heads before they could even react by swinging swords in his both hands. Another one came whose flesh had fallen off and was a mass of skeletons and nerves. Bodhi put his sword through its ribcage and pierced the heart and pulled it out. Manav took the scarf he was wearing and made the kids cover themselves and asked them to look at the other side. The older kid was sitting in the middle and he tightly embraced the other two.

Some of the undead army soldiers had by-passed Bodhi, these were two each who had gone from either side of Bodhi, Manav could sense the trajectory they would follow and he made a rendezvous with them. One of the Undead soldiers on Manav's right threw a spear at Manav, Manav had sensed that and he had moved and he had come in the direction of a soldier on the left. The spear missed him and hit the soldier in the left bang in the centre of his chest. This soldier tried to remove the spear but Manav took a step forward, jumped on this spear and put his sword in the eye of the soldier standing next to this one. He took out the spear, dived to his right and threw at the other two, the spear went like a missile piercing the belly of first and hitting the throat of the other. Then he severed the head of the one which was hit by the spear at first. Meanwhile Bodhi too had struck down a few more but the problem was that there were hundreds more, and one more problem the bodies he had cut were still wriggling around. This meant that they were still not completely dead.

The black magic was keeping them alive and if their body parts would be rejoined using the magic and replacing the damaged parts using the human body they would still regrow, Manav saw all this as the next move of his foes who were wriggling around.

"Fire" Manav shouted at Bodhi who was buddy cutting down his enemies

"What" asked Bodhi. " Fire, we need fire we have to burn them else they can become alive again" Manav told Bodhi the plan.

"You protect the kids, I will get something" Bodhi said and ran towards a rocky outcrop. The undead chased him, he kept on cutting any of them that came near. He picked a few stones and some dry twigs and rubbed them to create fire. But this was not enough to create any damage, there was a small tree which was almost dead. Bodhi jumped and gave a hard kick to the tree, it broke into two, he put it on fire. The fire became big and he kept on throwing the undead soldiers into fire whoever came near him.

Meanwhile Manav kept on defending the kids and fighting off the attackers. Bodhi took a piece of cloth and tied it to a spear of one of the undead soldiers, put the tip on fire and threw it at Manav and shouted " Catch it" . Manav got hold of it and used the fire to burn the attackers, his siddhi was still not working at full throttle since his attackers were only partly human.

The spirits accompanying the army were watching all this all along. There were a dozen of them but three were leading the pack and were also guiding the undead army. One of them said to the others. These are the same boys we had met and we moved ahead thinking that they were dead. "These are no ordinary humans. Humans lose their courage to fight after seeing these undead soldiers but these boys.. " a second spirit said."Yes, the way they are cutting through this army is unbelievable. Not even a hundred men could face this army"

But we cannot sit and enjoy this battle. At this pace this entire battalion will be annihilated and Khadim and the Master will be extremely unhappy with us" third one said, it was the oldest spirit of all and was the one which had spent most time in hell.

"I think this boy protecting the kids has some special powers as he can predict the attack even before it happens. Lets see what happens if we start whispering and mess with his powers?" the second one suggested the other two.

The three of them started using their whispering and it started impacting the siddhi of Manav which was already not working at its full potential. Their whispering was not heard by the ears but directly in the head via telepathy. Manav started hearing strange voices in his head "Don't fight us, Join this army and live forever, why are you protecting these children? What is the secret of your power? Your friend is about to die and you will follow him soon and so will these kids?" All the spirits started whispering at once and so many voices created distraction in his mind and siddhi could not work without full concentration.

He was now left to fight without the powers but Manav was an able fighter even without his powers but the soldiers kept on coming and slowly they had covered him from all three sides. The fire had also gone out and exhaustion was setting in. He could sense the sobbing of the children he was protecting. Bodhi too was almost getting circled by another horde of soldiers. It was at that moment of almost no hope, the two of them remembered God and slowly chanted the hymns they have been raised with, the Hanuman Chalisa - the one which protects men from the dark powers, and there was a huge thunder in the sky and a big bolt of lightning fell. The lightning bolt fell in the midst of the undead soldiers and the moment it hit the ground it led to a huge blast which took out many undead soldiers at once and the vegetation around caught fire. Sensing this as an opportunity Bodhi took a jump and landed on the skeletal head of a soldier crushing it in the process and then jumped off a few metres ahead navigating his way through the fire and the burning grass and plants. He reached Manav and he started chopping the soldiers from behind like a machine. This gave Manav a renewed vigour and now the few soldiers who were not dead yet were caught between the two of them. Soon all of them were cut and the ones which had not died were wriggling around the last one was stabbed by Manav and his head was cut off by Bodhi from behind. They then put these wriggling parts into the fire which was now all around.

The spirits watching this could not believe what had happened. "The undead army was invincible till this day and today just two boys killed hundreds of the soldiers" one spirit said.

"Yes but they got lucky with the thunderbolt , else they were about to be killed," the second spirit added the context of luck the boys had. " Whatever may be the case, even before and after the thunderbolt they managed to kill so many soldiers which no normal human could do" the first one again said. " Yes you are right" the third concurred " and we should not let go of the boys. Both of them would be prized possessions for the Lord if they are made to serve him"

"Yes but let's focus on one of them for now. I think we should capture this one" the first spirit pointed out at Manav. " Seeing their bond, if we capture one the other one will follow us".

The spirits came down, Manav was with the children and was trying to control the little ones who were crying after seeing all this. Bodhi was walking towards him when he saw many shadows in the smoke of burning bodies. He immediately recognised seeing similar figures in the dust storm. " Manav !!! The ghosts are coming back" he shouted. But before Manav could react and do something one of the spirits entered his body and Manav fell down and started getting convulsions. Bodhi rushed up to him.

Manav got up, there was no expression on his face and he started walking in the direction of the spirits. Bodhi tried to stop him, he called his name" look at me, I am Bodhi" he shouted at Manav but Manav did not seem to recognise him.Bodhi threw dirt in his eyes and chanted hymns but there was no effect on him. He suddenly stopped and turned around and started walking towards the kids. He raised his weapon, Bodhi held his hand and used his entire strength to stop him. Fortunately the kids were still looking in the other direction and did not witness this. "He is under the influence of the spirits. He is not himself and will fight with me without holding back but if I do the same he can get seriously injured" Bodhi thought to himself.

"I can protect myself by dodging his attacks but he will harm the kids" while he was thinking he got a blow on his face from the elbow of Manav. He fell down and went blank for a second, Manav raised his sword to behead him but fortunately he opened his eye just in time and saved with a cut on his shoulder by sliding under Manav. He quickly got up and kicked at the right ankle of Manav, Manav lost his balance and fell down. " This is my chance" he said to himself and quickly grabbed the hands of

Manav from his back and tied them up using a piece of cloth from his shirt. "I am sorry my friend, but this is the only way" Manav was groaning and trying to free himself. Bodhi ran up to the kids and tapped the oldest one on shoulder and signalled to go. He took the younger ones on his shoulders and held the hands of the oldest one and ran.

Manav after some struggle was able to break free but he could not see Bodhi who had used the cover of the still rising smoke from the burning bodies of undead soldiers to sneak away from him. "Should we get hold of the other boy too. He is extremely skilled without any superpowers" one of whispering said to the other, " Yes we should do that" but they saw the spirit coming out from Manav's body. " He has been resisting me for a long time, unlike any man" I cannot control him any longer" Manav regained his conscience and he rubbed his eyes as if waking up from a dream. " There is no point going after the other boy, even one is difficult to control," the first spirit told the others, and it gestured to two more to enter Manav's body. And when three spirits again entered his body Manav again got possessed.

Bodhi had gained considerable distance from them, so he stopped for a while and put down the kids under the shade of a tree. The kids were thirsty and hungry, so was he. He took a stone and hit the branch which was laden with berries, the throw was perfect and berries fell. The four of them ate the berries and went ahead after a few minutes but Bodhi was still thinking" My path is full of troubles, these children will always be in danger if they are with me" he managed to reach back the boat without taking any further risks and he kept on thinking of how to keep the safe. " There is one place that will be safe and welcoming for the kids". In a few days he reached AkhandaDweep Rashtra Rashtra. He was given a hero's welcome.

Kylie got to know of this and she rushed to meet her love. Bodhi was resting and recuperating in a hospital after many days of travel and from the wounds of his fights which had not healed properly. The children were being attended by doctors and teachers.

His eyes met Kylie's and for a moment he forgot all the troubles, she came up to him and held his hand while he was sitting on his bed " How have you been. I was waiting for you for so long"

She asked, her eyes were brimming with tears of joy and love.

He too held her tightly and they looked into each other's eyes for a few moments till a nurse entered the room and broke the silence. " The kids want to see you and are getting restless," she said. The teachers and doctors had managed to communicate with the kids using sign languages. "Kids?" Kylie asked in amazement. " Yes, it is a mind boggling story. Come I will make you meet them and narrate the story" Bodhi told her everything that had happened and how he had to part ways from Manav to protect the kids.

" So you will stay here with us and the kids" she asked him

" I did not know any other safe place for the kids, so I decided to bring them here. They can live and grow here happily" he again looked into her eyes and said while holding her hands" Take care of them"

"You are leaving again?" she said with dejection in her voice

"I have to. I need to find Manav and I need to find the reason behind the menace of this army of undead men and ghosts. If not stopped it will consume the entire human race"

Kylie knew her emotions won't stop Bodhi and he has a bigger purpose.

Next day Brahmbhatt too came to meet Bodhi and was apprised of the entire situation. "This is more than a personal mission now. I suggest you take some soldiers with you in the mission"

"The enemy we are dealing with I don't think soldiers will be of any help"

He paused and then continued after a few seconds "And I first need to find Manav, I hope he is safe" and started packing the stuff for his journey.

Brahm gave a hard thought "If not soldiers, then something else might work. Stay with us for sometime and let me find other ways to help you."

Brahm called up the learned folks he knew of for a meeting and he discussed the matter with them.

Meanwhile on Earth 1 the portal had started sucking up matter around it. It was just a two dimensional oval shaped dark circle but had become strong enough that the residents near it started experiencing gravitational pull. The geological authority saw unusual reading on the surface and soon a team of scientists gathered at the spot where the portal had formed.

The entire house where Carlos was hiding had been gulped inside the portal. "Whatever this is we must know about this in totality" said the senior scientist who was leading the team " but we must observe caution while approaching it". Two scientists who were wearing special suits to protect themselves against the pull went close to the portal along with their apparatus to observe the portal. " The reading on the device is nothing like I have ever seen. This is noticed in the extra terrestrial waves. It seems to have a strong gravitational pull around it but the gravitational pull goes on from positive to negative. It starts throwing out some unknown particles and radiation when gravity goes negative" said one of them on a transmitter. But his apparatus was not strong enough to handle the waves, it started beeping violently and became quiet and then its pieces were scattered and pulled inside the portal. " The device has broken down and its pieces are being pulled towards the object" he shouted on the transmitter but the voice did not reach anyone. The transmitter too had stopped working and he felt a sensation on this skin as if it was being pulled by someone. He looked at this partner and his eyes suggested that he too felt the same , they left all the instruments and ran towards their other colleagues who were a couple of hundred metres away inside a van which had a thick protective cover of lead. The scientists in the van saw their colleagues running and shouted on the transmitter " What is the problem? Why are you running?" but their voices were not heard.

The scientists came out of the van but the two men collapsed before they could reach them. "There is no pulse" one of the medic who was with the team checked and told the others. While an ambulance took them away the senior scientist of the team commented" This situation has become really dangerous and we do not even know what we are dealing with". Another one replied " You are right Sir. But what should we do now?" " We should inform the authorities and get this area cordoned off"

The dead bodies of the two scientists were taken to the lab instead of the morgue to analyze what had happened to them. The bodies and the protective suits were bombarded with rays and particles which seemed out of place and many restests were done to figure out the results.

The results were shared with ISVO and the erstwhile HRP chief Samarth. " They have been bombarded with dark matter particles and the dust on their protective cloth seems very similar to dust on earth but there is a major anomaly" said the chief of Lab on the video call which was being attended by the invitees"The composition of the dust is not what is present in this part of the World"he zoomed on an image" you can see these microbes, they are dead and are not found around here since the global warming lead to thawing of the polar ice and making it a hospitable place to live while submerging most of the landmass.

"They might have come from another part of the Earth where these microbes are still present," said one of the attendees.

"Actually they are not present anywhere on Earth" the lab chief paused to get the right words to complete his sentence and continued " but these were present thousand years ago and this dust the carbon dating shows that it is before the time of submerging of the continents"

There was silence all around, the fact was hard to digest " This means that this dark circle is throwing matter from a different time" Samarth spoke up. " As hard as it is to believe this but this is what the fact shows" the lab chief answered him.

"We had some inkling of this fact that this is a portal of sorts given that there were radiations coming out from this two dimensional object which is not possible for such a small object and that it was throwing out material also pointed to it. So I think we have something that science always wanted to create but it could not - a time travel portal."

Heavy cordoning of the area was done and it was covered with lead and anti gravity magnetic fields to reduce the impact. The material that was collected on the protective covers was collected frequently and the sheets were regularly replaced; their parts were sucked in by the portal. Super high resolution camera and sensors kept a watch on the portal 24x7

It was after about a month's time that the sensors caught something unusual, first the team of scientists felt that this was a glitch but it was seen again and again. The sensor images showed human shaped things coming out of the portal, the images were formed as these things were sometimes at much lower temperature than the surroundings or sometimes at much higher temperatures. These images were not always walking, they sometimes flew around in the chamber created by the cordoning, they observed the things around them, tried to come out of it and went back after sometime.

This was observed by all the scientists. " It seems that this time portal is acting as a gateway and we are being visited by some living entities who are able to access this portal. " said one of the scientists. " We should inform the Governments about it "said another one. "There is no other option, although there is nothing alarming as of now. We do not know if these visitors are friendly or malicious or maybe just observing" a scientist addressed the group.

The Director of ISVO, International Space Voyage organisation, had spent considerable time trying to find alien life and had approved many unmanned voyages to distant planets for the same but he could never achieve that. He was excited by this new discovery " I think we might be looking at some kind of alien life form which has the ability to alter body temperatures as per the surroundings and are not visible to naked eyes or maybe they have an advanced technology to make them invisible."

" You are true Sir and these possibilities cannot be ignored, especially after witnessing unbelievable turn of events at HRP" Samarth responded " but we should not try not to engage with whatever this is and maintain extreme caution while the covering sheets are being replaced"

The visits increased and at times multiple entities were seen but nothing more than that. The perimeter around the portal was widened since the impact of forces had increased until one day when one of the shields caved in due to sudden increase in the impact of the gravitational pull. Immediately a repair crew was sent to replace it but by the time they reached the spot the entities had managed to get outside the enclosure. These entities were none other than the agents from Hell who were sent by the Devil to do a reconnaissance on his Earth.

Any entity passing through a blackhole or timeportal has a stamping of the matter which can be used to trace them or find paths via these portals. Hence Carlos and others who were transported to Hell via the portal on Earth 1 became the source to track the path of the portal. Using the portal required dark arts and it was not possible for humans to pass through it since the gravity would crush them completely but the effect of gravity on the spirits was negligible.

The repair was made while the spirits roamed around. One of them who was leading the mission was a spirit which was one of the first few to get trapped inside the Hell created by the disaster of HRP, after getting trapped and tortured he was the first to accept the supremacy of the Devil and had been an ardent follower of him. He was given this opportunity because he knew about the place and could guide the others too. This group had come in and out of the portal but were not able to get past the strong barriers which were put all around the portal. The spirits waited till one day the barriers were being replaced and they got a tiny opening. While the group leader was visiting the places he had lived the repair was completed. The thought of coming back to this world as a human did come to him but he remembered his lonely existence outside HRP world and that by serving the Devil he had got a purpose and controlled thousands of spirits in the name of his master. While he returned back he looked with horror that the way to get back was sealed. It meant that he would be doomed to remain stuck here while not being able to complete the job given by his master.

He went back to the group he was commanding " The humans have sealed this thing back" he asked them. "Yes they have" all others were captured from Earth 2 so they had no idea what was to be done " We are stuck here then" he told them.

They continued wandering around the barriers for the next few days till the repair crew came to check the barriers. It was then the leader of the group came up with an idea and the spirits got to work. They started whispering and managed to possess two of the repair crew. These two possessed men stopped repairing the barriers instead they loosened it and a strong wave of particles and waves from the portal hit the barriers. It was strong enough that many parts of the barriers were sucked in the portal along with some of the crew. Others died due to sudden exposures of radiation. It was total chaos. The leader of the spirits sent two of them back to hell to relay the information that they had broken through and they soon returned with hundreds of their mates.

Many men around the area got possessed and many others started whispering. The possessed men started lost sense and all of them started walking towards one are, their family members tried to stop them but they violently shrugged them off and continued walking and they came to a market where many people were busy buying stuff, which was a new development post the fall of HRP when people mostly bought things through the HRP. The possessed men attacked the shoppers using anything they could lay their hands on. The shopper started running around in panic. Some of them were killed by the possessed men and some were badly injured. Many others got injured due to the stampede that was created by the panic of murderous men.

Police soon came at the spot and tried to control them but they could not control without using violence so they shot at these possessed men. They died and as soon as they died the spirits from hell attacked and possessed another person, meanwhile the spirits of the people dying at the hands of these men were being sucked in by the portal and were being transported straight to hell.

Devil was excited to see this new batch coming from the very place and time he had once lived in. He asked his servants to bring them to him " You all would have known about Hell in your religious scriptures. This is Hell and I am the ruler of hell…. Devil" He magnified his size manifolds and he looked at them with his glowing red eyes and bent down to come closer. All these newly captured souls trembled with fear and bowed down in front of him. They were lead by the guards to their cells and they faced special torture which gave sadistic pleasure to their new master.

Once the first batch of possessed men were killed a new set was taken up by these spirits, which included policemen who had firearms and hence the destruction became even more wanton. A reporter was shooting this with her cameraman " This is Kriti from Orca News bringing to you live coverage of sudden violence that has gripped the shopping centre of the city. Some of these people are under an unknown influence and are attacking everyone around them. The policemen who tried to stop them are also under their influence now. " The cameraman was capturing all this, the news reporter had her back to the camera while she was going towards one of the men injured in the violence to take his statement. She stopped suddenly and turned around , her pupils were white and she attacked the cameraman. The camera fell down and the live feed went dark.

The arrival of souls from the portal was captured by the sensors and the entire committee that was informed of it by the scientists. The emergency meeting of the committee members from different organisations and the government " It has now become clear that this is some sort of invasion that we are facing and these entities are taking control of the people and making them go violent" announced the head of ISVO. The Prime Minister of the country was also present along with the Defence Minister " This is the second disaster we are facing in a very short time. Our people cannot face so many troubles. The Defence Minister will personally oversee the operations. All of you along with the armed forces have to work together to fight off this invasion " said the Prime Minister.

"Yes Sir we will do that but before that we need to know what these entities really are?" Samarth said

"Yes, we will do that but before that I want the entire sector of the city to be cordoned off. No one goes outside the barriers. Anyone trying to cross will be shot dead " The Defence Minister ordered.

The sector was cordoned off and even the security personnel were a mile away from the cordoning to avoid getting possessed. Snipers kept an eye out and anyone trying to defy the rule would be shot on the spot.

Scientists were working to find out about the entities creating this havoc and research was going on the portal. Experts from other countries too had come up to help because they knew this could soon become a global problem just like the HRP incident. They were now certain that the portal had a considerable level of time travel properties apart from making things move from one place to another. All this while the sensors on the barricading around the portal had sent many images, they could identify many other entities coming out of the portal and many entities going in the portal. " If we see there is a certain pattern in the entities coming in and out. Most of those coming outside have appeared like someone walking through a door, they have come out with a lot of ease while most of those who had gone in seemed to have been pulled inside it" a scientist said.

A lot of theories had been put forward in terms of what these entities are which are coming from the portal and those going inside but they were all conjectures and had no evidence to back them. Believing in paranormal things like spirits was uncommon in a time ruled by science so despite some theories being put forward on the possession of the men by ghosts but the committee was not ready to believe it.

" We do not have any answer on how to stop this portal of fighting off the entities while people are dying in the Green city. Who knows if we will even be able to stop this" The Prime Minister said with helplessness in his voice.

Back on Earth 2 Brahm called Bodhi to his office. He came inside and was immediately greeted warmly by many people who were seated there. They had recognised one of those heroes who had saved their country from tyranny. These men introduced themselves , these were the most famous archaeologists, historians, priests, scientists and astrologers of the country. "I have told you about the things you and Manav have faced to the esteemed guests here. Hopefully some of them may be able to help you" Bodhi bowed down in front of them in reverence. The historian told him about the part of the world they had explored" After the great war many parts of the world were lost to darkness as mankind 's population became extremely thin. The radiation post the nuclear warfare created many strange creatures around the world. I think you might have come across such mutated creatures or humans" he ended by explaining his theory. " Or perhaps some strange virus might have affected the humans of that place" another man who was a doctor added this idea to it. Bodhi did not say anything, he tried to absorb the information. "These are obviously spirits and demons that we are talking about. And if they are devouring humans we should be careful that they do not reach our shores" the priest put forward his views. All of them continued debating and discussing for the next hour but none of the theories seemed right or wrong. They all left saying that they will consult more books and shall meet again in a couple of days to discuss the way forward.

When all of them had left except one Bodhi too started walking out of the room when one hand came on his shoulder. "Wait" he said. " There is something I need to talk to you about," he said. He was a man who was about sixty years of age, thin and had deep eyes.

"Yes Sir , please tell me, " Bodhi said." My name is Vishnu Gupta and I know about the Mandala. Bodhi felt that this is another of those theories that he had been hearing about all afternoon but he acted normally and let the man complete his narration. "I am one of the Navratnas, the group that was tasked with the safeguarding of knowledge, humanity and the power of Mandala for thousands of years since the time of the great King Vikram. Your teacher Acharya Prajwal and the Principal Tatwa were also two of them." he paused to let Bodhi soak this in. "I had never told the name of our teacher and Principal to anyone in this country. This man must be telling the truth" Bodhi thought.

Vishnu continued" We had been protecting the Mandala for many years and had also been looking for someone who could use its power to lead mankind into brighter days" he paused looked in the eyes of Bodhi and then said " it was then after hoping from many young students for centuries when we finally found Manav and you. Manav the one who will unlock the powers of Mandala for the good and you will be his overwatch and protector. Manav got his siddhi powers from the Mandala itself and this was when the Navratnas knew that the boy was the one we had been looking for."

"I believe you trust what I am saying" Vishnu asked Bodhi. Bodhi folded his hands in front of the old man " Yes Sir I absolutely do" and bowed down to touch the feet of the old colleague of his teachers. " The Navratnas had spread in different parts of the world after the attack on the Nalanda University when the Mandala was broken into two places and moved away from Nalanda. The bigger part part was in your Gurukul"

" Manav had submerged the Mandala in water before we reached the land of the undead army. I asked him about it but he did not tell me. I think he would have gotten the directions from the Mandala itself to do this and seeing what we encountered on land , it was best that he did it."

"He has bonded with the powers of Mandala completely" Vishnu told him

"But now I need to rescue my friend" Bodhi told him

"Yes and the two of you need to fight the evil that is about to grip the world. The city of Ashamura was recently raided by things which matched the description of the undead soldiers you had told. This means that they are all around us now and it is just a matter of time when they strike these shores" Vishnu said in a very serious tone.

" You are right, but I don't know how. I barely managed to escape from that place and rescue the kids and I don't even know where Manav is." Bodhi said with dejection in his voice.

" There are more Navratnas who are alive. We need to reach out to them and then go to the place where the Mandala is submerged. Hopefully we will find a way" Vishnu told him placing a hand on his shoulder

" Yes, at worst we will die trying. But that is way better than doing nothing at all" Bodhi stood up and was ready to go.

Thousands of miles away. In the city of Ghouls Manav was brought in. He was possessed all this while. He was brought in front of the Khadim where the whispering spirits told the Khadim about his powers. "He would be a good addition to the army," they said. " But he is stubborn as hell and we needed many spirits to control him" one of the whispering spirits said. " You have done a great job, this boy and his friend going by your description seems to be the same one that one of my captains had informed me about. What great luck the Devil provides us with" Khadim looked up.

"Now we have to control him and take him to the artefact that I was told about. Make him tell everything about it. We have to possess that power and once we do then the Devil will himself come on Earth and rule over it and we will be his legions of Darkness" he proclaimed and all the undead soldiers, mutated creatures and wandering spirits all started hooting in unison rendering a chilling music in the uninhabited lands.

On the moon of Saturn - Caliban , in Hell , The Devil was informed of this update, " Get the Mandala in your possession and harness its power. I will pay a visit soon. "The Devil was not in physical form so he knew he could not yet leave Hell." Very soon I will be able to rule over the multiverse. Be Omnipresent and Omnipotent. I will be the one people will worship because if they don't while being alive , they will do it when they are dead." he grinned and his minions laughed. The software which he had made created the hell to control souls but a portal like the Mandala will help him unleash his power and terrors in the physical world. Not only will his army of spirits be able to travel anywhere and capture anyone, he himself will be able to manifest himself and even link the HRP software of hell with the minds of people on Earth. Once he could do this even with a part of humanity he would control them completely and using the portal he would capture all the souls leaving the dead bodies. So he will rule over the living and the dead.

On Earth 2, In the Orca city. Everyone was puzzled on how to handle the situation because the snipers who were stationed outside the no-go zone of Green City too had got infected by the malaise and they had started shooting random civilians.

It was the meeting room where Samarth, his team and the Defence Minister were sitting, the Defence Minister knew that his idea to quarantine the entire city was not going to work and that whatever the problem was it was still spreading. It was then they received a call, it came from a source which was unknown to all of them. "Who got the access to our lines? These are the most secured ones on Earth" The Defence Minister said. He received the call, on the screen he saw a young man who was in what seemed like a lab, not the most hightech one and there was one more man behind him who was working on something. " Who are you?" asked the Defence Minister

"Sorry to barge in but this was important. My name is Jimmy and I am a scientist. Actually a junior scientist. My boss Martin was killed in the attack by these infected men in the Green City. We were working on an Android which had the powers to shrink to the size of an atom. We wanted it to help in treating diseases or research about micro organisms but I believe it can possibly help us in this situation."

"Why does it make you believe that your android can help here?" Defence Minister asked him

" I actually managed to get some information about this portal with the help of my hacker friend and he only helped me to patch into your secured line. I know that the extreme pressure and radiation will destroy any other object but the shrink tech as we call it will be able to withstand it and perhaps go beyond the portal to the other side and help us to know more about its origin and about these things that have invaded us. Once we know what these are we can defeat them. I am sure we will defeat them" Jimmy addressed everyone present in the meeting.

"First you hijack our systems and then talk about this invention of yours. I better have you arrested.... If you make out of the Green city " the Defence Minister got angry.

Samarth intervened" If you actually have the tech you are talking about then show it to us" Samarth had developed something which was unfathomable for the inventors before him so he knew there could always be such inventions which others don't believe in.

The Defence Minister looked at Samarth in anger" One of your inventions had put the world in jeopardy and now you want to entertain this gimmick?"

" My invention did not, but the people of the Corporation did and most of the top brass was composed of the people backed by the Government. I had no say over the fail safe. I was just the face of HRP when the Government started intervening in it" Samarth was in no mood to take crap from the Minister.

Minister went silent and Samarth continued" And with regards to the invention these fellows are talking about, what else do we know about the enemy. We are already in a hard place at least give it a shot" then he pointed to Jimmy "show us what you got"

The man standing behind him got a robot in front of the camera. It was about 5 feet high. They pressed a button and it started becoming smaller and smaller until it disappeared. He then again pressed the button and the robot came back in its original shape.

"Good but will this Android be able to make the journey on its own and make its own decisions while on the other side because I am sure what comms you use will be useless on the other side of the portal" one of the committee members present in the room asked Jimmy.

" It has artificial intelligence but we will need it to be more smart than that because this is the last piece that we have and the real creator of the tech is dead." Jimmy told him.

"Ok so why don't you just go ahead and use the tech to tell us where this portal leads to and who are these entities invading us?" another one present in the hall asked Jimmy.

" As I just mentioned, the bot has artificial intelligence so it will not be able to understand things which it might have not seen earlier. Also as one of the reports suggested that this might be a time portal it might be riskier to send a bot, the people on the other side might get hostile and we may not get to know. A human mind and body will suit our mission much more" Jimmy clarified his idea.

"So you want a human volunteer from us?" Samarth asked him

"No, not at all. I just want some help in terms of some neural programming. A news reporter was badly injured in the violence we rescued her but a lot of her body and brain was damaged. We believe we can merge the parts of this robot with her. She may live partly as a human and partly as a machine and we will be able to achieve our task. But there is one problem here, we will need some parts of the code of HRP to link her neural network with the bot. The tech was made at the time when HRP was operational and my boss would have figured out the way to use the HRP code but I can't do it. So I need your help to help us all"

"HRP has created so much destruction. There is no way you are getting the code?" The Defence minister rebuked him.

"I know it has but this is the only way HRP can make this work, we don't have much time."Jimmy pleaded.

"For all we know this may be a way to create the HRP or a spin off. You might be asking the code for your personal gains. A lot of industries went out of business when HRP was brought down , this code might mean fortune for you. And for someone who managed to hack into our secured lines…. Well the motivations do seem a bit shady" one of the scientists said.

"I don't know how to convince you all. What will I gain by having the code if all the world is destroyed by these things and more so to have something like HRP up and running enormous servers would be needed, which I dont have and neither have the resources to get them." Jimmy continued to convince the people on the other side.

"I think we need to end this meeting now, there is no point wasting our time here" The Defence Minister gave his judgement on the issue and disconnected the line.

Jimmy was disappointed but he knew he had to try so he went to his team and they continued working on making the neural connection.

Later in the night he got a call " This is Dr Samarth. Give me your address" the voice on the other side said

" My address?" Jimmy was confused.

" I cannot share the codes online, they are too heavy to transfer and will get intercepted. I will be sending them via hard drives" Samarth told him and Jimmy quickly gave the address.

" Delivering anything in Green city is fraught with danger, but I have some contacts to help me. The package will be delivered to you. The security password is a riddle to keep the package secure"

The city was barricaded but essential supplies were being sent to the city using drones. Samarth copied the code on the drives and used his contacts to get a drone and his drives were sent via it. It reached the address the next day. Outside there were people running around in panic, Jimmy quickly went out of the house and picked the package from the lawn. It was a big container, a cube of 2 feet x 2 feet x 2 feet. He took out the heavy drive from it which was insulated by a protective covering of fireproof material.

He plugged it into the mainframe. The drive was password protected, he looked into the package if there was some info on the password. There was also a small note in it which just had the word written in it in caps THE RATIO. All present there thought for some time and then Jimmy's friend the hacker said " this is the password, actually the ratio is the password"

"What ratio could this be?" one of the team members said.

Jimmy thought hard and said "This must be something which is important to this work and something that Dr. Samarth too might be aware of. This must be alluding to what Dr Martin had written about in his famous paper. His paper was titled The Ratio, where he mentioned the ratio of the amount of force needed to shrink the size of an object to the force of repulsion between atoms when they get nearer than their original positions."

The hacker continued him" Dr Samarth must have researched about the technology and Dr Martin and by this password he was also ensuring that we are not trying to cheat him by taking the codes for personal gains"

"Yes, this must be it. So just punch in the ratio" a team member said.

Jimmy entered the password , it was correct. They copied the code for the neural network linking. Soon the girl got up, she looked around and saw some unknown men around her. She moved her hands around it and she looked at it. It seemed as if she felt a strange feeling looking at her hands. " Don't worry, you are alright. You were badly injured and almost dead so we took you in and with the help of our tech revived you" she had lost some of her memory after she was linked with tech. The shrink tech had shrunk and merged with her body at a molecular level so she was part human and part robot. She had the human mind, emotions organs and the ability of shrink tech along with that.

Over the next one week she was trained on how to use the tech and she was programmed to reach the other side of the portal and know what is causing the trouble on Earth. She was given knowledge on most of the information that would be even remotely useful to her via a chip inserted in her brain. She was trained to fight through the programming . The tech in her body was stronger than any human could think of . The body was made to withstand extreme pressure while shrinking in size so it was strong enough to break any known material with its hands. An external suit again made using shrink tech was given which further helped to reduce the pressure on the body and had many gadgets which would be useful in her journey and fight.

"Kriti, the shrink tech bot which is part of your body was the fifth version of such a bot and now it is the sixth version after merging with you now you are truly a unique individual which combines the best of a human and tech. You are a unique creation - a unique *Kriti* " Jimmy told her while she was getting ready to go inside the portal.

———----

On Earth 2 Vishnu had sent his message to the surviving Navratnas of what was coming.

Navratnas had managed to safeguard the Mandala and the knowledge of the world from human attackers for millennia but this was the first time they were dealing with supernatural forces. The Navratnas used ravens and pigeons to send their messages. They would send more than one carrier to avoid the loss message due to the death of the carrier. The coding was known only to the nine men.

He had started the preparation of the journey along with Bodhi. Kylie pressed Bodhi to take her along " I don't know what perils I will encounter so I do not want to risk your life in this and besides you have a purpose here in this country, helping the Orphan children. That is a fight as worthy as any." Kylie knew that however hard she tried Bodhi will not budge and deep down she understood that if she will be with him it might slow him down as her safety will remain a priority so she let go of the matter. While he was loading the boat she got him arrows and a bow. " Take these". The arrows had stones on them, not a metal tip. " These stones are explosives, if you shoot them from this bow at maximum strength they have the power to blow up a small island.

Bodhi smiled and picked up the bow, it was very heavy and the strings were actually very tight, no average human could use it.

Just before the commencement of the journey Vishnu received messages from the other Navratnas, he decoded the message. " What do these messages tell you?" Bodhi asked him

" All the protectors of the Mandala will come to help us but hey are all around the globe and we don't have much time for reach out to them all so we first need to reach to the Mandala and see if it is safe"

Vishnu and Bodhi went towards the direction of the spot where the Mandala was submerged. It was many days of journey from Akhand Dweep Rashtra, and on the way Vishnu told Bodhi about one of Navratna who was the master of history came to this land and started a Gurukul here. He then passed on the legacy till the time he was chosen as the heir to the knowledge and responsibility of preservation of Mandala. The nine men remained scattered so that they could monitor what was happening around the world and also keep the torch of humanity and knowledge lit. The ones who were away from the pack also learnt the martial arts to defend themselves, some of the teachers of Bodhi could avoid that since they had people around who could fight whenever the need would arise.

Two days later, at dawn time Vishnu was standing at the deck. The sea was calm and he was observing the beauty around when he saw a wooden boat at a distance which had a saffron colour mast. He took out the binoculars and looked at it and asked Bodhi to move their boat towards this one. Bodhi did as instructed. When they came near the wooden boat he asked Bodhi to slow down but move closer. They were now within touching distance of this boat.

A young man showed up and waved his hand. Vishnu made a hand gesture to him to speak up and the young man shouted out loud " *Gyanasya Rakshanartham* ", to preserve the knowledge. This was the motto of the Navratna. Bodhi turned off the engine and Vishnu went on the boat " You were expecting an older man?" the young man on the boat said. "Actually yes. I am surprised to see someone so young taking this massive responsibility" Vishnu replied.

" My name is Angad and well I am not that young as I appear. Apart from being the protector of the knowledge of warfare I have managed to learn mystic arts. Warfare needs to adapt and my Guru had advised me to learn the mystic arts to combat any opponent who might use dark magic against me. So when you told me the problem that we are dealing with I knew I had to come to help in the fight both as the master of warfare and magic. So I managed to hitchhike my way to meet you before your rendezvous point."

"Now that there are three of us we should be able to retrieve Mandala and the boy who possesses the power to use it" Vishnu tried to boost the morale of the group. Angad picked his stuff from his boat and dropped its anchor and jumped on the boat of Bodhi.

In the next two days they reached close to the point where Manav had dropped the Mandala in the sea. Vishnu who was standing on the deck felt a stench, and asked Bodhi " Do you smell something other than the sea, like something rotten, rotten flesh". Bodhi slowed down and came out. He smelled the stench, " They have reached here" he said, trying hard to hide the tension which was creeping on his face. "This means that they know about the Mandala and with Manav in their control … " Vishnu did not complete his sentence because he was about to state the obvious.

Angad had been busy with preparations all this while since he had joined them. Getting his weapons ready to face the undead army. He asked them, " Have we reached the battle ground?"

Bodhi and Vishnu came inside and said " Yes we have."

Angad smiled " Good, I am done with my preparations and would have been bored to wait for the fight"

He picked his sword and his backpack "So let's go and get your friend and the Mandala back."

They were in the middle of the sea and no land was in sight but they went full throttle in the direction of the stench, and a few minutes later Angad spotted a large ship from his binoculars. The mast of the ship was made not from cloth but skin and many other parts of the ship were made using bones , " I can see a ship, which is surely one from hell" but to his surprise he soon saw two more behind this ship. They were even bigger. " Actually there are two more, and bigger than this one. It's a big army gathered there"

"So three men against three ships full of half dead men and ghosts which can possess humans." Bodhi said " The odds seem favourable to us" Angad tried to lighten the mood trying to lift up the mood.

"We must drop the anchor here and go ahead on the dinghy," Vishnu suggested to them.

They put their weapons on the dinghy and started rowing towards the ship. Brahmbhatt had given them lots of supply for the journey and possible battle. He had given them camouflage sheets. So they took out the one which had a bluish shade like the sea. They covered themselves and the dinghy boat with it. " This will help us get closer to the ship without getting noticed," Bodhi said.

"A lot of undead soldiers are scattered around the sea and swimming in it" Vishnu told everyone while viewing it from his binocs while Bodhi and Angad were rowing. "They must be searching for the Mandala. It would have been hard to remember the exact spot in this vast ocean" Bodhi told them. "Yes you are right" Vishnu said but he observed something and his face became more tense " It seems they have got whatever it was that they were looking for. The undead men are swimming back to their ships"

"Oh shit, they have got the Mandala and they have Manav too. We don;t have much time to get both with us" Bodhi said and he started rowing faster. After going a few metres ahead Angad said " Wait" Bodhi stopped rowing and Angad jumped in the water. The other two were surprised , they waited and saw a couple of minutes later Angad came out of the water and he was pulling out something. Bodhi took out his sword because to their utter surprise Angad was holding an undead soldier in grip "He is completely dead now. Nothing to worry about" he said. "But why did you get this thing here?" Vishnu asked him. " We can go only so far with the boat but to get on the ship we need better camouflage" and he tore the limbs, bones and flesh of the undead soldier and tied it to his body.

" Yes, we can become a part of this army and remain undetected as much as possible" Bodhi agreed to his plan. " He too dived in and got hold of one more undead soldier who had gone away from his troup and did the same as Angad it. "So let's go ahead. Vishnu can remain here and wait for us" Angad said" Yes, I am not much of a fighter but a guide" Vishnu agreed to stay back " but there is one problem" Bodhi said before going ahead " What?" the other two asked.

"The souls. They can smell humans from a long distance. I don't know why they did not trace us today, perhaps they were busy with the search of the Mandala"

" Yes and no" Angad said " I had put holy water on all of us without you all realising it which has made their ability to locate us weaker and they being busy on a different hunt too helped us"

The other two smiled "and I have made some adjustments to the weapons too" he told them while unsheathing his sword, " I have added a slight coating of silver to them along with holy water and the power of holy Mantras. Your bullets too are adorned by this. A slight touch of our weapons will burn these evil creatures". Bodhi smiled looking at him and so did Vishnu he too unsheathed his sword and looked at it with confidence.

They swam ahead and soon saw themselves surrounded by the undead soldiers who were all swimming towards the ships. They swam clumsily due to their disproportionate bodies which were made by joining parts of other humans. Bodhi and Angad swam slowly and awkwardly to avoid anyone noticing them, some distance ahead they saw that the Mandala was being taken out from the sea using chains tied to a pulley on the biggest ship. The two of them looked at each other saying they are still in time to get it back. They moved ahead and joined the queue which was getting up on the ship using a rope which was hanging from it.

They went up the ship, they saw on the edge of the ship there was Manav standing , his clothes were tattered and his face was pale and gaunt. It seemed he had not had food for days. He was surrounded by undead soldiers and some mutated creatures. Over the ship there were spirits hovering who were barely visible to the naked eyes but Angad could see them using his magic.

The plan was simple: Angad will try to rescue Manav and Bodhi will get the Mandala because it was too heavy to move. Once they get it they will send out a smoke signal to Vishnu who will get the bigger boat to carry them away. The wooden ship of the Undead army could never compete with the hightech boat of AkhandDweep Rashtra.

Some of the undead soldiers were going to their posts and others were going down to start rowing to take back the ship. Bodhi was standing on the other corner and standing close to one of the undead soldiers who looked into his eyes and realised that he is a human. Bodhi realised that the soldier was about to open his mouth to speak but Bodhi took his sword and put it inside the back of the skull of the soldier and killed him before he could speak. Angad stood in front of this execution so that no one could witness it.

The Captain of the ship was directing his undead men and the mast was unfurled and the ship started sailing. It was the right time to make a move, both of them moved forward to their targets. Suddenly all the undead soldiers turned and looked at them, the spirits had now sensed human presence. They were too close and even with the magic that Angad had tried it was impossible for them to escape these spirits who had been controlling human minds for hundreds of years now. An alarm was sounded and all the undead men surrounded them, one of the spirits recognised Bodhi "He is the same boy, friend of the one we had captured " it told its fellow spirits. " Good he came here by himself, he will serve our cause well" another one said. " Let us not get him away, we should just capture him instead of letting the undead soldiers die at his hand"

The spirits swooped down and hit the body of Bodhi. But they could not penetrate him and got a shock while trying to do that. Angad had given Bodhi an amulet to fend off evil spirits and that combined with mental, physical and moral strength of Bodhi it had created an impenetrable armour. They tried again and failed, Bodhi did feel a slight impact of spirits trying to get inside him. They tried to possess Angad too but failed ," They have come with preparation and have used magic to protect them against us"

The spirits immediately alerted the undead soldiers and directed them to attack the two men. They stood with their backs to each other to face the soldiers. The soldiers attacked them, both of them had their swords unsheathed. Bodhi's sword landed on the neck of a soldier and the moment the sword touched the neck it turned to ash and the soldier was beheaded. In the last encounter, this army of Satan was not dying easily and their bodies continued crawling even after being cut in half till their heart or brain was severed, this time they are not getting this liberty. Bodhi smiled seeing the efficacy of the weapon. He attacked the enemies even more violently. He whispered to Angad " You make the move, I will handle them here". At that very moment four soldiers thrust their spears towards Bodhi , all of them were at different corners. Bodhi took a leap and landed on the head of the tallest of them, while all these soldiers stabbed each other and they remained stuck in each other's spear, Bodhi took out a boomerang from his belt and threw it at one of the soldier and this Boomerang which had a silver tip hit all these soldiers and they all got burnt to death. This soldier that Bodhi was standing on was over seven feet, Bodhi took his sword in both of his hands and pushed it between his legs going through the skull of this tall soldier whose head went up in flames. He then jumped off, grabbed the boomerang and then landed on the shoulder of another soldier and he kept on jumping from one point to another making it impossible for the soldiers to land a single blow on him.

Angad ran in a straight line towards Manav, cutting down everything that came in his path. The spirits were all watching this. Manav was still under partial impact of the spirits and he was standing still in a trance. The other spirits swooped inside him and his eyes lit up as if a switch was turned on. He picked up a spear and threw it at Angad with all his strength who was still fighting an undead soldier. Angad was unaware and he was saved because an undead soldier jumped in between to fight Angad and met his end. While the soldier was falling Anagad saw that Manav was picking up another spear to launch at him. This time Angad was ready, he deflected it by his sword, another one came his way and he moved aside while severing the head of a soldier but he kept on moving closer to Manav.

The spirits had ordered the soldiers on the other two ships to help their comrades. The two ships had come closer and a rope was thrown on the deck of the ship where the action was happening and more soldiers started coming through. The ones who were rowing the ship too started coming up on the deck to fight. The weight on this ship increased and it went a little deeper in the water. Many of the undead jumped in the way of Angad to stop him from reaching Manav. Bodhi saw this incoming from the corner of his eye and he climbed a mast. He then took a knife and threw at the edge rope which the soldiers were using to get on to this ship. The soldiers went down with the rope, he did the same with the rope which was tied from the other ship. This certainly slowed them down but would not stop them as after falling in the sea they started swimming slowly towards the ship.

Angad realised that the enemies are too many and even Manav is fighting against him he will sooner or later get over powered, so he took out the last weapon he had. It was a pistol he was carrying. He started shooting it, the spirits looked at it and laughed because it was shooting plain water " He is planning to drown us in that" said one of them laughing. But soon the laughing stopped as it saw that the water was making the soldiers burn. The other soldiers who got in touch with the burning soldiers too caught fire, and they started running away, some of them jumped in water to save themselves. The water that Angad had used in the gun was not ordinary water, it was holy water. He kept on firing it while holding the pistol in left hand, small drops of it were enough to burn the evil, and he held the sword in his right hand and was cutting anyone who escaped the holy water. He was now close to Manav, Manav picked his sword to fight Angad. Manav was no longer in control of his siddhi since his body was controlled by the spirits and with a corrupted mind or body siddhi would not work. The spirits had been trying hard but they could not make it work and it had drained Manav of his physical strength making him an easier opponent for Angad to fight but there was one problem while Angad was fighting to make Manav free of the grip of the evil, Manav was fighting to kill Angad while being helped by many undead soldiers. For the next few minutes Angad and Manav kept on exchanging blows and undead soldiers making their regular presence in the fight. Angad had run out of holy water and the soldiers from other ships kept on coming in. Fighting between the two continued, at that moment a huge tide came into the sea. The weight on the ship was too much for it to properly balance itself and the ship started rocking, many undead soldiers who tried to climb up fell down in the sea again. Manav and Angad too lost their balance and two soldiers collided with Manav making him lose sight of his opponent. When Manav was shoving them aside some blood from these soldiers fell on his face and while he was clearing it Angad went on his knees slipped and got behind some soldiers took out a pouch from his pocket and skidded to get behind Manav while he was looking around for him, he took out something from the pouch and smeared it on the head of Manav using his right hand while grabbing his body from his left hand. Manav let out a loud cry , it was *Vibhuti* , the sacred ash which he had put on Manav and then Anagad took out an amulet and tied it on Manav. Manav kept on letting out a loud cry but the voice of the cries were not his, these were spirits who were inside him. The sacred ash and amulet burnt these spirits who were controlling Manav. Manav fell down on his knees exhausted, Angad grabbed him " Don't worry you are safe now" he whispered in his ears. He took him in his arms and ran to the edge of the ship and jumped in the water before jumping, he shouted at Bodhi " Bodhi…My part of the mission is done ". Now Bodhi had to retrieve the Mandala, the second part of the mission.

Bodhi had decimated a huge chunk of the undead army but he was still nowhere close to reaching out to the Mandala. Though his task was to get Mandala but for him Manav was more important than Mandala or anything else, he decided to move ahead to reach to the Mandala he jumped over the combatants and was about to touch the Mandala but that very moment the wooden floor of the ship deck broke and he fell down and slipped till the edge of the ship. From beneath the deck, out came a beast, it had broken through the deck with its horns. It had the face of a bull, body like an extremely well built human and tail like a crocodile and the blood was so hot in his body that it appeared all flushed and red. It was more than 8 feet tall and weighed more than a ton and there was another man standing next to it. A gaunt figure whose face was covered, it was the Khadim who was looking at everything that was happening and he realised that with Manav being taken away from them it was time that he came to the fore to handle the things.

The creature let out a loud roar while Khadim just stayed back and watched, the creature tore bodies of some of the undead soldiers with his bare hands and ate the head of another one. This was the pet of Khadim which he would use only for extreme situations because of this reason, it was too violent to control and would attack anyone except Khadim.

Bodhi was taken by surprise to see this giant. Khadim raised his fingers towards Bodhi and the creature ran towards him. Its hands were as big as the torso of a human and the thick sharp nails were longer and sharper than a knife and it kept swatting away the soldiers who were in between, it wanted no help from anyone to get to his prey.

Bodhi threw his boomerang at the creature. It easily swayed out of the way, and looked at him with anger and arrogance thinking that this puny creature was trying to hit me with a toy. Bodhi did not react, the boomerang came back and hit it at the back of his skull. It was the silver coated boomerang which had taken out many of Khadim's soldiers, Bodhi knew that the creature might get away from the first strike of the boomerang but it won't be able to see the return. But to his utter surprise the silver on the boomerang had no effect on the creature because he did not know that it was created by magic of the spirits and mutation due the nuclear radiation and was a fully functional living creature unlike the undead soldiers.

The creature raised its hands and Bodhi was barely able to avoid its nails which tore through the wooden rails on the edge of the ship. For the time being the best strategy seemed to Bodhi to stay away from the reach of the beast. He tried on doing the same for sometime and the beast kept on destroying things on the ship which was no longer in a shape to set for sail again. The beast got angrier when it was not able to catch Bodhi and he kept on throwing things at him which included pieces of ship and soldiers. Bodhi had been fighting for a long time and with this running around he was soon losing his breath, he was thinking of his options which included making a retreat by jumping into the sea but the creature who had the tail or crocodile seemed more than capable swimmer and Bodhi would lose the option of jumping and dodging if he would get chased under water.

He finally decided to take the creature head on and he came in the middle of the broken deck and waited for the beast to come to him, holding his sword tightly with both hands. The beast stopped for a second and then came charging at his full speed. When the hands of beast were about to reach Bodhi swung and threw his sword at the neck of the beast and moved out of line of attack at the last second once again but behind him this time was the Mandala and the punch of the beast was about to hit the Mandala, when his entire body completely froze like a statue with the hands inches away from the Mandala. Bodhi had observed the gaunt figure had his eyes fixated on the beast and he was continuously making some hand movements. He had sensed that he is the one who is guiding the beast in some manner to keep on attacking Bodhi. It was obvious that the Mandala had meant a lot to him so he had released his most powerful soldier to protect it; he could not never let any harm come to the Mandala. So before it could hit Mandala and destroy it the man stopped it.

So without wasting a second Bodhi picked up his sword and used beast's arm as a step to jump, the mouth of the beast was open while it was frozen because it was bellowing while making the charge, Bodhi put his sword inside the mouth of the beast cutting his throat and the sword coming out from the back of its neck while he was standing on the shoulder of the beast. By then the beast was unfrozen as Bodhi saw the pain in its eyes and it tried to smash Bodhi by clapping its hands but Bodhi evaded it and jumped off the shoulder and stood behind the beast and held the part of the sword which was protruding out of back of his neck and pulled it further towards himself, it was a rain of blood and the beast fell down choking and hitting his hands all around and while the man was trying to control it he could not and the beast ran over the edge of the ship and fell in the sea, it could not swim with all the blood coming out of its throat , it drowned to its death. Khadim could not believe that his most powerful beast was slain. It took him a few seconds to absorb this and he decided to take things in his own hands and took out a sword which was burning with electric blue flame and started walking towards Bodhi.

Bodhi was on his knees trying to catch his breath and his eyes fell on his arm. The amulet which was given by Angad to him to protect from the possession was broken when he was fighting the beast. " If the spirits realise this I am gone. If Manav could not resist them with his siddhi I stand absolutely no chance and I no longer have the strength to keep on fighting for long. Running away while carrying the heavy weight of Mandala would be impossible for me now." He made up his mind, took a few steps back, ran and jumped into the sea. Angad and Vishnu were now on the boat and were observing all this. They immediately went full throttle and reached close to Bodhi while he had swam only some distance away from the ship. Vishnu gave him a ladder to climb on and he grabbed it. Khadim had come on the other ship which was still intact. He was ordering his men to chase down the boat but the boat was smaller and powered by solar electricity, the ship was no match for its speed and it soon was disappearing from the eyes of Khadim and his men. "Slow down" Bodhi told Vishnu, "but" Vishnu was about to reason but Bodhi gestured with his palms to stop and he ran inside and came back with a bow. It was loaded with an arrow, it was the arrow which Kylie had given to him. He aimed towards the direction of the ships chasing him and fired it. The distance was a lot and he was tired, he missed the shot by quite a distance and the arrow was about to fall more than a hundred metres in front of the ship. Some of the soldiers laughed seeing this but Khadim realised something. He shouted "stop and turn" seconds later there was a huge blast inside the sea and ships were blown. Khadim had jumped out safely from it.

———-----

Kriti came out of the house and went towards the portal. The entire area was strewn with dead people, body parts and blood and the air was full of such a strong smell of decaying bodies that any human would faint. But this did not impact her and she moved quickly ahead. No humans were in her sight, it seemed most of them were dead or in hiding. Jimmy and team were looking at a screen which was showing the status of the organs and tech of Kriti using heat waves of her body and seeing everything around her via a small camera attached at the shoulder of the suit. She was about to get inside the portal when all of a sudden many possessed men came and attacked her at once. Her physical mind recalled something from the past, how she was possessed and almost died before she was rescued by Jimmy and his team.

The team sensed an unusual spike of heat through the sensors in her suit. " She is probably in a state of panic after seeing these men. We have programmed her mind and gave her a super strong body but she still has emotions and she can't win without overcoming them. This is her first test" Jimmy told his friends while they waited with anxiety on what will happen to the girl, to their project, and to the last hope to get rid of the invisible attackers. The men came near her and one of them attacked her with an iron bar. She tried to block it at the last second and got her arms between her head and the iron bar. Iron bar hit the arms and was twisted. She was surprised but her programming told her she has even more strength than this, the body temperature went down and she calmed herself. She slapped the attacker and he immediately went down. In came two more attackers from both her sides and she grabbed them both and threw them away and then without wasting much of her time jumped towards the portal. The portal sucked her inside like she was made of a paste which is being squeezed inside a tube. "Off she goes" exclaimed everyone at the lab. Jimmy sent a message to Samarth " Package sent across the portal. Fingers crossed now" Samarth saw the message while he was still surrounded by many men who were discussing every other solution to stop the invasion.

He knew that his hopes rested on the people who were far away from that room.

———————

On the boat Vishnu gave medicines to Manav to help him recover from the physical suffering he had to undergo while he was in control of the spirits and then took over the controls of the boat. Bodhi and Angad too were resting and nursing their wounds. About half a day later Manav got up and called for Bodhi, " So like always this time too you managed to get me out of the trouble" Bodhi smiled "Yeah now I am leading 2-1" Bodhi then narrated the entire incident which he knew and introduced Vishnu and Angad to Manav. " The Mandala had instructed me to drop it in the sea to safeguard it but the evil forces were still able to get it,"Manav told them with regret.

"Don't worry we will get it back now that you are with us" Bodhi tried to console him and then asked " What had happened with you all this while and what are these evil things and what is their plan?"

"It will be important to know more about them if we have to defeat them" Angad said

" After I was possessed by the spirits I tried hard to fight it off but I could not. Most of the things that happened seem like a dream or rather a nightmare which I was in but could do nothing to wake up from. Even while I was fighting Angad ji , I felt i was seeing a nightmare and I am just watching someone fight and I could not feel my body which was being controlled by the spirits"

" But how did you get defeated, you have your siddhi and see the move of your opponent beforehand" Vishnu asked him. " While I was being possessed my siddhi state did not get activated because my body was being controlled by the spirits and siddhi would not activate while I was impure" Manav told him.

" Good for us it was, otherwise it would have been impossible to get you back," Vishnu smiled.

" Tell us more about these things" Angad again asked

"As I was telling, I was under their control and I went with them to a far off place. We crossed the land on foot and then continued the journey on a ship and reached a strange land. There were no humans or animals to be seen while we traversed through it. Till we reached a place which seemed the capital of these undead soldiers. They had strange animals guarding the fort and their leader was the same man who you had encountered, the gaunt man who they called the Khadim. I had seen these visions when I first tapped into the powers of Mandala." he paused for a few seconds and gestured for water. Bodhi got up and brought him some water. Manav continued after drinking the water "These undead men were humans who bowed down to the dark powers in exchange of life but to sustain their life they needed to harvest the bodies of other humans else they would decay and die. They serve the Khadim, the spirits guide Khadim and oversee the activities of the army. To increase their number they keep on attacking human settlements just like what we had encountered and they would not stop until they have enslaved the humanity so that they continue to harvest the bodies without any resistance"

Manav told the plans that he heard during his stay around Khadim.

"But what are they trying to do with the Mandala?" Angad asked him

" I think they wanted to use me to tap into its power but fortunately I got away but what I heard once was Khadim talking about his master wanting to get the powers of Mandala. I think there is someone who is even more powerful than this guy and I fear if someone is so powerful he might unlock the power of Mandala even without me and more than I ever could. We do not know what havoc it might create "

"It seems we do not have an option but not only to retrieve the Mandala but also destroy this evil empire of Khadim" Angad told all the others around him.

"Yes we have to do that, but before that lets come back with a plan because now even the opponents know that we will attack and they too would be ready for us." Vishnu told them "also I had asked help from the remaining Navratnas when I met Bodhi and came to know of the peril. We all would need to meet again to plan out the next course of action together"

" So where are we headed to? " Manav asked the two of them

"The Navratnas would come to the AkhandaDweep, that is where we would go and make the strategy for the attack" Vishnu told him.

Back in hell, Devil had got the news of the chaos that has ensued on Earth 1, the Earth of his universe. " This is something that calls for celebration. You have successfully managed to leave my footprint on Earth and I have so many new slaves in hell directly transported from Earth 1. Soon more and more will come in my dominion and I will unleash this terror till the time even those alive accept me as their God"

Over the hundreds of years since the time crystals of Electronicium fell on Earth, many spirits which came with the crystals kept on wandering on Earth and many others got lost in the void of the universe but a few of them managed to travel back to hell. The spirits could travel at nearly the speed of electricity and became messengers and hunters for the Devil but they were very few . Now with the portal opening up on Earth 1 this problem was solved. So he finally decided to make his presence felt on Earth 1. He was in technicality a spirit , a ghost himself whose simulation had become powerful enough to capture other spirits so after walking out of Hell he was not sure how the physical world would treat his non physical form. There was only way to know, to walk out of the realm of Hell into the realm of Earth. He kept his dummy, using simulation, in his castle to cover for him in his absence and he went through the portal and came out of it on Earth. He saw the same Earth he had once walked upon and looked around it. He had been to this part of the world and it was not many months since the day that he had managed to cause HRP servers to malfunction.

He saw there were a lot of dead bodies lying around which he understood was the doing of his own minions .He tried to smell the air and feel the Earth, he was used to these sensations while walking in his dominion- Hell, but those were not real only simulations. He tried to change his shape and exert control on the surroundings but he could not do it. So he wandered off and finally saw a man on the road. He decided to enter into his body and take control. For the next few days he roamed around, had food whichever he liked, went to the brothels and had a lot of sex. He went to the old places he knew of. To satisfy his desire of control and violence he joined a group of rowdies and indulged in arson and theft and while the police chased the group he tried to escape by jumping over a bridge, he fell down and died and both the spirits that of Dr Oz aka Devil and that of the man who was possessed came out of the body.

" This was fun while it lasted," Devil thought to himself, " but I cannot do much if I am shapeless and by controlling only one person at a time will not get me what I want. So while my minions are controlling more and more humans I have to plan a way to unleash the same terror on Earth that the spirits that I had captured had faced in Hell. But for the time being I need to get back to Hell and then plan for it ". Over the next few days he managed to retrieve more information about the Mandala and how to use its powers and then when his work was done he asked one of his messenger spirits " What is the news of Khadim and the mission he was assigned?"

" We have good news. They have got the artefact, the Mandala but" the messenger stopped

" But what?" Devil asked sternly

" The army of Khadim had suffered heavy losses, hundreds of his soldiers had died when they were trying to get the Mandala because they were attacked by some men who too were armed with powerful magic" the messenger gave the entire news.

"Hmm. The soldiers are expendable, inform Khadim and the spirits to make more soldiers and they have to unlock the power of the Mandala and for that I am sending a dark magic chant and the method to use it. Deliver it to them"

Just the way crystals of Electronicium were the physical manifestation of the realm of Hell which no one could see by naked eyes, the Mandala was the physical form of a portal which could transfer thought and spirits to anywhere in the multiverse. So having the power of Mandala and the control of Hell would mean that Devil could link the two and then he would be able to make the realm of Hell part of the physical realm on Earth and he can control reality just as easily as he was controlling the simulations.

Now with Mandala in the possession of his forces and a possible way to unlock it meant that the Devil was only a step away from controlling the entire multiverse and all its timelines. To what extent could he control it? It was something that itself was hidden within the wombs of time.

The messenger spirit was still some time away from delivering the message of its boss to Khadim. When the arrow was shot by Bodhi Khadim knew that a warrior like Bodhi would not miss by such a distance and there would be something else about the arrow, he noticed the arrow had a crystal head. Centuries earlier he had used the power of a crystal - Electronicium to plunge humanity into the abyss of World War 3 , he knew this crystal could be something similar and took evasive action but the ship was blown to pieces and many of his undead soldiers died. Mandala was safe on the other ship and he managed to repair it to start the return journey.

The messenger spirit reached Khadim with the code to unlock the power of Mandala while he was about to reach the shores. The magic required an elaborate setup and meditation. Preparations for the same began.To tap into the powers of Mandala huge antenna like structures were being constructed in the fort of Khadim. He was also making a special crown made of eight metals so that his mind can use the power of the Mandala.

Meanwhile one troupe and some spirits set out to new lands to recruit more soldiers and the rest of the soldiers started working on increasing the fortifications around the capital. Khadim had sensed that there might be another attack on them by the men he had encountered on the sea so the preparations for that had to be done.

Kriti had crossed the portal and was about to enter the physical realm of Caliban the moon. At the very instance the messenger spirits who had been travelling between Earth 2 and Hell were crossing the portal to reach Earth 1 to deliver the message of the Devil to his minions who had possessed men of that World. The messengers left the imprints of Earth 2 in the portal and a link was created which transported Kriti to Earth 2. She stepped into an unfamiliar territory. She looked around and saw trees , it was a dense jungle she had landed into and there was no human in sight. She started making her way out and walked for many hours. "What is this place?There is no information of such a dense and vast jungle anywhere in my database. Many trees and animals too look different from what I have seen or known. How do I navigate my way and get to the things who were making people go crazy and murderous?" She had many questions in her head but was not finding any answers around her.

The spirits who were on the hunt for new humans to make them slaves along with the soldiers came across a scent which was very new. It was human but something else, they started tracking it and saw a female dressed in something metallic." This is something different , not entirely human. We should seize it" the spirits talked among themselves. They asked the undead soldiers to attack it. The soldiers ran towards it, the female was Kriti. She spotted these things from a distance, at first there was dread within her but it soon changed to excitement because she noticed that these ghostly men are a reminder to the possessed men she saw back home. "I was searching for clues and a clue had walked up to me. All I need to do is to track them and know their origins"

The soldiers came very close" I cannot engage in combat with them, I have to hide from them and follow them." but she could not think of anything so she started running away from them. Her speed was much more than the soldiers so she was able to outrun them , so the spirits came to attack her as they were swifter but could not take control of her as she was only a part human but while spirits tried to enter her body she did sense some malfunction inside her and presence of external energy which was entering her. " This might be the same or similar entity which had taken control of the people and made them go mad. It is trying to do the same with me" but she kept on running till it realised she is no longer feeling the sensation, the spirits had given up their effort " This thing only looks like a human but it is made of metal, it is something else. We cannot possess it, better to head back and recruit soldiers "the spirits discussed among themselves and went back to the soldiers.

All this while Kriti was thinking of the way to track them, then she realised she has the power of shrink tech and she immediately became small enough to remain hidden in grass and follow the undead soldiers.

The smaller size meant much lesser scent for the spirits to sense which without her knowledge eased Kriti's work to keep following the undead soldiers. The undead soldiers went to a village and started injuring the people and making the injured accept the dark powers. Kriti the cyborg just kept on observing this. She wanted to help the people but she did not engage, the scenes were horrific but she had to watch this to understand the power of the enemies and then trace from where they are coming and their possible weakness.

The undead soldiers captured about twenty villagers and took them along. They were tied with ropes and were made to walk a long distance for more than 12 hours. The villagers were then made to get on a boat and were taken to a place which was more than 2 days' journey. By the time they reached the shore these people had all passed out. On the shore some more undead men and creatures came to gather the hostages. Some people had died, others were still breathing. They immediately placed these people in separate glass chambers, each big enough to contain one person and it was filled with smoke. They then loaded all these chambers on carts and took them in a place which seemed like a makeshift prison cum army base with tents around the and cages to keep prisoners.

A big fire was lit in the middle of the place, along with wood some stones were put in the fire. Then she saw up in the smokes some human-like shapes which looked like ghosts. Some undead soldiers danced around the fire and a man who was wearing a long cloak chanted something. He then poured blood from a skull into it and then some leaves. After that the undead soldiers opened the caskets and cut the thumbs of all these people who were still asleep. One soldier made a garland of the thumbs and gave it to the man in the cloak who smeared it with a black powder and poured more blood on it and again chanted. Then he moved his hands around the fire and it subdued. He took a stone and wood from the fire in each hand and pressed it on these sleeping people and made a symbol. People were too deep in sleep to react. The ghosts in the smoke entered some of these people. She saw that a new thumb grew instantly and the man in the cloak raised both his hands. The soldier shouted in happiness . Same happened with the others, they all grew new thumbs.

–Few days before the encounter of Khadim with Bodhi and Angad—

The undead army needed more recruits and also more and more recruits would need more and more humans to supply them body parts and humans were getting difficult to find. Khadim informed his master about this problem via a messenger spirit " Why did he not tell me this before? That entire planet is full of radiation, radiation acts as a turbo-charger for magic and these two powers will combine to create mutated humans which would help Khadim to farm body parts. "

Khadim had gotten busy with finding the Mandala till this day when he managed to use the power to harvest human bodies by making them grow body parts instantly. Now he would not need thousands of humans to supply body parts to his undead army. A few dozen will be enough.

———————

Few days had gone since the battle with Khadim, Manav and Bodhi were able to meet the other Navratnas too who were called by Vishnu. All the existing Navratnas had also selected their next in line to preserve their knowledge since they knew with the power in hand of Khadim many of them may not survive the battle.

They were discussing how to get back the Mandala, the information given by Manav was vital as it helped in understanding the defence and offence capabilities in the city of undead. The group met Shashwat, the new general and told him about the enemy who could even destroy the peace of his country. The General consulted the new Prime Minister " Over the last hundreds of years we have maintained a policy of minimum interaction with the outside world. It helped us to preserve the technology and knowledge from the time before the Great War and go beyond that. We did not interfere in any problem of the world or invaded any nation, which was something the Dictator wanted to do. But all that you all have told me makes me rethink this policy. The enemy is too powerful to ignore and if left to chance we may find ourselves in bigger trouble in near future, one we don't know how grave it might become. So I have decided that this time the best soldiers from AkhandDweep Rashtra too will be a part of the war with this enemy and would launch the offence on this Khadim. We will also make preparations for defence in case the enemy comes close to our shore. I will also alert the navy to send out patrol boats far and wide so that we can keep on monitoring the activity of the enemy."

Angad was to oversee their preparations and was also busy making the necessary artefacts and weapons to counter the magical power of Khadim's army. He chose the men who were not only physically strong but were brave to stand in the face of any supernatural attack on them and have strength in their hearts to not accept the supremacy of Khadim for immortality by becoming his soldier. Hundred men from infantry and another 50 from the Navy were selected for this. They were divided into small teams. One of the team was to gather intel on enemy movement, Arshad came to meet his old friends after knowing about this development. Manav, Bodhi and Brahm were excited to see their old mate back. He had got a prosthetic leg and offered to lead the team which will spy on the enemy using his expertise in this field. The other team was to launch a guerilla attack on the army which was being led by Manav and Bodhi. The defence preparations were being monitored by Brahmbhatt and Mark. Mark had gathered the engineers to strengthen the security systems around the islands. Floating bombs were placed around the islands which could be triggered by the defence team whenever they would spot enemy ships.

After seeing the creation of the humans for perennial harvesting Kriti decided to follow the man in the cloak but he disappeared in a thick mist while she was still a bit distracted in looking at his human victims being turned into a crop, she looked around but did not find him so she again decided to follow the undead army to get to their boss in the next meeting. The undead army was aboard a boat to find more recruits , the spirits accompanying them told about human scents coming from the ocean. " There are some humans around and the scent has been at a constant distance. Some people are following us, these could be the same people who had attacked us a few days back"

The boat continued on its path and crossed a narrow strait which had rocky outcrops all along. The boat which was following it soon crossed the strait. Many soldiers of the undead army had hidden themselves behind the rocks . The boat of the undead went ahead with some soldiers. These hidden undead soldiers made a surprise attack on the boat which was chasing them. It was one of the patrol boats which was to follow movement of the undead army, they had heat sensors. The heat map of undead soldiers was different from humans or animals making it easier to locate them, the patrol boat had made arrangements to cover the human scent to avoid getting detected but they had recently crossed a sea storm and the spray they had done of the holy water had gone away, but they were not aware of it.

This was being led by a Navy captain. Arshad who was in command of the overall spying operations, was back in AkhandDweep Rashtra making plans for the next move and activating spy networks in other countries too to track Khadim's movement. The captain and his men had never been so far away from their homeland and this part of the ocean was unknown to them. A hidden soldier jumped on the deck and then another one. The Captain and his team were inside but they saw it from the windows and he asked the boatswain to immediately put the brakes `` They have spotted us and now we are being ambushed" he said to his men. " This is the time which separates boys from men. I know you are horrified to see these things but we shall fight to our last breath"

The undead soldiers were trying to break in and when they finally did they were met with bullet shots, the captain was standing in front of them. The bullets which hit them were silver bullets and it burnt them to ashes. The 4 soldiers accompanying the captain were motivated by seeing this and took their positions, more undead soldiers entered they were shot at by the soldiers of AkhandDweep. Captain and his men saw from their positions ash flying in the air. Soon everything was silent ," it seems they all are dead " said one of the soldiers to the captain. The captain gestured to them to wait, in case anyone was waiting. They waited for a few minutes and then slowly came out. There was smoke and ash still around them. They looked around and did not see any enemy soldiers and smiled at each other on their victory. They still had a smile on their face when a spear came flying and pierced the throat of one soldier and entered into the chest of another one standing in front of him. The captain immediately asked his men to rush inside, he had realised that the enemy was not dead yet while he shot at the direction from where the spear had come. He saw that two soldiers were carrying heavy metal shields big enough to hide themselves completely behind it and were able to stop the bullets using the shield , the others who were without it had succumbed to the silver bullets " I know you are friends of the men who had attacked us earlier. Since then we had prepared ourselves and we have been building shields and armour for the soldiers, to protect from your silver weapons. " They walked ahead," without the silver you cannot do anything to us" The captain took out his sword but he was not a sword fighter, but before he could fight the two soldiers plunged their swords in his chest and the captain died on the spot. The other two men saw that the boat they were chasing was now coming towards them " We cannot fight so many of them but we need to send out the message to the Headquarters". They spoke to each other, one of them switched on the boat and went full throttle. While the other one took a flame thrower and went outside. The one riding the boat shot a torpedo, the only one that the boat had, on the enemy boat. It went up in flames but the soldiers jumped out while burning. The sea water doused their fire and they started coming towards his boat. He went at full speed so none of them were able to climb up. It was only two undead soldiers on the deck who had to be dealt with. His friend came out and threw flames at the undead soldiers. They protected themselves with the shield, he then shot at them with his pistol but nothing happened as the shots were blocked by the shield. He threw his pistol and took out his sword. The undead soldiers got up and ran towards him, they traded blows but the soldier of AkhandDweep could not stand them for long and his body met the swords of the Devil's soldiers. The two undead then went to the last man who was in control of the boat. " You have destroyed our boat so we will use this boat to take us to our destination. We will not kill you if you do our bidding and be our boatswain" one of them said." The other one continued " If you this we will not only spare your life but we can give you immortality if you accept the supremacy of our King"

Kriti too had come on the boat and had witnessed the entire event of the death of Captain and his men " These people appear to be more advanced than other people on this land and seem to be in war with these monsters" she understood this and thought "If I help them perhaps I can find some solution to my problem and they too will be able to defeat their enemy" she was not sure if she should help them or keep on tracking the undead soldiers and reach their leader but before she could finally make a decision the last remaining soldier of the Navy took out his pistol and took a shot at one of the undead man, it was a headshot and the undead soldier could not do anything before completely dying. The other one was enraged , the Navy soldier fired another shot at him but by this time he had picked up his shield and was able to block it, and he continued to hide behind the shield till the bullets ran out. The human soldier picked up his sword to fight , at this point Kriti could not hold herself back and she came back to the normal human size, she was some distance away from the two of them and she rushed to help the human but he had not noticed her presence amid the fight. She took her first step by then the undead soldier took out a knife from his belt and threw it at the soldier, it hit his chest. Kriti reached closer and the undead soldier saw her and threw another knife at her but she dodged it easily and picked up the sword of the fallen soldier and beheaded the undead soldier in a single strike. She then picked up the human soldier, she saw surprise in his eyes. " I am a friend. I am not from this place, but I will help you to go back. The soldier was unable to speak but he guided her to the compass and the map. She took out the medical kit and tied up the wound of the soldier and then took over the boat and went towards the land pointed in the map.

The soldier was barely alive by the time they reached AkhandDweep. Kriti was held up by the coast guards, who immediately understood that she was from some other place. But the injured soldier who was unable to speak gestured that she helped him. But the guards still accosted her and they took her to the newly formed emergency council comprising Brahm, Manav, Bodhi, Vishnu, Angad and the other surviving Navratnas.

She was surrounded by the soldiers. " This girl had brought the last surviving soldier of Patrol team 7 which was attacked by the undead army" one of the soldiers told. " She looked a little different and we were not sure if this is not a trick of Khadim or of any other enemy country so we wanted her to be questioned by you all"

It was obvious to them that there was something different about the girl. The suit she was wearing had gadgets. Manav remembered the time when he and Bodhi had arrived on this island and they were too captured " Who are you and how did you get to the Patrol boat" he asked her "

" My name is Kriti and I have come from a place far off. My city was attacked by strange entities who were taking possession of people and making them go mad and murderous. I was also attacked but was saved by a group of scientists who added their mecha and tech to me to not only revive me but also give me special powers" she told them

" Looks like she is speaking the truth" Manav thought to himself but the very next minute he remembered how he was once betrayed.

"I had stepped into the portal through which these entities had entered my city and then I came into another place, a forest. I came across these strange half dead creatures and followed them around till they attacked the boat where I was able to save one soldier who asked me to bring him home"

"How did you follow these undead men without getting noticed? They can smell human scent" Vishnu asked

"Because I can do this," she said while shrinking her size.

Everyone was astonished and she again came back to normal size " This technology is shrink tech"

Brahm whispered to the other men, "I think she is not lying, because someone with this power could have easily infiltrated the country and would have gone unnoticed and fulfilled her nefarious purpose if any". Everyone agreed

"As of now we don't have a reason not to believe you. But we will obviously keep an eye on you. These two men will accompany you. We will regroup again to know more from you" Brahma told her. Manav and Bodhi were to accompany her and keep an eye on her. He gave them a small chip which will help them track her and Bodhi slyly attached it to her suit.

" Where can I get food?" She immediately asked them before getting into introductions " I am starving"

"I will get it right away" Manav told her and asked some attendants to get it for her. A lavish meal was spread and she ate voraciously like a child, when she realised after a few minutes that the two men are watching her she felt a bit embarrassed " It's been days since I haven't eaten anything proper, just managed with some fruits and roots whatever I could lay my hands on" and again began eating. Manav smiled at her, Bodhi saw the shine in his eyes which accompanied the smile. " It's good that this place has electricity, I could not find any place with it. I need to charge the mech attached to me. "They accompanied her to a room where she went to sleep and attached an electric wire to a socket on her back. It sucked in so much energy that the lights flickered for a few seconds, Manav switched them off and waved a bye and closed the room.

" You realise she is not completely a human" Bodhi told her sensing that his friend might develop some feelings for her . " Yes I do " Manav spoke plainly thinking that Bodhi is just mentioning a fact.

The group reconvened the next morning, and Kriti was asleep. " To fight the undead- the half human and half ghost we have someone who is half human and half machine, she is a good addition to our army" Brahma said to the group.

"Yes you are right" Angad said " I think the magic of the dark too might not work on her"

" Meanwhile I am getting the patrol parties to report back. It is too dangerous out there and even with full preparation they fell into the ambush" Arshad told the group and all of them agreed.

Kriti got up and one of the attendants informed Manav and Bodhi. She came and met the group who wanted to know more about her. " So which is this place you came from?" Brahm asked her

" I am from Antartica. I was a reporter for Orca News Channel. "She looked at them and was confused to see their astonished faces so she continued talking "Even I was surprised to see so much land and greenery. I have seen the world via HRP but did not know so much land mass was not submerged" The group was even more confused.

" Can you tell us everything from the beginning about your place? All the history you know about it just everything" Vishnu asked her, he sensed something is not adding up. Antarctica was never inhabited , he and the other Navratnas would have known if such an advanced civilization lived there.

Kriti sat down and told her about her life, her city , her work and then she went back and told about HRP. People were intrigued and they asked more about it. She told how the entire world was connected by it and the major countries of her World which had survived post the global warming.

"Thank you so much for telling us all about your place. Manav and Bodhi please take her around the place and make her familiar with the things here" Vishnu thanked her and then he went to another room and gathered the Navratnas. "Did you think the girl was lying?" He asked one of the Navratnas who was an expert of psychology and humanities. He was present there to judge her response and understand if she possessed any threat. " I am sure she wasn't lying. Also the clarity with which she explained everything it is clear that she is not delusional "

Vishnu went into deep thoughts" What I am about to say might sound difficult to digest. But given that the knowledge that we possess as a group about anything and everything under the sun hearing something like this makes me come to only one conclusion" He took a pause and then continued "she is from a different dimension or another Universe. She is from another Earth which is plagued by the similar entities as we have been "

There was a heavy and uneasy silence around the room. Angad broke the silence " We have seen many things which have been difficult to believe and as has been told in the scriptures that where we live is just one of the many universes and there are infinite universes like this and we finally meet a person from a different universe"

Vishnu continued seeing that the group is ready to buy his idea" Kriti's coming to this world and the fact that even the other world is troubled by the same problem means that the enemy has come up with a way to travel from one universe to another. "

"Yes, she said about walking through a portal. This portal must be the door to the other world. We need to find it and find it quickly before more chaos ensues" Angad completed Vishnu's statement.

"Do you think that the Mandala is the portal?" Vishnu asked him

"Thinking about the timelines, the time since Kriti's Earth was attacked was earlier than when Khadim got the hold of the Mandala so I think this particular portal is not Mandala but what I am sure of is that Mandala has a connection to the portal" Angad expressed his views.

The other Navratnas agreed and this group then went to meet the other officials of the country to make the plans post this new development.

"Another Earth" this sounded impossible to everyone but with all the facts they realised that this is the only possibility how impossible it might sound. Even Kriti was told about this " So I have come into another universe on a different Earth" she went silent and then added in her head the pictures of places she had seen after coming out of the portal" I think this might be true, there is nothing like the places I have seen on my Earth"

"Where is the portal that got you here?It might hold the key to knowing how all this is happening" Vishnu asked him.

" It was a dark circle-like thing which had alternating gravity, sometimes it sucked mass and other times it threw out dust particles and those things which controlled people. It was only about a metre in diameter. I went inside and there was extremely crushing pressure inside and complete darkness. I felt I was being sucked inside this dark tunnel at the speed of lightning and suddenly there was light and I saw myself on this planet in the middle of a jungle. I looked around but did not see where did I come from"

Khadim all this while had been meditating and due to his powers he could concentrate more than any human could and finally he was able to bond with the Mandala. He saw everything right from his childhood to his becoming of Khadim in a matter of seconds. It had been so long that he had forgotten much of his past life. He concentrated again and now he felt a presence around him and the presence asked him "Who are you?"

" I am Khadim, the ruler of the Empire of the Devil on Earth" he replied and he heard a laughter on the other side followed by a "Welcome" now Khadim saw that he was in a large room and a tall figure was standing in front of him who had large red eyes and a horns for his crown. He stretched his arm "So now you have started tapping into the power of Mandala through your subconscious. This is great news. This is Hell , I am your Lord the Devil"

Khadim bowed in front of him " It is an honour to finally meet you after having ruled in your name for centuries "The Devil came down from his throne and walked up to him and held Khadim's shoulders "You have done great work now I can talk to you directly without the need of messengers and I can view things from your eyes of all that is happening around you. Soon you and I we will rule all the Earths"

" All the Earths" Khadim asked with confusion. The Devil smiled, "Let me show something" he said, and he made him walk from the portal which was inside the hell to Earth 1. The consciousness of the two of them walked out of the portal " See this new world" Devil said to Khadim. " This is completely different from what I have seen, this place is more advanced than what the world was before I started the great war" Khadim replied with surprise.

They moved around the city a bit and the Devil told him about the multiverse and how using portals scattered in the multiverse one can travel from one universe to another and even between the timelines. He showed him the destruction that his spirits had created in this world " Very soon this world too shall fall under my feet just like your Earth and soon all other Earths too but to achieve that I will need to get the control over all the portals linking the multiverses and the timelines. But to master them the power of Mandala has to be controlled completely and once it's done there is no power strong enough to face us".

At AkhandDweep the preparations to launch the offence were completed. The armada consisted of 3 big ships accompanied by small boats to easily manoeuvre and get greater speed. More soldiers were added knowing that the danger is grave, the attack team consisted of 500 soldiers now. Entire silver of the country was bought back by the Government and was sent to the arms factories where it was melted to give silver coating to the weapons that would be used by the army. The soldier who was saved by Kriti had narrated the entire sequence of events and how the undead soldiers had shields. So after knowing armour piercing guns were perfected and silver coated bullets were loaded in these guns. Hand Grenades with silver shrapnels were given to all the soldiers. The Soldiers had flamethrowers too along with these guns in the arsenals and the boats and ships had missile launchers, flame throwing canons and harpoons all around.

All the soldiers were also given pistols which had holy water and they had sacred threads tied on their wrists to protect them from the spirits. The army men wore green armour and the navy men wore blue armour. Armours were made of strong fibre which could withstand a few sword blows before the body would be harmed and had an inflatable pocket in the back which could be filled with air to give them buoyancy while swimming or fighting in water.

Manav, Bodhi and Nagad also wore green armour as they would go ahead on the terrain to take down the fortress. Kriti's gear and mech were an armour itself so she did not need another armour.

The ships had tanks and armoured vehicles to transport the soldiers over land since the fortress of Khadim was away from the sea as Manav had told them. Similar arrangements and arsenals were also given to soldiers who were protecting the borders and the coastlines of the country.

"I think we have prepared well to fight the army. We have numbers and all the weapons to deal with the enemy. I am sure that we will come out victorious." The Prime Minister said to Brahma and his general, he had come to see the final leg of preparations before the troops left for the war.

The armada was about to leave and the entire harbour was crowded because the families of the soldiers had come to say goodbye to them. This was the first time that the Navy and Army of AkhandDweep Rashtra was going to undertake such a big mission in a foreign land. The soldiers were both excited about being part of this opportunity and were nervous too. The newspaper reporters too had thronged the place . The Prime Minister addressed them "We have never embarked on such missions earlier but this time the enemy is too powerful and if we do not take action then tomorrow our own existence might be in danger. But we have made sufficient preparations to defeat the enemy. We know all that is to know about them and our men and technology will be enough to defeat them easily."

The reporters wanted to interview the men who were going on the mission but they could not , one of them was able to identify the heroes who had a few months ago toppled the Dictator. They swarmed them to get some info about the mission but were not lucky enough to get a word "Sorry. We are in a rush " was all that Manav said, while Bodhi remained tight lipped and they went on to the ship.

In the biggest of the three ships all the leaders of the troop assembled in the central hall. Manav, Bodhi , Angad, Colonel of the army, Admiral of the Navy and also present was Kriti. Vishnu, Arshad, Brahma and others Navratnas had stayed back in AkhandDweep and were not part of the attack.

All of the leaders gathered around a table which had a 3D map of their route. " This is the route that we are taking. Our team of analysts have made this 3D map of the entire route and the places around it using our knowledge of the geography and the information we have got from Manav and Kriti"

The admiral told the group as he moved the image of the armada around the route. He pointed at the archipelago "This is the place where the boat of ours was ambushed. We will not be taking that route and instead be using another route where there are no such small islands. We will travel mostly through the open seas where it will be easy to locate the enemy and our Naval superiority will be able to destroy them immediately. Then once we come to the land, " He pointed out the continent in the South western quadrant of the Earth. "We land here , this is a fair distance away from the enemy's den and there is no natural harbour so the enemy would not be using this side of the continent for his ships. Then the armoured vehicles take you all ahead, meanwhile two of the ships will go towards the side of the continent which the ships of Khadim have been using as harbours. While the army would attack the fortress, the navy would take out Khadim's ships and any soldiers returning from their raids to completely annihilate the empire of Evil "

All of them looked at each other with appreciation and a sense of belief. Then the Colonel took the map and then he showed the map his team had prepared. " Here is the terrain that we will traverse to reach the fortress. The drones will lead the way helping us to intercept the enemies and avoid falling into their booby traps. Kriti too would be moving along with the drones, since she can reduce her size she will not be seen while helping us with the navigation"

He then zoomed the fortress" we have tried to make it as close to your description as possible" he said to Manav. " The tanks and armoured vehicles will clear the area around by wiping out the soldiers.

Direct one to one engagement of the soldiers with the enemy might not be needed till we reach close to the fortress, after that we will smoke bomb the entire area so that Manav, Bodhi, Angad, Kriti and ten of my best men will storm inside to take back the Mandala. I will be in touch with you all and if more manpower would be needed I will keep on sending more teams inside."

"While we keep the men and creatures of Khadim occupied, Kriti can reach the Mandala and get it close to me. Once it happens I will be able to bond again with it and it will be easier to get out. Once we are out we can bomb the entire fortress and go back" Manav told the last leg of the plan.

"Just one more thing" Kriti interjected. "Yes, please say" the colonel said " there are many humans who are held captive in a vegetative state and are being harvested for body parts. We should free them too" she told the group.

Everyone nodded and appreciated the humanitarian thoughts of Kriti, the Colonel told her" I will assign a team for that, to free the prisoners and help them escape. Along with them a couple of medical corp members will also be there to help the prisoners get back to senses"

"We should now get back and get ourselves ready. Meanwhile I will inform the captains who will be leading the teams and tomorrow I will introduce you to my men who will storm the fortress" he told them and the meeting was dismissed and all of them went back to prepare for the battle.

Manav took time to meditate while Bodhi practised his martial arts. After that both of them did some target shooting using the guns and sparring in the practice range which was there on all ships for the soldiers. Kriti checked his entire mech and charged it completely and took rest. Angad spent time reading scriptures and making some more weapons, charms and amulets. The Admiral and Colonel met their men and motivated them while doing the last minute checks of their preparation.

Almost two days had gone by and the fleet was hundreds of miles away from the homeland. Manav was standing on the deck all alone and looking at the open sea. Kriti too was taking a stroll around and she saw him and went to him " Hey, what are you doing here?" she asked.

"Nothing really, just thinking about the last few years since the time everything has gone topsy -turvy in my life" Manv told her.

"What about you?" He asked her while trying not to stare at her, because she was pretty. A perfectly proportioned face, blemish free skin to go along with her tall, slender body which was strong enough to break a tree in a single kick.

"Thinking the same as how the last few months have been. I was a reporter living my dream but then there was a tragedy in the biggest tech company which claimed the lives of so many, my beloved fiance was also in that. Took me months to recover and then the city gets attacked by possessed men and I am almost dead but then I wake up with these powers and then reach a planet where I am going to fight someone who I am not even sure holds the key to my return. I can't even fathom what physical mode could take me back to my home. Sometimes I think maybe I am just sleeping in the arms of my love and I will just wake up realising this was just a crazy dream and nothing else" her eyes were wet.

Manav felt a slight sting when he heard about her ex but later felt bad about her misfortune. He gave a slight tap on her shoulder while her head was down. She raised her head up and he saw her beautiful eyes were red due to weeping. " I never wanted to be a warrior or a person with super powers, all I wanted was a happy life and love. Why can't it be all normal, people trapped by Khadim harvested for their body , people on my planet getting possessed and murderous, why Manav why?? "she said while leaning on his chest. " You will get all that you want and you will go back home. I promise you that, whatever it takes. By now she had started crying loudly , Manav felt her warm tears on his chest " She is an accidental warrior, one who has hardly spent a few days fighting unlike other people on this ship who have been doing it for years. Her body can take it easily but for her heart this is too much pain to see" he talked to himself and not knowing what to do in that moment he put his arms around her and she completely sunk herself into his chest and when he looked at him he wiped tears off her cheek, she felt such a warm assuring touch after so many days, she kissed his lips. Manav reciprocated and hugged with all his strength and soon they were wrapped in each other's arms and made love.

The two of them woke up a couple of hours later. Kriti had fallen asleep in Manav's arms. Manav was not sure on how to react but Kriti assured him by gently holding his hands he again kissed her "When you find the way to my world. I am taking you with me" she said. He smiled, she again said " You will come, right?" She was serious now. " I will, " he said, holding her body in one arm and her face in his hands.

They got dressed up, the waves in the oceans were rising due to strong breeze and the moonlight had gone dim due to cloud covers. Their ship was the one in the middle of the other two. The admiral was in the ship which was ahead of them and the Colonel was in the ship behind. They saw alarm lights on the ship ahead of them and they saw many soldiers rush out with weapons. To know what was happening they rushed inside to the captain's cabin and they got to know that the sonar in the ship picked up signals of a huge creature probably a whale coming towards them. They were relieved " I thought it was something dangerous" Manav said to the Captain who said with a smile " Yeah, the animal or fish whatever it is will pass by and if it creates any trouble the ship has harpoons and torpedoes to blow it into pieces. You should now go and rest, it's late. We too have our weapons ready for any such animal attacking our ship"

The two went outside the cabin and Manav was closing the door when they heard a very loud sound, it was a blast. He looked at the captain who was viewing on his screen, the first ship had been hit and there were flames coming out. Manav, Kriti and many others rushed out to see what was happening. Bodhi too reached the spot. Many of the sailors took out the boats and started rushing towards the first ship.

The Captain over the PA system announced " Everyone please remain calm, we are trying to connect with the Admiral's ship and trying to know what has happened" It was obvious to all that a whale or any creature however huge it would be cannot create such a destruction and there was something else to this. Angad was in the ship behind them, Manav saw him via binoculars which he asked from a soldier who was standing nearby, he was safe and was surrounded by the soldiers who had come out to see what was going around.

Manav got into his siddhi state but did not find anything , soon they all saw the floating carcass of a dead creature who was blown to pieces and there were many other fishes which had died. It was gigantic and probably the same one which was spotted by the sonar of the ship. Manav guessed that the creature had explosives on it and that it had managed to hit the ship despite being targeted by missiles and torpedoes.

The boats were taking out the people from the first ship, when another thing was spotted by the sonar of the second ship, something coming from deep down. The men got ready and fired torpedoes at it, the soldiers who were on the boat aimed their guns and spears and shot in the direction of this thing , then came out a huge wave like a tsunami and a monster appeared which was a like an enormous crocodile it was the size of the ship itself, its skin was so tough that the torpedoes were not harming it. "Perhaps the creature which had hit the first ship too had such a skin," Manav conjectured.

Manav went into his siddhi to predict the next move of the croc, he saw that it would hit the ship from below using his tail, so he ran to the Captain and took over the controls to manoeuvre the ship. He was a little late. The tail did hit the ship but fortunately it was a partial hit and no major damage was done, the ship rocked and people on the deck fell down.

Seeing that the ship was able to evade the attack the croc got agitated and devoured one of the boats which was on the way to pick men from the burning ship. All the six men and the boat were gulped down, it froze most of the people who saw this visual. The Captain shouted on the PA " keep on firing at it and distract it using the drones " the drones were launched and they too fired at the croc from all directions and so did soldiers on the boats and ships.

It got slightly disoriented and swam around in circles and gave some respite to the ship but the ammunition was not making much of an impact. The third ship too had come close to help the ship under attack and it kept on firing at the giant croc.

Seeing that nothing was working, Kriti jumped in the water, Bodhi tried to stop her but she was already in water before he could do anything. She shrunk her size and went close to the croc, she was so small that the beast did not notice her and she went inside its mouth. She had a small torch built in her wrists, using it she navigated and then went inside the body via the food pipe, it was big enough for her to get back to the normal size, she took out a knife from her waist and started cutting the food pipe. The Croc now feeling the pain started going up and down the water surface violently while Kriti kept on going deeper inside the body cutting through every organ she encountered , when the croc could not bear it anymore it went inside the water.

It was now all calm, people from the first ship came to the second and third one. The injured were getting first aid, Manav came out and asked Bodhi about Kriti. " She jumped in the water and went towards the animal, I tried to stop her but before I could anything she had made her move"

The water soon turned red "That thing is dead now" Manav said to Bodhi, he could see it through his siddhi, but Bodhi knew he wanted to know about Kriti which his eyes were searching for. He kept waiting and suddenly felt a tap on his shoulders. He turned around and saw Kriti, standing there. His joy knew no bounds and he hugged her tightly and she reciprocated the same.

Bodhi smiled looking at them.

Few minutes later, the three of them were sitting together in Manav's room and Kriti was telling them of what all she saw inside the body of the giant croc when Angad joined them. The three of them could make out from his worried face that he had something important to share and wanted to discuss it with them.

" I think these creatures are not inhabitants of these waters, they were mutated by magic. I took the samples of the carcass and blood and when I mixed with the holy ash and the reaction it gave told me that something is not right . " he told them.

"Do you think that…?" Manav said but before he completed his sentence Angad gave him a nod and completed it" yes, we are under attack by Khadim, he perhaps knows that we are coming and he even knows the route that we are following and these are his pets which he had sent to attack us and slow us down. He is coming at us with full preparations, we might see more such things pretty soon"

There was a tense silence around in the room, they now knew that they were up against an enemy who is one step ahead of them "Does this mean that he has got the powers of the Mandala and can look into our movements?" Manav asked about the thing he was fearing the most. "This seems to be the most possible explanation and even if this is not the case we should be prepared for such a scenario" Angad told everyone in a grave voice.

This was the worst fear of everyone, now with Khadim able to keep a watch on them they have lost any advantage of the surprise attack they had. Also they were not aware of so many dangerous creatures in his command. "What should we do now ? " Bodhi finally spoke up

"What can we do? He might be tracking our movement for all we know " ,Manav said ,"I guess we just have to wait and watch for his next attack"

Khadim had gained some powers of the Mandala and he was able to see in his visions the movement of his enemies, the visions were blurred and he saw that a fleet is coming to attack him and he was able to predict the direction from which they would come from, so he sent out the army of most dangerous ocean dwelling beasts to stop the enemies in his track.

One more day had passed since the attack of the croc and the whale, many of the men who were on the first ship had died or were badly injured, the Admiral also was in the list of the injured. The ship too was beyond repair and the armoured vehicles in it too were of no use to anyone now. All this had slowed down the movement of the fleet but they were much more alert of any attack coming their way, they spent the day preparing for the attack and thinking about all the possible foes that they might come across.

The next dawn they were all woken up by alarms and the sudden slowing down of the ship, the drones and some of the patrol boats had been sent well ahead of the ships to give them an extra few minutes of preparation once they spotted the enemy. The information was relayed, the enemy was about an hour away, coming on a large wooden ship.

Every soldier got ready with the weapons. The gunners came at the post and the cannons were loaded and the torpedoes were ready to be deployed once the enemy ship was in range. The gun fitted drones were launched to both monitor and shoot at the enemy soldiers.

The first ship was visible now, a huge ship which was just like the previous ships they had seen, made of wood and skeleton. It came closer to them and the cannons fired their shots. The ship jumped out of the way, everyone who was watching this from their binoculars were shocked. What looked like the ship was actually a living creature, it was a humongous thing which had a wooden ship tied to it. The creature was of the same colour as of wood making it difficult to view it from a distance. It raised its head and its dark black eyes saw everyone in front of it, the undead soldiers standing atop the thing jumped out in the water and started swimming towards the fleet of AkhandDweep Rashtra.

This giant creature now opened its arms and then stood upright, swimming in an upright position, it looked like a giant bear or a hairy human. Humans were smaller than its fingers, the cannons shot again and he jumped inside the water to avoid being shot. The jump sent out huge waves in the sea, the ship got rocked and the cannon shots went in the wrong directions.

"It is avoiding fire, this means its skin is not impermeable to our ammunition, so if we keep on shooting we will be able to bring it down" the injured admiral told the Captain. Manav, Bodhi, Kriti and Angad, who was on the other ship, were all standing on the decks with their weapons, ready to meet the enemy.

What they had not realised was that the waves which were generated by the giant were used by the undead soldiers to ride them and they came very close to their two ships which were now parallel to each other. The soldiers started firing at the undead army, soon many of them died but, in the background a few hundred metres away they saw another ship, it was so huge that its mast casted a shadow on the ships of Akhandweep and with so many undead soldiers on it that it looked like it was an entire floating city. The swarms of soldiers started jumping down in the water to take over the ships of Akhandweep.

"The fortress never had so many soldiers," Manav said with worry on his face to his mates.

The guns started shooting and the big cannons too started firing, Khadim's soldiers were getting burnt like insects around fire but they were so many that they kept on moving ahead.

Fire the torpedoes " The Captain ordered,"This ship is made of wood i am sure, we will burn it and all those riding it"

Torpedoes were fired at the giant ship by one of the ships of Akhandweep, it was a hit and the navy men shouted with joy but the hole was not massive enough to sink a ship of this size but another hit would create considerable damage. The second one too shot a torpedo, but before it reached the ship the giant who was hiding in the sea leapt up and caught the torpedo and deflected it away.

Another torpedo was fired by the first ship, but before it came out the barrel the ship was toppled. The giant had gone deep down to the surface of the sea and then leapt up at full speed and its impact toppled the ship.

Manav and the ship's sonar had sensed this just a few seconds before, so the soldiers on the deck along with Manav, Bodhi and Kriti jumped in the water. While the ship was toppling the captain had communicated to the other captain over the coms" The giant will topple us so as soon as you see it , shoot him with everything you got" and the giant came out of the surface of the water. The other Captain bellowed the same message, the giant had come out with such a speed that it was in air for many seconds, he was a big enough target to not miss. The Cannon and the giant gun on the ship and the soldiers all aimed at him and kept on shooting. The giant had agility and tried to stop the missile by grabbing it but it was way faster than the torpedo he had deflected underwater and it hit him in the torso and the blast injured his hands too. The bullet wound was like a needle wound to him but hundreds of needles were enough to give it pain. By the time it fell back on the water it was bleeding and it charged the ship. The first ship had managed to avoid capsizing and it regained its balance by now and fired at the head of the giant who was looking at the other ship. The shot hit his temple and it lost its balance and went down in water and drowned. Water turned red. But this blood invigorated the hordes of the undead soldiers coming at them. Many of them had reached close to the ship and started climbing up by creating stairs using their bodies, they were so much in number that at a distance it looked like termites were attacking a piece of wood and were about to cover it.

The human soldiers standing on the ship kept on shooting with their silver bullets and flamethrowers . They were burning the undead soldiers but the undead kept on coming. There were over a hundred undead soldiers for every human soldier, despite all the preparations and having the ammunition to take down the enemy, the soldiers of AkhandDweep Rashtra were facing such a huge swarm that it was difficult to control.

The twenty odd soldiers who had jumped in the water while the ship was toppling were completely surrounded by enemies. To fight so many enemies while swimming was almost impossible for them. One soldier was pulled in the water and he tried to get up but there were three undead soldiers pulling him down from below the surface of the water and another two who were pushing him down from top. Bodhi rushed towards him and cut down the ones who were inside the water and then the soldier shot the ones above, then Bodhi saw a hundred more coming to pull down the other soldiers.

Bodhi came to the surface to help another soldier and freed from the clutches of undead. He smiled at Bodhi but the next minute the soldier was hit by a dagger thrown at him which broke the shield of his helmet and hit him in the eye and he died.

Seeing so many undead soldiers grabbing them, many soldiers panicked and started shooting all around, even hitting their fellow men. Two brave soldiers looked at each other, they were friends since the day they had joined the armed forces, knowing the end was nearing they removed the pin of the grenade to take as many undead with them as possible.

The others were getting pulled down in the water one by one. Manav Bodhi and Kriti were looking all around seeing this, they tried to help but their help was not enough in the face of the enemy swarm. Manav who was already in his siddhi state was shooting using the pistol loaded with silver guns when he ran out of bullets he reverted to his preferred weapon the sword, this one had silver coating on it. Bodhi took the flamethrower of a soldier who was killed and he was using it for burning the enemies. Kriti kept on shrinking and growing back to make the enemies blind sided to cut them using the long and sharp silver claws that she had put on. Realising that all soldiers are dead around them, Manav and Bodhi came together having each others' back and Kriti giving them the cover by swimming around them. The three were now like a whirlpool where the enemy kept on coming like water and kept on getting drowned to bottom.

The spirits of Hell were also watching the entire thing, they were not able to do much since all three had amulets and holy water with them. But the ones who were getting caught by the undead had their protection spells broken by the undead and some soldiers accepted to join the enemies to avoid being killed, the spirits immediately worked their black magic and the human soldiers were converted to undead soldiers. One such soldier walked up to the Captain's cabin in the first ship, he was not harmed by any of the sides, the undead recognised him as their kind and the humans just looked at the green armour of the army and let him pass through, he opened the door and shot the captain, and before anyone could act he threw a grenade and ran away. This soldier who had switched sides, used a flamethrower and burnt the engine room before killing the unsuspecting men working there, the ship was set on fire and so the first ship was now destroyed by Khadim's undead men. Some soldiers who were caught in the fire jumped in the water to douse it but were met by the undead who stabbed them before they even touched water.

Angad's ship, the second ship, was still sound so far but was under heavy attack, a large chunk of undead army was wiped out but it was still enough to bring down the ship. The Captain decided to go full throttle and move ahead rather than waiting for the ship to be captured. His idea was to give less time for the undead to climb up the ship and take it down as there were not many options left. Lesser enemies to fight at a time might just help them, so he did that and in a few seconds crossed the burning ship. The speed went on gaining speed " we are going too fast, the ship has never gone at this speed it will be difficult to control " warned his deputy- the first mate but Captain was in no mood to listen, his eyes had become bulged and red and he was not even blinking. Witnessing this battle and the events of the last two days had driven him crazy and finally after deciding to make this move, once the ship started accelerating, he lost his mind completely and he kept on going full throttle. The gigantic ship of the Undead army was up ahead, the human soldiers were still fighting with the last bit of ammunition and the cannons were still roaring and it successfully made a shot on the enemy shit, but the Captain no longer able to manoeuvre his ship and it rammed straight into the ship of Undead army and there was a huge blast and both the ships were blown to bits. All the human and undead soldiers who were still on the ship or near it were torn into pieces. That very instant the first ship which was already on fire too had a huge blast and was blown apart.

Back in his fortress, Khadim who was in his meditation watched all this. Once the ship was blown off, he smiled while meditating and then went off to work on his new project along with his helpers and whispering spirits.

Even before he had started harvesting humans for the body parts by regrowing the body parts he had tried regrowing the parts of an undead soldier. He cut the arms of an undead soldier and did the magic charm but instead the arm regrowing, an entire body regrew from the arm but the body was dead.

He sent the information of this new discovery to his master, and then experimented with live humans which started regrowing the fresh body parts needed to supply for the undead soldiers decaying bodies.

When the Devil heard of the creation of undead corpses, he went to the prison in Hell" To all of you who are rotting in this prison. I give you an opportunity to be free"

Initially there was a silence because some of these souls had been trapped for hundreds or even thousands of years, and were surprised to hear such an announcement. Sometimes few souls would be selected as minions of the Devil but never ever there was mass recruitment for the same.

"Yes, you heard me right. I will give you the freedom. All you need to do is to fight for me"

The Devil had gone to the prison which had the souls of those who had lived a life of crime or violence when they were alive, so it was an easy option for these souls to accept the offer.

On Earth Khadim created the undead corpses by thousands and Devil let out his prisoners to occupy those bodies. And then the undead corpses came back from the dead and thus the Khadim created such a huge army which overpowered the fleet of AkhandDweep.

Angad and Manav had figured out ways to kill the undead but they had never expected that they would face such a huge number of them. The undead army had a few thousand soldiers which they would have defeated easily with the help of the army and the Navy but what they faced was close to half a lakh soldiers.

Over the next two days, having lost most of the army, Khadim and the Devil created another army of a few thousand undead to replenish for the lost soldiers. Then he went to Hell through his consciousness to meet the Devil and the two of them crossed the portal to reach Earth 1 . Devil asked his spirits tofind a suitable person whose body could be taken over by Khadim's consciousness.

On Earth 1 some people had figured out that this problem plaguing them was not aliens but ghosts or spirits and they started trying using exorcism to cure the possessed although Samarth and the Government had warned the people not to try anything at all . They had asked the public to disengage with the infected population but some still went ahead with it owing to the desperation of the time. This Earth was far away from properly using the power of magic , and hence most of these exorcists and priests died while trying the exorcism. But there was one who had managed to perform an exorcism with some success and he cured three possessed men. He was a priest and was a wrestler before he became a priest.

The Devil got to know of him and asked all his spirits to attack him and take control of his body. " A person who can use Magic on this Earth will be useful for me and his physical strength will help dark magic flow through him."

Once he was successfully possessed by spirits he was made to bow down to the Devil. Khadim's consciousness got into his brain and then he used this man to create undead soldiers and then the spirits from Hell started taking over their bodies. He did this for next one day without any break and his life energy got consumed in creating the undead soldier, the priest died but by that time Devil and Khadim had enough foot soldiers along with the spirits who had been a trouble for this Earth.

Now the Empire of Darkness started spreading on this Earth too. This new batch of undead soldiers created on Earth 1 started killing the humans and those on the verge of dying were given an option to choose the dark side and get immortality by becoming an undead soldier of the Devil and Khadim.

The plague was spreading thick and fast, and there seemed no end in sight.

While in the jungle of Earth 2 there was a camouflaged team moving deeper towards the fortress of Khadim. It was Manav and team who had come on to the mist-covered land of the undead.

------------------Back to the day of the battle at the sea----------

Manav, Bodhi and Kriti were in the middle of these two blasts and they went inside the water to save themselves from the fire and the debris. A minute later they came out and saw the smoke had filled the sky and it had covered the sun and there were body parts falling all around. There were still some undead around them, some had lost limbs and were not in a fighting shape, the others were alive but seemed to be too un-bothered by the existence of humans because they did not want to remain stuck in the middle of the sea. So they started swimming back in the direction of their ship.

In the smoke Manav saw the shape of the spirits, who had spotted him and his mates. They were probably building their nefarious plans on trying to possess any of these, the amulets of Bodhi were damaged, the spirits swopped in towards him along with the smoke but there was a strong flash of light which left everyone blinded for a few seconds. Manav removed his hands from the front of his face when the light had died down. In the water a few feet away from them was Angad, Manav was delighted to see him " We thought you.." he and the others had thought that Angad too had perished in the blast but here he was holding a small lamp like thing which had emitted this powerful light. It was still glowing and had a light blue shine in it. " You never fail to amaze us."

" I had realised that the captain had lost his senses when he was going full speed. I took my stuff and jumped in the water" he told how he was able to save himself

"Great that you did" Manav smiled at him

Bodhi continued. "What was it that you did a minute back" and he took some of the stuff of Anagad that was carrying in the back pack to lighten his load

"Look up , do you see anything ?" Angad asked them" I still see the smoke but the spirits, I could see them, now .. they are gone or may be are again invisible now" Manav said

Angad gestured at the lamp and smiled" So you have managed to capture them?" Yes" he gave a calm reply but seeing a bewildered look on the face of others he replied" I knew the spirits will create trouble so I had created this charm and contraption to capture them. I will see if I can make them reveal something for us" Angad told his plans

" This is great, at least a small victory for us" Manav said

Kriti swam close to him and whispered" You are safe and that is a victory for me"

He smiled.

"I was worried for you but then I saw no one could land a single blow on you" she said while holding his hand under water and floating using the air pocket of the armour.

" We should look out if there are any of the spare boats or anything that can help us take to some land," Bodhi told the group.

" Look that side" Angad pointed on the other side where they had come from" there is a boat, before jumping I unhooked one of the boats from the ship" just a small hitch that some undead are using right now. "

It was a small task for the group to kill the undead and take the boat, they rowed it for many hours. Fortunately the bag packs had extra food and a small desaline kit to help them drink sea water. They found the land that they were looking for.

Khadim could see the battle from far but he could not see the minor details, when both the ships of the fleet of AkhandDweep were destroyed, he assumed that everyone including Manav and Bodhi would be dead or even if they are alive they will not bother to move ahead and would rather go back to regroup during which he can quickly rebuild his army and expand the empire on the other Earth.

This overconfidence helped the team to reach closer to his fortress, but Khadim's hunches tingled and he meditated using Mandala and he saw the group alive and closing in on his fortress. He was shocked,"How in the Devil's name did these pests escape and reach here." he shouted in anger. Few seconds later when he calmed down slightly, "it was an oversight from me which I will correct immediately " he said and got into action.

The four of them were moving swiftly towards the fortress when they heard footsteps of a large group approaching them. " There are barely any humans left in this part of the world," Manav said " It means we are about to meet the undead again," Angad said.

They took positions on tree tops separated from each other by a considerable distance , Bodhi kept on leaping from one tree to another till he even crossed the undead troops that were coming. Kriti too shrinked her size and went behind. These were barely a hundred undead soldiers

Bodhi and Angad attacked from the front. It took them a few minutes to kill the undead. Then they continued moving for few hours and then decided to make a short halt and while they were catching their breath they saw some more undead coming from far away, they were running towards them and when they got spotted they jumped high and then to the amazement of all there came out wings from their backs and they started flying. They had dark black wings like eagles and when they got a closer look the face too looked a little avian" Another wretched creation of Khadim, made by combining undead soldiers and birds" grunted Angad. "He is watching our movements" Manav said " The first batch of the undead soldiers we just encountered was only to slow and tire us down while he was working to send these flying monsters"

These flying undead soldiers were about fifteen in number but they were quick so it was difficult to strike them, they were carrying bow and arrows and were shooting at them from all directions.

"If we don't move ahead quickly more of them will come and will keep on coming till we collapse and die" Manav told the group. They kept on moving around taking covers of the trees and bushes to avoid being shot, it was not very difficult for Kriti who had her powers to avoid it but Bodhi and Angad despite their agility were finding it difficult to avoid so many arrows coming their way that too in the mist which was hovering over this entire marshy land mass which was ruled by Khadim and the undead army. Manav too felt it difficult to view the trajectory of a dozen arrows coming towards him. Khadim had by now known their powers and knew how to counter them. It was only Kriti's power he was not aware of because had not fought her in a direct battle so far.

"Shouldn't they be running out of arrows?" Bodhi shouted and asked Manav while still taking cover and narrowly avoiding an arrow shot. Manav who was viewing the attackers through his powers told him " Their bows are made of a long bone and so are arrows. The tip of the arrow is also made of bone and their quiver keeps on getting filled with the arrows" it was then Bodhi and others noticed that the arrow head which looked like stone was actually bone. "How do we fight them?" Bodh asked Angad, he so far had answers for these questions " I do not know" Anahad replied and was about to be hit by an arrow which he defected with his sword.

Kriti went up the tree and then while still being small in size jumped on a flying arrow and then on to next till she was able to reach one of the shooter, she then came in her normal size used her strength of grab his hands and change the direction of his shot to hit in the middle head of another flying demon. The other demon fell and his head hit a tree on his way down and his skull was smashed into pieces. One down still fourteen more to go. Kriti again did the same again and one more was down. One of the flying demons shot at her from behind, fortunately it did not do much damage because it hit her shoulder which had a strong metallic protection to cover the mech underneath it. She turned around and used her full strength to throw the one she was holding at the one who shot her. They collided mid air and fell down while Kriti again shrunk her size and jumped on another demon, the two falling demons tried to balance themselves and they regained balance metres before hitting the ground but when they went back up time Anagad and Bodhi jumped on them from the trees. They used these demons to shoot at their mates. Manav picked up the bow and quiver of one the fallen demon and climbed up the tallest tree around in a few seconds. Sitting on the tree top and using his siddhi to know the movement of his enemies he started shooting arrows at the flying demons.

Soon all the flying demons were down except the three Kriti, Bodhi and Angad were riding, seeing that their work was done Bodhi pressed his demon to go lower and he jumped on a tree and immediately this demon was shot by Manav. Angad and Kriti's demons shot each other and they too jumped on to the trees. Some of the flying demons were lying on the ground injured from their fall but not yet dead, Bodhi and Angad finished them off by beheading them.

The stench of death had now increased and the mist too had thickened that it was difficult to view more than a few metres ahead. Manav was leading the pack walking ahead of everyone while being in siddhi state to view any attack that could come along their way, the forest had given way to marshy lands making the forward movement slow.

While moving in the marshes Manav spotted the image in front of him which was only slightly visible when the mist reduced for a few seconds. The fortress was now visible, it was still like a spec of dark far away but Manav was able to recognise it due to the harrowed experience he had of being a captive once. "There it is, " he shouted at his mates. There had been no attacks on them in the last couple of hours. " Has he run out of tricks and his army or is he trying to lure us in?" Bodhi asked Manav. I think Khadim is now waiting for them to come to his den to attack.

They reached closer to the moat surrounding the fortress, " Beware, the moat is filled with strange creatures" Manav told everyone. There was no way to cross over to the other side, it was deep and wide, and impossible to jump over to the other side. The only way was to swim through it without knowing what is lurking beneath.

" At our speeds the fifty metre wide moat should be a couple of minutes of swim" Angad reassured the group.

"I will go first and look for dangers, meanwhile all of you keep on crossing" Manav told the others " I will come along with you. I will shrink my size to sit on your shoulder and if you see any danger alert me" Kriti told Manav.

" Seems a good plan." he agreed and they proceeded as per that. He jumped in water with Kriti sitting on his right shoulder, her size reduced to that of a thumb.

―------------------

On the other Earth, in the dark of the night. People saw from their windows the moon getting slowly covered by a shadow. First it seemed like a claw was covering it, then they saw a face like an image too. Rubbing his eyes again a man first thought that it's the clouds but he used binoculars and saw the shadow on the moon. He then reached out to a friend in another part of the city to confirm if what he was seeing was real or not.

"Are you seeing something strange?" the man asked his friend.

" What is it?" the friend asked.

" There is a strange shadow covering the moon, look out of the window" The other man rushed to his window and gaped in amazement " Yes, I am seeing it too"

The Devil now had enough spirits and slaves in this realm that he was able to extend his influence in the physical world. By linking the portal with this universe he showed his image to the world not in a physical form but as a shadow only. But to send out his voice to every part all his slaves spoke together in unison who had also taken over the broadcast channels too which were sending out their message. Their chilling voices created a resonance which instilled fear in the hearts of all those who heard it

"I am the one you have read about and have feared all your life. I am the one whose coming on Earth was always spoken about. I am your master, your new God, The Devil. Kneel and pray to me if you wish to live or else I am waiting for you in hell too" it was followed by a spine chilling laughter. Just by listening to this over broadcast many people around the world went hysterical , some of them jumped off the buildings and committed suicides " The world is paying for its sins" said the ones who still believed in God. Many others came out of their houses and kneeled on the roads and prayed to the Devil and accepted his empire.

The armies and technology were now futile, they did not know who the enemy was and whom to target. The entire cabinet of the Antarctic resigned in helplessness.

The Devil was looking at this while sitting on his throne and smiled " All the great kings and Dictators of the past tried and failed to rule over like a God over the same planet that they were once born. Now I am the ruler of Earth and Hell. If there is a heaven too somewhere I shall rule over it and if there are real Gods somewhere I shall make them also bow to me soon"

There was no one or no power that could stop him.

―-----

The others too jumped in the water, Manav did not sense any trouble " Water seems surprisingly clear. Nothing in it " Anagad and Bodhi moved till the middle of the moat, the calm water started shaking and it felt a tremor was rising from deep. Thousands of piranhas came up from the depth of the trenches. They saw these little death machines were only a few seconds away from them. Bodhi took out the last grenade which he still had in the armour that he was wearing and dropped it in the water. The grenade went down the surface and hit a piranha and blew up. A few dozen piranhas died but the number was still huge. "Throw me to the other side, quickly " Kriti saw something and immediately asked Manav to do this, he did the same using his full strength, she reached the other side and before hitting the ground regained her size using the impact of which she cut the chains which were holding the door which acted as the bridge over the moat, it fell down and Manav Bodhi and Angad latched on to it with Piranhas having reached the surface of water, some of them jumped up but were cut down by Bodhi. They walked ahead and Manav said " My powers are no longer working it seems. I could not sense this danger that struck us"

" You and your enemy both have the power of foresight, it is cancelling each other out" Angad replied with the probable reason behind it.

They went inside the fortress, there were some big slug-like animals hanging on the walls which jumped on them but were duly cut by them. They came into a wide and dark hallway, some undead soldiers came out to attack them from behind the pillars. Manav even without his siddhi was capable enough to fight them using the silver coated swords and so were the others. After crossing the hallway , there were rows of pillars which were separated by some distance creating different paths. " Which one do we choose?" asked Kriti to the group. They all did their best to look ahead but it was dark and nothing could be seen. " We will need to split," suggested Angad. " It is dangerous but it seems the only way. Others nodded but before splitting the group they re-adjusted the communication device on their armour to communicate to each other so the one who finds the right path can inform the others.

Kriti walked ahead, she switched on her torch to get some light in the dark. She saw a small opening from where the light was coming, she came closer and it was a hole in the wall on the other side was a garden. She bent down and came outside. She took a few steps and realised that this was the same garden she used to visit as a child , it was in her own world. She walked ahead and soon saw a familiar face. It was the face of an old friend, her old schoolmate. She was smiling while taking a walk in the garden. Kriti went up to her but she was not able to reach out to her, because many undead soldiers came into the garden and attacked her friend. She shrunk her size and reached close to the undead and then hit them hard. All the soldiers fell down immediately, one of them got up and tried to attack her from behind but she was alert to it she took her sword and swung it to behead him but he shifted in time, the sword did not behead him but he got a big slash on his torso and it sent out blood which hit her face. The blood was warm, much warmer than that of undead soldiers. Suddenly she saw that her friend had disappeared and then there was no garden around her. She was still standing in the alley of the castle. The two undead soldiers were tending to the one who was injured, they turned into humans, she saw it was Manav and Bodhi and the injured person was Angad. She was trapped in an illusion and was not able to recognize her friends. Angad was losing blood fast, Kriti stood there in shock unable to comprehend what she had done. Manav and Bodhi managed to tie up the wound but Angad was not in a shape to fight and Kriti was too shocked to fight. " It was not her mistake, she was trapped in an illusion and she could not see us" Angad told the others, he then whispered to them " Neither she nor I will be able to fight much, it is up to the two of you now"

"Don't worry, you will be alright" Manav told him. " We need your guidance in this battle without that we cannot defeat the evil powers"

Kriti was standing motionless, still in shock and silently uttering " I never wanted to be a warrior , I never wanted to be a warrior" in a loop Manav held her arm and shook it, "He is fine, just look after him as he wont be able to fight much now" . Kriti carried Angad on her back as they came out of the alley and went into another one which was the way ahead.

" The evil powers are too strong here; we must tread carefully" Angad warned them. They walked into a large hall which looked like the central hall of the palace.

Khadim was sitting on his throne which was on an elevated platform which required about ten steps to reach the throne.

" I knew that it was impossible for any of my minions to beat you so I decided to take it up upon me" Khadim said without any hint of discomfort in his voice.

" His powers are too strong. He can create illusions and telekinesis won't let you come close to him," Angad told Manav and Bodhi. "Kriti could have reached out to him by shrinking her size but she is in no mental state to fight"

Manav and Bodhi were thrown away by a flick of his hand. They tried again and failed. Khadim let out an evil laughter, he was toying with them. Angad wanted but he could not help them at all. Khadim then raised his hands and both Manav and Bodhi went up in the air and they were close to the ceiling which was more than ten metres high and he pulled his hands slightly back, he then rolled his fingers. Manav and Bodhi now felt as if they were being tied up with an invisible rope, they were not able to move their hands , then they rotated and their heads facing the floor. Khadim then stopped for a few seconds to gather some more strength to throw his victims with full force on the floor which was made of hard rocks. Angad saw in horror, knowing what is about to happen, the hit would kill any human however strong and if someone is saved miraculously he will live in a state of coma.

The hands were about to come down, there was a sudden cacophony and everyone was surprised, there was fluttering of wings. Angad believed that some new minions of Khadim were coming to attack them, so he warned Kriti who was holding him. It was a swarm of crows who had entered the fortress.

Kaagbhusundi, the great crow who watches over every universe, the crows who would come on the behalf of deceased forefathers to eat food in the month of *Shraddh,* the crow that would bring news of the visitors by coming to house and sitting and cawing on the balcony. Crows which would circle an animal which was about to die but not yet dead or the crow which would sense an impending calamity before it would happen. Crows are the messengers of Kaagbhusundi and this creature was made in the shape of Kaagbhusundi .

Kaagbhusundi after being hit by the arrow of Arjun vowed it will never blink an eye or miss a movement of importance on Earth. Not only that, as an atonement of this sin it promised it will intervene through its messengers whenever needed. So using crows it would send out signals to help the humans.

Today was one such day, a day which would decide the fate of humanity which was surviving on its last legs. But only the signal was not enough today. Something more had to be done.

With hundreds of crows blocking his vision the telekinesis of Khadim was broken and Manav and Bodhi fell down in a free fall with their hands untied, but there so many crows between the ceiling and the floor that the speed at which was reduced and they came on ground without any injury.

While unable to fight still as the last resort, Angad made an offer to the souls he had caught. He spoke to them " If you help me I will let you go else if I get killed you can never come out of this prison, even Khadim's magic won't help you come out" The captured souls had spent hundreds of years tormenting humans and now to be in this prison just like they were in Devil's hell was impossible to bear.

The crows threw around stuff in the castle,they picked up artefacts and they broke many of them. All this while the soul whispered and Angad using his entire strength crawled up to Bodhi, who was trying to get a look at his nemesis to attack him.

The crows on their way out plucked the eyes of some undead soldiers they encountered on the way, the entire place was again quiet now and Khadim was furious with this interruption in his killing business.

Bodhi saw the shining crystal while he was lying on the floor .The crystal was inside a thick glass case. He took out his knife and threw it at it, the knife broke through the glass and it hit the crystal, the crystal broke. It released electric waves all around and it hit the walls of the room which were blown to pieces at the spots where the charges hit them. Khadim who was standing closest to the crystals had the most powerful hit from it. He was thrown away and hit the wall with full force, his telekinesis to stop himself from being flung away did not work because the electric shock had stunned him and his neural connection to use the telekinesis became slow. He broke through the wall due to the impact and his clothes and body were on fire. The shock and fire was enough to kill a normal human many times over but Khadim was not human. He used his entire strength to get back up again. His skin had now completely burnt off along with the clothes and he was only flesh and bones and his body.

He finally again stood up while his body was still on fire and he raised his hands to use his telekinesis. Angad used his entire strength and threw a sword at him which sliced away both his arms. Khadim went mad with anger and put his strength to regenerate his hands. The flesh was growing back again in real time.

Manav and others were lying on the ground which was much lower than where the crystal was , the electric waves travelled straight parallel to the height of the crystal and they were saved by its fury.

Bodhi and Manav ran up to Khadim before his hands had fully regrown. Bodhi stabbed his heart and Manav came from behind and chopped off Khadim' s head and fell down on his knees. The century old empire of Khadim was now over.

"How did you know about it?" Manav asked Bodhi while still on his knees.

"In the cacophony created by the crows Angad crawled up to me and told me to hit the crystal which was in the glass case." Bodhi told Manav while still looking at the dead body of Khadim and ready to strike again if it was to wake up again.

"The souls told me the crystal has so much energy that it can bring down the entire palace, break it into two and it can even incapacitate Khadim" Angad told them how he managed to get Khadim down. "

Khadim 's body was still burning and turning into ashes.

Angad kept his promise and released the souls. How they had once started the kingdom of Khadim, the crystals and whispering souls now ended the kingdom. The undead soldiers who were alive even after the death of their human bodies due Khadim's magic started collapsing and died. Those who were in the countries far away from the fortress and on the last dance of destruction they too fell like a pile of dolls.

"The next task is to locate the Mandala. It was the primary reason why we have come to the fortress, to ensure it does not fall into the hands of evil again. " Angad reminded the boys.

Manav and Bodhi ran around in the collapsing fortress and finally Manav located the Mandala; he felt that he was guided towards it despite it being located in one of the hidden corners of the castle. With Khadim dead, the powers of Mandala again started helping Manav and it guided him towards locating itself. It was glowing when Manav reached close to it because Khadim had unlocked some of its power which had helped the Devil to travel to Earth 1 and now with evil gone from its vicinity the power of Mandala got unlocked to such a level which was never done before. Manav immediately went into the siddhi state.

His consciousness now moved out of the physical realm and moved to another dimension, the dimension which could not be seen or felt, the Mandala was part of the realm, a realm outside time and space. But a realm through which one can see everything in every universe.

He within a few microseconds saw how Khadim who was once a normal human became the ruler of the undead empire on Earth. His consciousness was then flown away, it was nothingness all around but at a distance he saw the souls which were released by Angad and next second Manav saw himself outside another castle.

There were huge steps leading to the giant door, he ran over the stairs and reached the door. There were two guards standing over it, they stopped him by using their spears. Manav waved his hands and the guards became unconscious. He looked at his hands and was surprised to see what he could do, he raised his hands towards the door and the giant door opened.

In the castle of Khadim, everything was collapsing. Bodhi was looking around for Manav but he came across the prison where the humans were kept in captivity to harvest them. He opened the containers they were kept in, Kriti and Angad too had come there. Angad chanted some mantras and the people regained consciousness "You had been kept captive here, you all better run away from there the fortress is about to collapse" he told them and used his gestures as sign language since some of them did not understand his language. The prisoners started running away. " Manav is still inside" Bodhi told Angad" I need to go and find him" and he went inside

The Earth beneath them collapsed, Kriti lost her balance but managed to hold Angad and keep him from falling. She finally came back to her senses and realised the situation, that if she did not act now it would be too late to save Manav" I am coming with you " she said to Bodhi and rushed inside.

The building was collapsing. Bodhi was able to save himself using his quick reflexes and Kriti had her super strength, they cried out for Manav but he was completely oblivious to their voices in his deep meditation. His physical self was there but his consciousness and soul were billions of miles away, he entered the castle. It was huge and very different to the one where his physical self was, there was no rotten stench of undead men or blood and body parts around. It was a piece of perfect architecture. He walked ahead and saw many guards coming towards him. They wore horn-like head gears and capes and were huge in size. One of them shouted " Who are you?" Manav did not reply because he was still confused about where he was.

Before he could think more , a huge fist almost hit his face but his siddhi was back and he avoided the punch in a nick of time. " This guy was quite some distance away from me. How did he come so close in a fraction of second? " Manav was a bit perplexed , but he had encountered many strange creatures in the last few days to keep this thought for long.

Manav jumped and gave him a hard kick which broke his neck. The next to who came close to him Manav pushed them and they fell many metres away. He then jumped in the air and kicked the others without touching the ground and then he moved ahead.

One person was watching all this melee and he was waiting to greet Manav. Few moments later Manav entered the large hall where this person was seated. He was twice the size of a normal human and his huge horn and red eyes were scary to look at. " I have heard quite a lot about you from my minions" He smiled and told Manav " You defeated Khadim who no one could touch. Your powers will now help me with what Khadim was doing earlier. "

Manav remembered" Khadim had talked about someone he was serving, this must be that person. Khadim's lord"

"Welcome to hell" the Devil told him " and I am its ruler the Devil"

Manav was frozen with panic " Am I dead, the building was collapsing when I went into siddhi state. Did that kill me?" He also understood why the normal laws of physics were not working in this place.

"But If I am dead then why have I come to hell? I was a good person" he was still thinking

The Mandala had picked up the traces of origin from the electricity blast from Electronicum which had charged it to full power and when it activated the consciousness of Manav the first place it went was into the realm of Hell.

"Since you have killed my servant Khadim I will use your power to go into other universes and rule them just the way I have been ruling over your Earth and the one from which your beloved has come from" Devil spoke about his plan to Manav.

"And what makes you think that I will be a part of this ?" Manav spoke back.

"Because , you don't have an option my dear" the Devil walked up to him and smiled.

Manav saw two serpents suddenly appearing in the air and they floated up to him at great speed. He had seen this seconds before it happened using the siddhi and he jumped back doing a somersault but as soon as he came on his feet the serpents tied his wrists and then he too flew with them and he was stuck on a wall , the serpents had now changed to handcuffs.

"This is how you had reawakened your siddhi, when you were tied up in the prison of Rajgarh" Devil reminded him.

"He knows everything about me" Manav thought " Afterall he is the Devil but I need to escape from here"

A portal showed up " Look inside it" the Devil ordered Manav. He looked inside and he saw people being devoured by undead soldiers but this Earth looked very different from the one he knew. It was the Earth from where Kriti had come from. He saw a huge gathering of people dressed in white robes and chanting the name of Devil and making human sacrifices in front of a statue which looked similar to the Devil."He is indeed speaking the truth. He is destroying all of the creation and I need to stop him…. But I no longer have my friends around and this place ruled by him is filled with magic"

"Magic..he thought"

Devil walked up to him, towering over him he bent down a bit and placed his palm on Manav's head. He suddenly started shivering and the surroundings around Manav started blinking and blurring. This happened for a few seconds till Devil did not remove his hand away from Manav.

The Devil then smiled as if he was intoxicated " Ahh… I could see the multiverse" he then smacked his lips gesturing to Manav that he intends to devour these universes.

Seeing the worry on the face of Manav the Devil said " Don't worry I won't destroy them completely, just enough to make them accept me as their ruler , their God"

The Devil walked away and in the next second he was back at his throne sitting and smiling at Manav. He summoned his deputy and other soldiers. Manav noticed that some were floating in the air like spirits " Well it is expected , this is Hell and these are souls in here. Some of these were the souls who had gone to my Earth and helped Khadim create the empire of darkness on Earth. Soon he saw that hundreds of spirit soldiers of the Devil had gathered outside the court of their ruler. The Devil again appeared right next to the face of Manav. He placed his long hand on the head of Manav and he stretched out the other hand in the opposite direction. It opened a portal , he then moved this hand slightly away and it opened another portal and he did this for a few seconds till about ten portals were created. He then removed the hand from the head of Manav and spoke to his army "Go out my soldiers to the new Universes and rule them in my name. Make everyone tremble with your fear, kill and destroy as you please and make sure they bow down to me" The soldiers then started jumping into these portals and started vanishing as they crossed it.

They all reached these universes to bring death and destruction.

"I am so incapacitated, my siddhi is working but I can't do anything to overpower this magic"

"Magic" he again thought and paused " The crystals which knocked out Khadim, they were having the souls within them, those crystals were basically the pieces of Hell. This means that this place is not in the physical realm. This is a different dimension, just like I am just a soul and the Devil could touch me. It means that nothing is as it seems."

Then he heard a familiar voice.

Back on Earth the fortress of Khadim had collapsed. The ground underneath had sunk in and Manav too went in the ground and the Mandala too was with him. The debris and mud was covering his body slowly, since he was in the state of deep meditation his breathing had slowed down and he needed less oxygen but it was a matter of minutes before he would be completely buried and the oxygen around him would run out.

Bodhi and Kriti were running out in panic, Bodhi was clearing the debris to look for him. Kriti had shrunken her size and went through every space to look for Manav. They were frequently attacked by the creatures who, unlike undead soldiers, were made partially by mutation and magic. Bodhi and Kriti dealt with them but it stalled their search for Manav.

Angad was sitting outside, " I too need to look for Manav and help them but how can I? I am in no state to run around, and even if I try I will get caught in the collapsing building". He thought hard and got into meditation and tried to look for life signs around him. Manav's consciousness had peaked to a high level and he was easily able to telepathically connect with it " Where are you Manav? He asked. " I am in a place far away?" he replied.

"You were stuck in the collapsing building, we are trying to locate you." Angad reminded him.

" I don't know where my body is," Manav replied.

"What do you mean? Where is your consciousness?" Angad was confused

" I am in hell," he replied.

" I get it that this place is like hell but where are you actually? We need to find you " Angad was a little agitated that Manav was talking in puzzles.

"No, I am actually in hell, the Mandala got activated and my consciousness flew to this place. The crystals which killed Khadim had souls trapped in it, they are part of hell, where the Devil the master of Khadim lives and controls these souls who cause destruction on his behest.Using my powers he has opened portals to many universes and is now trying to destroy them all . The Earth from where Kriti has come from has already fallen. It's all magic here and this place is not in the physical realm even I was able to throw away guards by barely touching them.But now using his magic the Devil has tied me up"

Angad thought about all that he had learnt about in his life, this was the culmination of all of it "Listen to me. You have the power of Mandala, if it can help the Devil open the portals I am sure it will help you to beat him.Remember the training you had in your teenage,concentrate hard on the Mandala, all the universes today are dependent on you."

He concentrated hard enough and focussed to push his siddhi , he looked around he saw that the soldiers, the minions of Devil and Devil himself looked like air. The walls of the court and the castle itself seemed to disappear and all that was there was the electric blue wall all around,which was electronicium." Everything is a mirage" Manav realised and looked at the handcuffs. The handcuffs were gone and disappeared in thin air. " I was able to magically throw away the guards of the Devil without even touching them. I can control some magic of this place because I am not a dead person whose soul has been trapped here. My body is still alive and this is my consciousness which can act on its free will and can fight magic with magic."

He then walked ahead and waved his hands and pulled something out of thin air, all the souls which were sent into these portals were dragged out in the middle of the portal he then closed all the portals trapping the souls where they could go nowhere.

The Devil who had retired to his library during this time where he was trying to find ways to gain control over the new universes. He came back out and was surprised to see Manav out of his chains and closing the last of the portals. There was no trace of any portal that he could see, full of anger, he increased his size furthermore and now became a twenty feet giant and stretched out his right hand and grabbed Manav with force.

Manav who had not noticed the Devil was caught unaware but he teleported himself to another corner of the room, away from the grab of the Devil who was bewildered seeing this.

Seeing the amazement on the face of the Devil, Manav gave him a smirk and said, I know nothing is real in this place. It is an illusion which appears to all your slaves and prisoners as magic.

His connection with Angad had broken now, who was trying to still reach out to him desperately " Can you hear me Manav, can you hear me?" he kept on shouting. Manav had focussed hard on his surroundings to see through the magic of Khadim and he was no longer able to have telepathy with Angad, he for the moment did not feel the need to do so.

The devil looked at him and then after a few seconds laughed " Standing in the very place I have ruled for a billion years , you are a mere human trying to scare me. I am the very fear that every religion has made people afraid of. The darkness that every child fears is me. I am the origin of fear, the creator of the supernatural. And you dare challenge me"

He laughed and laughed so loud that the entire place started vibrating, the huge chandeliers started shaking. Manav saw the next attack of the Devil using his siddhi and he tried to fend.

The falling pendants from chandeliers became projectiles and they hit Manav at such speeds that he did not have any time to fend. He was thrown many feet away and blood started coming from the wounds created by the projectiles. " Your powers which make the Earthlings marvel are nothing here. Get up and fight. Let me end it here for you, once your consciousness is dead you will cease to exist in any form"

If the body dies he will only be a soul and if the consciousness dies even the soul would perish and there would be nothing left of Manav. Now both body and consciousness were on the verge of dying.

Manav gathered his strength and got up , the entire place was spinning and he was not sure if that was due to the wounds or due to magic. " Focus, focus" he said to himself." If I die today all the sacrifices done by my Gurus to protect the magic of Mandala would go to vain. The deaths of billions of humans who were killed by the designs of Khadim and the Devil would go to vain. I cannot let that happen. I was the chosen one by the Mandala to get its power and I will remain worthy of it"

He felt a strong surge in his body as if he had gotten a health boost, the ties of his consciousness and soul had broken off from his body. Now he knew that he actually left his mortal body behind. But it also made the consciousness stronger than before.

" I need to take this fight on even grounds, I will make him fight outside his home turf" he thought. He raised his hands and opened a portal and ran into and disappeared. The Devil too ran behind him and asked his minions to follow him. He needed Manav's powers to control the multiverse. Manav jumped from one universe to the other and from one time to another and the army of the Devil kept on following him. Every Earth was different, some of them had dinosaurs coexisting with the humans, others had humans and androids in coexistence, while there were some where humans were extremely different, one had humans who were too tall and other one had very short humans. In one of the universes where instead of apes, reptiles became humans. Manav had a look at all of this but he kept on running with the Devil's army on his tail and they kept on getting lost till the last one was left. Manav kept on thinking about the plan to defeat the Devil because the time was running out, he could not stay as a consciousness forever. If the body was still alive the consciousness would return to it which seemed improbable and if he was dead he would either attain the moksha by reaching heaven or would again become part of life and death and will be born as a new human. So he did the final time jump which none of the servants of the Devil could do. He kept on running and he kept on seeing the various timelines now simultaneously, he now could sense the presence of Kagbhusundi around him. He had made so many jumps from one universe to another and from one timezone to another that he ran outside the dimension of time and multiverse.

He could now see all the universes like thousands of screens in front of him and every screen had infinite layers behind it which too he could see, these were the entire past of these universes leading up to the present point and he could see dim projections in front of the screens. These were the future of the universes and the Earths in them, Manav looked at them. He spotted the universe which was his home, it zoomed up and he saw that Kriti and Bodhi were looking out for him, he looked at himself buried deep in the ground along with the Mandala.

He had died a few seconds ago, exactly at the time when he was able to make the final leap to cross the boundaries of time and space.

He then saw the universe from where Kriti had come from and how the people were killing each other to please their new God the Devil. He saw the projections of these universes growing dimmer and dimmer, and for some universes it was completely wiped out. Wiping out of the projections meant there was no future for these universes, these Earths would be devoured by the Devil. His army of souls would finally reach the Mandala and then will find someone who can use that to unlock the portals. Then there would be no humans left, it seems that the Devil does not understand that he will have no one to rule over if he continues the destruction that he has been causing.

He looked all around, he flipped through the projections, seeing into them, he looked into the past of all these universes. "Who made the Devil, was it God?" he asked himself. " It must be, there have been many myths and stories about him. Right from being a fallen angel to being the brother of the Devtas. All the religions had different stories which were taught to us in the Gurukul. The stories lived though the people and their culture died. I need to know about him." He flipped through the past of his Earth. He found out nothing. The Devil had been there since the beginning of time even way before there were humans on Earth"

It took him hundreds of hours to shift through the past but time on Earth was still the same when he had jumped out of the dimension of time and space. I am stuck here forever, if he would jump back to Earth at any other time he would be a soul of a dead man and he would not be able to come back to this dimension. He had one chance to make things right, he thought about all the things that the Devil had told him " He showed me the Earth where Kriti had come from and how he was destroying it. Of all the universes he chose that one. Also Kriti coming to my Earth means that there has to be a connection between him and that Earth" and then he started looking through the time panels of Earth 1, he saw the recent destruction that was caused by the souls which had crossed the portals, then he went back and saw how the Earth came to a standstill after the HRP fiasco. He looked at all the things and people connected with HRP, he saw how Dr Oz created the mess and the flying of the spaceship which had taken out the HRP server. He looked inside the HRP HQ and in the HRP universe, he saw the trapped consciousness and he saw a person controlling all of it and calling himself the Devil.

" He was a human who had gained powers in the virtual universe which later became Hell " Manav saw all that had happened.

Making any changes to the timeline could mean creation of new universes or destruction of existing ones, any change will have a ripple effect and its implications were difficult to understand because they would compound over millennia. But he had to act, so he took his final jump.

He was in his childhood home, celebrating Holi with his family. He was applying colours to his friends and then his uncle was carrying him in his arms giving him sweets. He heard a knock and then the scream of his mother. His father gave him a compass and a book and asked him to run. But Manav was frozen, his father shouted again " Run Manav run" but Manav could not run, he saw his father being hacked to death, he saw his friends being killed, his relatives and neighbours all of them being killed. Manav shouted seeing all this at the top of his voice "someone help us" but there was no one to hear. He was spotted by a soldier of King Bhutshikhan, he told the other soldiers about Manav's presence and they all rushed towards him with their naked swords smeared with blood. He turned around and ran away from them to save himself, his heartbeat was racing, his face was red hot with tension. He ran with all his strength but the distance between him and the soldiers kept on reducing, his legs were hurting and he was running out of breath but he put all of his strength and the soldiers kept on coming closer and closer but they never reached him. Physical pain and exhaustion was reaching its limits but nothing else happened, neither did he get away from the sights of the soldiers nor did he get caught. When he wanted to give up and let things take their course he still couldn't do that because he was now in the simulation of HRP which was being controlled by Dr. Oz This continued for days at a stretch and Manav was facing his personal hell of emotional agony and physical pain.

Manav took the jump inside the HRP, before it became The Hell and had passed through the black hole during its journey in space." The best place to fight the Devil is not in the actual Hell where he will easily defeat me nor is it in the physical world where I will be just a soul or the implications of any change would be great. The safest place to fight the Devil is HRP which has neither become hell right now nor is it in the physical world," Manav had pondered before the jump.

Like everyone else who was trapped in Hell Manav faced his biggest nightmare and he felt powerless to do anything about it and it kept on going for days. Before the jump he had been chanting the Mantra given by the old man Sudama to make him remember his past and break free from the hyper reality, his subconscious which was still chanting it came to the fore and now he could hear it. The subconscious mantra had been repeated a million times and it had become an armour now which would protect the wearer. He remembered that this was a hyper reality projection in which he was caught, he remembered the purpose he had come for and he threw off the spell of virtual reality which was overpowering him. He saw the HRP as it was, wires and chips and he was so small that he could see the atoms around him which constituted the HRP, he saw the binary numbers; the strings of 0s and 1s which was behind the software of the HRP. He saw the brainwaves and consciousness trapped in it which were running like electricity in it. He himself was an electric signal in this giant machine, he now had to find the signal which was controlling the entire HRP making it the hell. The most powerful signal, he could feel its presence and he ran towards it. The image in front of him kept on alternating between the actual physical HRP system and the billions of atoms making it and the virtual world. But he kept on moving ahead. As he moved closer to the signal of Dr Oz he felt a strong force which was pulling him away. It was due to signals of the same charge trying to come closer. The Images of the virtual world too became stronger with that, he saw how he had crossed a valley and now he saw the all familiar castle which was surrounded by a dense fog.

Moving forward was getting difficult, it felt like he was moving against a strong wind but he kept on pushing. The guards on the gate tried to block him but he threw them away by a gesture of hand, in reality he was using the repulsion which pushed away these electric charges which were acting as the guards.He entered the circuit, the castle and ran into the courtroom of the Devil. The Devil was surprised to see someone entering his dominion; it was impossible to break away from the mental trap he had set for any consciousness entering the hell . He immediately stood up from his throne " What are you?" he demanded an answer. Manav just looked at him with anger and did not say anything " Are you a virus which has entered the system? Nothing else could enter this place. But HRP is incorruptible, no software or virus can penetrate it."

"I am the one who will stop you from destroying the universe" he said and before the Devil could comprehend anything, Manav ran towards him and collided with him at full speed. Overcoming the repulsion between the similar charges it released a tremendous amount of energy and within a split second the entire HRP system became gas.

There was a huge blast and Manav was thrown off. He was blinded by the flash for a few moments and then it was only pure light " It is time to say goodbye to the ghost realm too". And he closed his eyes. His soul passed through the Mandala which had earlier transported him to Hell and then into the realm of Kagbhusundi, the Mandala exploded and the mortal body of Manav was blown to bits. Bodhi and Kriti saw the blast. Bodhi fell down on his knees and Kriti disappeared, he looked around but she was not to be seen anywhere. All the portals scattered all over the multiverse closed forever along with the destruction of the Mandala. Time was again a straight line.

Bodhi and Angad went back to the homeland and they established the Gurukul with the other Navratnas. Kylie joined them and took care of the children at the Gurukul.

Kriti was back in her world at a time many years before HRP was made. She was a normal human and had no powers or mech attached to her. She was surrounded by strangers but it was her world. Though she missed the people she had met on the other Earth, the brave soldiers who laid down their lives, the wise Navratnas, the magical Angad, strong Bodhi and the man she missed the most, Manav, she often told their stories to her son Samarth.

Manav opened his eyes, it seemed like it had been centuries since he was asleep. "Is this rebirth?" he thought. He looked around him and it looked as if he had seen this place in a dream. It was a castle, he remembered the place and immediately took a step back ready to face an attack from his foe, it was the castle of Hell. The Devil was nowhere to be seen, his head felt heavy, he was wearing a crown and he was seated on a throne. Kalyuga had finally ended and Satyuga started, the Hell needed a just ruler and the one to defeat the King was made the new King as per the rules of royal wars. Hell was a necessary part of the creation to catch the polluted souls and create balance in the universe. Manav was the new ruler of Hell.

*****

www.ingramcontent.com/pod-product-compliance
Lightning Source LLC
LaVergne TN
LVHW061542070526
838199LV00077B/6872